~ SHORT LIVES ~

*Also by John Fraser
and published by
AESOP Modern Fiction:*

Animal Tales
Black Masks
Blue Light / Starting Over
The Case
Down from the Stars
Enterprising Women
Happy Always
Hard Places
An Illusion of Sun
The Magnificent Wurlitzer
Medusa
Military Roads
The Observatory
The Other Shore
The Red Bird
The Red Tank
Runners
Sisters
Soft Landing
The Storm
Thirty Years
Three Beauties
Wayfaring

~ SHORT LIVES ~

John Fraser

AESOP Modern Fiction
Oxford

AESOP Modern Fiction
An imprint of AESOP Publications
Martin Noble Editorial / AESOP
28 Abberbury Road, Oxford OX4 4ES, UK
www.aesopbooks.com

First paperback edition published by AESOP Publications
Copyright (c) 2017 John Fraser

www.johnfraserfiction.com

A catalogue record of this book is
available from the British Library.

First paperback edition 2017

ISBN: 978-1-910301-45-6

CONTENTS

I

O THE POOR HORSES

'COMMUNISM,' the old guy says, 'is the spirit. It never dies. That is its problem. The Party, necessarily, is the body that it seeks, inhabits. The body has the force, it fights, it thinks, manoeuvres – putrefies, and dies. The spirit – it wanders on again, like a butterfly, a ghost.'

'Yes,' says Julie, much enthused.

'Ah, Julie,' says the dying man, 'your mother had in mind to call you Aurelia – but she found that was what they called a road. So, it was Julie – after the hero, stabbed in the back. A messy life like they all did then. Epicurus morphing into Stoicism. Lots now start with a religion. You need be a good reader, even if your nose is stuck into a book – to see what's going on around. But – inside that paper ball in front of you there nest a thousand wasps. It doesn't matter where you start – the seminary, the foundry – it's where intelligence can take you...'

'Yes, of course I see,' says Julie, swept up, excited, in a history that won't be hers.

'It sounds precarious,' the old guy says – some relative of hers, she at first constrained no doubt, to tolerate – 'The tumbler you're attached to. Can he catch you when you fall?'

'Oh no!' she shouts. 'They set you up, to talk you off my Pierre! They are a team – Pierre and Dora! I am with them both. They bear me up, they cast me down. It's passion, stupid!'

'They're acrobats,' the old guy says. 'When you fall, you stand again and bow and smile. It all fits in the act.'

'Just like you say,' she shouts. 'The spirit's in the air, you weave it round. If you are slippery, well – into the sand you go, your time is up. They bind you like two snakes with ruby eyes, they're warm and leathery, the sex fleets like a cloud...'

'Is there an audience?' the old communist guy asks, quite greedy for the scene.

'I'm always hidden,' Julie says. 'If the elephant goes mad with must – I have the rifle, and will shoot.'

'That means you're some kind of spy,' the old man says, seeing communism slip away. 'Everything is falling down. There's war everywhere for silly things, all will end as heaps of stones... So, Julie, you're not bombing, so you must be in intelligence.'

'We have to be around to build it up again,' she says. Maybe she wonders who's trying to split her from Pierre – perhaps it's his girl Dora, whom she loves...

'I know,' the old guy says, 'the circus goes round everywhere, it's made that way. Travel with them – you're the dross that finds out everything.'

'It's not about fooling gravity, and climbing the stairway up to heaven,' says Julie. 'That's maybe how it looks – but really, it's about the other body twisted round you, it's monkeys in the puzzle tree, it's hanging on to creatures with no tails... It's all sex, and everybody holds their breath until you reach the ground. Tossing the fruit, chasing the tails, hierarching, picking nits...'

'You? You've been up in the cradle, Julie?' asks the old earthbound guy.

'What's remarkable for humans,' Julie says, 'is nowhere near what monkeys do. You applaud – but you should cry, in shame, frustration, for your kind.'

'That's what I was telling you,' says the old communist guy. 'Shame, frustration. With falling on the floor, trying to run up the air, without a branch... When it happens, you think there must be a way to start again. Mankind, Julie: is there more to come?'

Now, neither is listening to the other. 'Monkeys are cruel,' the old guy thinks. 'I love Dora too,' thinks Julie, 'But I don't want Pierre screwing both of us.'

★

'Another premature,' shouts Pierre. 'You slither, Dora!'

'Oh,' she says. 'They clap, whatever happens. Using the powder makes my skin come off in scales. I oiled ... a little. Your grip – it's slack.'

'I'd train Julie up,' says Pierre. 'She'd do the act like you – except she doesn't bend.'

'She's not been to the academy. They don't let you in, if you can't kick your height,' says Dora, quite indifferent.

'If you're not concentrated, Dora,' says Pierre, 'you'll fall. No one will pick you up. That is the rule. Even if you're dead and smashed.'

'I've the world to choose from,' Dora says: 'I don't believe in falls, nor being caught, nor being held. It's a humiliation. Better to pretend our act's against our nature. See them far below, men and women, the whole world.

High above the wind – no longer earthbound, so long as you hold tight. Up on the rope, you're left quite free to sing whatever song you want.'

'We'll go up higher,' Pierre says. 'Do or drop – it'll help you focus.'

'There's some old guy,' says Dora, 'trying to have Julie sign up for something. She'd be better with the animals – that way, you may get love.'

'She's back in the paper centuries,' says Pierre. 'We're not bound. We have no words, no language. There's nothing choreographed. Just bare bodies and treetops. No meaning. What we are – a frolic with tears and fractures.'

'There's compromise,' says Dora, stroking Pierre. 'The tent. The arena. Sand. The camels and the lions. We have a place.'

'Yes, Dora,' says Pierre, 'but there's no rain. No hunts. A desert with no sun, oasis waterless. True, we've a place and a programme – but they don't exist anywhere, on no map, no globe. Tomorrow – we're in Aschaffenberg. Nowhere. It could be Bactria, or where there's yurts. Ours is the only art that's painted on with arnica.'

It's lovers' talk. Julie's pushed back among the clowns and floormen, the hoopers and the wirestrollers.

'Julie's old guy – it's on to a future primitive, no cash, no banks,' says Dora. 'And no employers, so he says.'

'We're primitive already,' says Pierre. 'Just hands and toes. No monotheism – no idolatry at all, no heresy. No punishments – just accidents. No faith...'

'Pierre – we must have some belief – or else they wouldn't make a booking for tomorrow's show,' says Dora. Pierre says,

'There's trust. Belief in gravity That's it – we are not humanists, we do what Julie cannot do, our act, no juju and no miracles.'

'That Masha, the Cossack from Prague – she says we're like copulating caterpillars,' Dora says. 'Why can't you explain yourself, Pierre?'

'Their horses are too tall,' says Pierre. 'It's so the riders get to do their tricks. Steppe ponies – they're the ones that spread the fear. It happens so – first the panic, then you make them worthy enemies, vainglory comes in – then, they're noble losers. Like the Tuaregs. Those Cossacks – good at sabering Jews, then, just another curious minority. Good for the circus. We're not like that, Dora. We go way back, as we go up!'

She sniffles, unconvinced. 'You can't use a sabre from a pony. You need a high horse. That's your trouble – you're approximate, Pierre.'

*

'I don't see the fun in communism,' Julie tells them. 'And I'm too tall to climb a rope.'

'Build up your mass,' says Pierre, 'Then you can carry me.'

'Julie should come with us,' says Dora. 'I'm keen on her. She's quite outside our show.'

'I'm super-strong,' says Pierre, 'but I can't support the pair of you.'

'No nakedness in Germany, Pierre,' says Dora. 'They think it's fascist.'

'I try to hurry things along,' says Pierre. 'Julie's old communist – it's baby steps and cover up, for him. Besides – there's no one following. It's just an evolutionary trial – it lands you with those beetles that can jump like kangaroos. The secret of all life is there, revealed – but it's an obscurantist way to carry on.'

'You're wrong, Pierre,' says Dora. 'It's true, we don't do epitaphs. But what we do is celebration, not departure. Dominating animals, training ourselves to poise and slide. It's regression, confirmation. No one sees your face. It's a rite, in masks, with death lying on the floor, impermanence flitting on the trapeze. If you want more, Pierre – don't climb and embrace. Granite and gristle, Pierre – those are the marks, not fur and furbelows.'

'In that case, Dora,' says Pierre, 'we must do something else. Forget the curtseys, the prissy running on and off, the show... The clowns, mocking it all down. The beasts – who must submit. All vanity, Dora – vanity, the training and the trainers. We should try everything extreme, beyond the limits, beyond natures – further and further, colder, hotter, more lonely, more hugger-mugger, more profane, tighter chained to the holy book, more idolatrous, more iconoclastic, more modern, more reactionary... Then we must leave these couplings – the high, the low, the opposites – every contrary, we must have both and neither. Break the fetters, Dora. No pairing off, no individuals, but finding the vital nub, the fuse, the burner – then blow! Blow it out, extinguish, find what there lies beyond the nothing you create, make it a world, and then destroy it! Light! Snuffed. Snuff – inhaled and with a mighty sneeze – splatter it all out!'

'We don't have time to try each one of those extremes,' says Dora. 'Someone thought of that, your plan. That's why we're given these short lives. That's why our arms tire, our heads crack open on the floor, we need a net – we fall, we're caught, we're hooked, we end up in the freezer or the fire.'

'Then we must find whoever designed it so,' says Pierre. 'Confront them. Kill them, probably – they have no genitals – or maybe a whole stock – no family, or everyone is child to them. Destroy them – it's the only way – malignant polyp, each one of us their sucker in this crap design.'

'It's useless, Pierre,' says Dora. 'Smash the machine – you'll die. That's how it's made.'

'That's your fear, Dora,' says Pierre. 'I'm prudent, but I'm not afraid. I have no fear. If I did – I'd drop you, fall – to show I had it, fear. I don't and so – I'm not afraid.'

*

Dora tells Julie, 'Pierre's full of air. He's lucky – he performs where it never rains. If he goes on like this, I'll start a school of dance, a gym, a yoga haunt.'

'I'm with you on the yoga,' Julie says. 'It's sport, religion, and it loosens up your spine. Those are my three goals in life just now.'

'It's the same with all my enterprises, Julie,' Dora says: 'You need to concentrate, that's all. For me, anything I do for myself would mean Pierre's not dragging me along – he wants to go up higher, near the roof. You can't be seen up there, and it's much further down.'

'Pierre's not the state, Dora,' Julie says. 'Not your religion, a disease, a famished beast, all saying you must die to feed their appetite. He's a guy with high ideas, strong arms and legs – that's all.'

'Oh Julie,' Dora says. 'Those things, the beast, all that – they ask you to die for them, and if you don't – you have no choice.'

'It's true,' Julie says, 'you shouldn't go to places where there's questions without answers.'

'Not so,' Dora says. 'If it's not a physical thing, a torment, then living impossible situations, even for years – it's a good thing. It straightens up your face. But what I'm in – it's physical too. You must keep concentrated, but if you have to think too much, it starts to hurt.'

'You're not telling me everything,' says Julie. 'Or, if you are, I can't follow you. Living a logical life – it doesn't need a spiel, and doubts and doublebacks. If it's not easy to set out, explain – it isn't right.'

'The risk attracts,' says Dora. 'The perfection too. But – what does it produce, our act? A frisson and a giggle.'

★

Wearing their clothes – Dora and Julie lose some height. In a beautiful crowd, they'd fit quite well – it's all a question of their symmetry. That's beauty – everyone that looks the same. No crumpled-paper faces; all striding out, no hobbling along. It has significance.

'I've been thinking, Dora,' Pierre says. 'I should do the act alone. Its meaning becomes clear when there's no man-woman stuff, no strong, no weak, no apelike dexterities and suppleness – just me... No responsibility for someone else, no glam.'

'It's a relief,' says Dora, 'to be cast off. And then regret. And bitterness. You are right, of course. A double act – it is ambiguous. So – throw in one hand – another will be dealt. Julie and I – we'll start another life... She spies on people. Most people do that work. We'll start again, instead, knowing nothing about what we'll do.'

'That could be treachery to me, of course, though it's quite bold,' says Pierre. 'What I do has failure and success imprinted in. Your wandering – it's failure, relatively, from the start.'

Julie thinks of the old guy. 'The spirit,' she starts to say, but sees she doesn't know what spirits do, what they get up to in the dark. Put on sailor suits and walk the promenade – at Kronstadt or at Biarritz? Who knows – they are invisible, though probably they could buy their clothes from Yves or Coco, or just run naked up and down, no need to cover absent genitalia, or risk a fine for nakedness, or a sore throat...

*

'Acrobats don't have a good name,' Dora says. 'Now I'm not one, I see it clearly. Pierre – is a hero. I used to read about them, in the caravan, as we nomads – the dromedaries padding, the tigers nodding, side to side, for the eventual sparking out, their chase – we went jogging on... Heroes don't all end smouldering on the pyre. Some just disappear – errata. Some linger on – Erwartung. Some – it's apotheosis. Which is the best? It isn't clear. They say it's us, who pay, mark up their points, and are beholders – we are the center, sages, the knowing ones. That's crap: being a hero's best. If you only plan a looking on – you can be life-trainers for other clueless souls. We could do that, Julie.'

*

'You can be a hero, Pierre,' says Masha. 'But it's quite juvenile. If you want to impose yourself – you need a sense

of where things go. Use your resource! That emperor – the
wrestler – in Byzantium. The Romans – soldiers, gladiators,
boxers. They all started off like you – resistant bodies.
Carapaces. Now, in the time of broken logics, of chaos –
that's all gone. A fad that no one mentions now. We know
things are quite desperate – looking for a saviour's gotten
serious. Nations or continents? Bankers or bishops? West or
East? That's where you must make your choice, take your
stand. Climbing your rope and twisting round – surely,
Pierre – the limitation strikes?'

'Our animals – they're under threat,' says Pierre. 'The
only people without rights – is us. We're every nation here,
and citizens of nowhere land. We can go round and round,
apolids, apolitical, free as the glass fragments in
kaleidoscopes... Higher and higher up my rope – I'll
cogitate some way to shift us from our metaphor – make us
that tiny planet of the good – the Greeks were sure they saw
it, reflected in a well. We are already beautiful – the good
awaits!'

'We've no defence,' says Masha, tugging at her leather
pants. 'They'll take our tigers, lock them in a zoo. They'll
forget their tricks – and so shall we. We'll have to learn the
patter over, and do theirs too.The bad morphs into bad,
and we go round and round. All I've to show for being free
– is barnacles on my bum.'

'You guys,' says Pierre. 'May not be worthy of the plan.
So – that leaves me to think things out...'

'We centaurs,' Masha says, 'we're statues. We never
make things on our own. You find us everywhere, but we're
not real. We're nothing without our mounts. You, Pierre –
now you've lost Dora...'

'Yes,' says Pierre, 'I'm supreme. I've climbed the wall,
I'm on the top and reaching up. I feel I've given birth and

dumped the kid. I didn't use my partner, but we were a hybrid, no one saw me climb without me humping her up, my sack, my slithering worm. She's beautiful, Dora is – but what's two bodies clamped together? She's not your soul, your spirit. She is not your twin, or your disease, your tone of voice, colour of your eyes, your smell, your seed. So what...? I love her, Masha, and it's best she should go off, and maybe with that other one, Julie – maybe as twins they'll feel for what the other needs.'

'You're granite, Pierre,' says Masha, not much liking him.

'It isn't what I am,' he says. 'It's what I want.'

*

Those Germans – they're supposed to be tough guys. They organise shows, carnivals – to show they love parades, colours, and peace, and spitting in the eye of order, and disorder. They organise quite thoroughly. This city where the circus comes to rest – it used to be a US base. Americans brought in the food they liked, their trucks and planes. They made the place a target once again ... no one felt like bombing it – but that would have been a different story.

Performers – they've no nationalities, no history at all. They are perfection, entertainment too. Pierre's powdering his hands.

Empires gather people from every place, they churn them round, they come out nearly uniform. They bring literacy and metalwork. They bring uniforms, and sonnet form.

'They don't bring what I do,' Pierre says. 'I'm unique and quite unlike – that's why all these people come to see me. Even if,' – he's nearly ready to stick on to the rope – 'they've seen something almost identical when the last circus came.'

Pierre's act – you mostly see the women do it – they're more lithe, there's guys who like to watch their breasts plump up or disappear, as they hang up and down the rope, or see their hair stream out as they spin, or watch it dangle down – then, in your mind, there's that mix of athletes and the naked dazzlers in the clubs, doing the pole dance...

'You screwed it, Pierre,' the manager says. 'Fall was disastrous. Kneeling before the crowd, arms in the air – was genius. Then – hopping off – the end.'

'I invoked a higher power,' says Pierre. 'My heel is shot – it's congenital for heroes.'

'Here, you're through,' the boss of the ring tells Pierre. 'What were you thinking of?'

'I wasn't sure I fit,' Pierre lies. 'I sought a guide. There wasn't one.' The boss says,

'There never is: it's all up to you. No project, no ambition, nothing counts except – just landing soft, and right way up.'

What can you say, thinks Pierre – what breaks your concentration, lets you drift – sex or the Rheingold? A clown that makes you laugh? Reaching the top – open the canvas, open the kingdom. Burst out – excelsior! Instead, you see the whitecoats strolling up, they give you serum up your nose that makes you tell the truth. If you don't know the formula expected – that's you, for life – a cripple plastered up, hobbling and seeking chairs.

'I have to start all over,' says Pierre. The boss pushes him, away from the caravan, no farewells to yaks and poodles, the human cannonballs leaden, expectant, in the breech. The boss tries to inspire – he says,

'And you're the lucky one! Who else has that chance? A clean start... Heels, toes, legs – it's congenital, the heroes suffer, mostly it's their mothers. Who pulls you down? You drown – it's worse, though probably that is the likeliest end. On the earth – you shatter. One experience that doesn't leave you just the same.'

'I did it all mself,' says Pierre.

'Yes,' says the boss, 'it doesn't count. There's no tragedy, no context. No good done, the bad done to yourself. Pierre – there's no way out. No hero – a clamberer, brought down by inattention.'

*

'You could stay, polish the horses,' Masha tells Pierre. 'Don't go back to Dora. To her, and Julie – you're no use. Don't be a clown – they cry – it comes out of their hat, it's water. When they die – remember Grock – then everybody cries. The clown – he should be Jedermann – but Jedermann is off, crossbow in hand, hunting everything before him. Don't trust them, Pierre – yes, you've come to that. It's where we all end up – distrusting our neighbours, their designs upon our animals. You were high, once – now you are brought down, where we all are... You wanted to con us, think those contortions were the magic, the rope trick, appear and disappear. It's never so, Pierre. We pessimists – we pretend, we shout and clap. We see you practising and falling off. You're just another oracle who doesn't know, smokes too much pot, and takes our cash.'

'Round and round you go,' Pierre says, 'like goldfish. Up and down the helix – guys will scramble up and down, stand on each others' heads, cry "Hupp!" – and some are caught and some come softly down, spreading their wings,

burst into "olés!", run off. There in the wings is Julie, with
her gun – ready to shoot the lusting animals, the clowns
tipping over their edge, horses with broken legs...'

'She could have shot you,' Masha says. 'You fell, were
wounded, cannot be restored. You're you, it's clear, but in
the spirit, wandering.'

'All right,' says Pierre, 'Masha – your advice is good. I'll
set to, polishing the horses.'

'That leaves me with the camels,' Dora says.

'Remember,' Pierre says, 'this way – we don't make up a
team. We're not in metaphor here, though Masha and the
Cossacks, maybe they are – they spin round and round –
ah! their costumes, red, beautiful – *krasnyi* – their sabres
sing in the air like 'cellos, I've seen them pluck the horses'
tails, string for their bows... What can I do? It's ritual that's
left – a ritual for show, without belief...blacken the hooves
and plait the manes...' He weeps.

The others wring their hands: 'I can't run,' he says.
'After my tumble, I can't do sex. I'm happy, though.
There's other fields lie stretched before me, full of flowers.'

'Just curiosity, Pierre,' Dora says. 'Why can't you do sex?
You don't need your heel for that.'

'A circus child, Dora?' asks Pierre. 'Would you want
that? Fired from the cannon? Tossed by clowns? Suppose
my heel's transmissable – the progeny, a heroine disabled.
Suppose she becomes an oracle? A vestal waiting for the
rape? Those are places you can't escape from fast – caves,
temples, groves...'

'Julie has a gun. That old communist guy is dead – or
moribund,' says Dora. 'She can be a subversive, as she
wiles away her life... But me – I don't have her
philosophical twist. I'm not a mystic, not like you, Pierre.

I'm normal. I want to be carried through existence, like on the Mississippi, slow and warm.'

'Remember, Dora,' Julie says. 'Those camels will not walk unless you sing to them. Remember the caravaners, on the road, their bundles bound with birch-bark, those prayer-wheels made in Lanzhou – how they all sang, the cosmopolitans, Manichaeans, Nestorians, Zoroastrians! That's your destiny, for sure.'

'Can we take a trip, then, Julie?' Dora asks. 'You'd have your arm...'

'No, Dora,' Julie says, 'It's much too dangerous. Mountains, deserts... Then, there's the boundaries. And customs. Besides, Pierre would slow us down.'

'I'd have in mind to ride,' says Pierre. 'It takes no special skill. It's Masha and the Cossacks, make it all seem complicated.'

'There's fun guys, wry guys, if we are a caravan,' says Masha. 'They'd keep us cool. And warm. The head clown...'

'The pasty one? The pointy-head?' Dora asks. 'I'm going on no trip with Mister Death, whatever jokes and rounds he knows. The guy who's law and order – but likes his little joke? No, Masha – and no tophats, no black horses, or I'm not in.'

'There is no trip,' says Julie. 'Pierre knows. You'd need some stuff to sell. Stealing the animals – there'd be cops in wait...'

'Oh Julie,' Masha laughs and pirouettes. 'You can shoot them down. Freeing the animals – that would be our thing.'

'We could be minstrels,' Pierre says. 'In them, there's no paradox, no bondage and no freedom. A band of jongleurs, juggling our repertoire from classical to humalong. But – even as I say the words – it's so banal. It's sleeping in the hay, and shovelling straw to pay our way. Street furniture, that's what we'd be.' He weeps again. 'It's all so different from when I could aspire...'

'It's acquired tastes,' Julie says. 'We can imagine it, how it would be, no clowns, no deaths, no dwarves. The rancid tea. Yak meat with bits of twig. The mountains, balding, snow-cannons and people skiing down. The truck-stops with TV. The caves with frescoes scissored out, and full of shit. Waiting at the borders – writing in your log about the blue, the quiet.'

'You're so snide, Julie,' Masha says. 'You want to sit inside, not ride shotgun.'

'There's no inside,' says Dora. 'We're used to having the machinery around – the ropes, the ring, the special sand, the mountains made of oriental men – how'd we manage, when it's all outside, raw and rude?'

'Forget the scenery,' says Julie. 'That's always scuffed and full of emptied tracks. This could be our act. A Recessional, like Buffalo Bill. I could shoot, Pierre aspire. Masha on the leading horse, Dora with cartwheels bearing up the rest of us. With cameras and moving photographs as souvenirs.'

'What would be the point of that?' asks Dora. 'Why's the hard work mine?'

'It's our life,' says Julie. 'What we can do, have done.'

'It's too sad for me,' says Pierre. 'Besides, it means we have survived. That's not so sure.'

'That would be just us,' says Dora. 'People looking on – they have real lives. We're not part of that. We're figures, dancing on the spinning wheel. Not masters, and not slaves.'

'Our horses,' Julie says, 'they are our slaves. I hate this gun. I guess I'll have to use it, pacifism notwithstanding.'

'They're Arab, Julie,' Masha says. 'They're not our slaves – maybe our pseudo-slaves. And you, Julie – you have the gun, that makes you warrior. But – more mercenary than master, I suspect.'

'Fuck you, Masha,' Julie shouts, 'I'm not a bought soul. For me, the cash springs up like mushrooms – I stoop to pick it up, but I don't bow my head.'

'A typically fascist view,' Masha shouts back. 'More bread for you and screw the rest of us. You stuff with truffles, wave your gun – it's true, my horses just go round and round but... If I told them, they'd be free, dash off in straight lines, plunge into the sea, dragging Apollo's chariot... I love the Arabs – let them leave the oil beneath the sand... I'll ride my stallions...'

'Are you Plague or Penury?' asks Dora. 'We are sporty types. We go on foot, love everyone until they do us down...'

'You're back on to my fucking foot,' Pierre shouts: 'I have to go by cab, whether with horse or engine. I'm mister moderate, I'll cuddle with you all...'

'Enough,' says Masha, firmly. 'This way, before we have a destiny we'll all split up, and Pierre will lie helpless in the hedge. Or – he can hop, I guess. A little ludicrous, but still...'

'Yes,' says Pierre. 'I meant to reach the height, if not the pinnacle. But now – all this commune stuff, the trip, the new society – it's all pissing up a rope, you guys.' He waited, but the others cannot laugh. 'We're already bound into our round, the horses – if they had a wish, an easy one to grant – they wouldn't chose to gallop on and on arriving at no place, just to get their hay, with prancing on their backs, makeup, and applause... Their fate – becomes our way as well. Where's the dignity in that? for them, for us?

And freedom: they've no use, except for dissolution into glue and turning into leather pants...'

'Oh Pierre,' says Dora, 'you've been brought so low... You lived without the truth so long – now it's overwhelming you...'

'There's too few of us,' says Julie, 'sitting here clueless in this caravan, that doesn't move unless it's towed. There's the riggers...'

'Oh, they're sailors who have lost their ships,' says Masha. 'The ships have lost their seas – they're in the depths. The matelots – each port we reach – it's treasure island. They go off and rob. To them, it's all in nature – the houses, the people like savages, you take what you want because they don't know ... not about property, or retribution. What can we do with them, the sailors, up there on the masts? Or – there's the elephant man, Dora – try to speak to him...'

'You're racist, Masha,' Dora says. 'It's true, we have no common language. And just for now – no common plan.'

'Then there's the cannon,' Julie says. 'Maybe they'll take a person, load them in – and fire them at this caravan, and we'll be pressed, quite flat and one-dimensional, like green beans in a can that's squashed.'

'Then use your gun,' Pierre says, and laughs. 'Shoot back!'

'Listen!' Julie says – there is a roar, a crash, the caravan is rocked.

'Someone must go outside and see,' says Pierre. 'A scout. I'll be the wounded warrior you call upon when all else fails. Be sure I'll save anyone of you who's left alive.'

'It's arms and legs,' says Masha, peering out. 'It's clear we are suspected, and someone else has volunteered to make a show. They call it suicide – but really, they make themselves a projectile. It requires a better name – human cannonballs go far far back, into the dawn of antique times. Or else – maybe it's an execution: a person even more unpopular than us – for after all, we're innocent.'

'Yes,' says Julie; with her gun she pokes the mess. 'It's arms and legs for sure.'

'No doubt, it's just the lions' lunch,' says Dora. 'Who it was, the meat – it isn't clear.'

'The lions have had their day,' says Pierre. 'Back to the forest for them. Free and unwanted.'

'It's Julie's fault,' Masha says. 'Her dalliance. The communism. It doesn't fit the circus.'

'Not me!' Julie shouts. 'The old guy – communism, the camp fire – was his primal scene. It never lived. It roams, a ghost, quite unrevivable. Like Pierre's heel.'

'We all must have a ghost,' says Dora. 'That lives inside, that makes us die, a progeny that never lives.'

'I don't have one!' Masha says. 'The cannon – just a nuisance, or a joke.'

'It could have been a chimp,' says Pierre. 'They load the gun and crawl inside. They cry at night for better lives...'

'Maybe when we all were chimps,' says Julie. 'We could have had the communism.'

'Maybe we had it,' says Dora, angrily. 'So! But I'm for civil life, society where it's all cut up and specialised – fruit in boxes, art on walls, nature on the gelatine.'

'The dismemberment,' says Julie. 'It was a powerful portent. It could be Dora's cutting-up, everything in fits and parts. The circus is a perfect circle, where we show we can be perfect, cooperate with the rude beasts, even those poodles, and the clowns... When it breaks, the crystal bowl...'

'It was Pierre's fall,' says Dora. 'It broke the symmetry, the roundedness.'

'It was nothing biblical,' says Pierre. 'Just distraction. Maybe a hero doesn't think of anything but heroism – but an epic has its scansion; an up, a down. Second chances are abundant. You griping monsters – paladins of golden youth! Accept it – you grow old: perfection – up leaping like a silver salmon, turns into king otter, brown and fusty – those baccy-yellow rabbit teeth – down in the mud. Age makes you into clowns – those pink potty pates, the hair that sprouts like pampas grass from ears and nose – ah yes! – the nose; pores stretched and ready to release a spray of pepper ... that noble nose ruined with a blast of partridge shot, a stream of inconvenience, of baby snot... Yes, my friends, that is to come. If you stay here, of course: accept the golden loss, your plating wears and bares the copper core... And none of it my fault!'

'Your cripple's foot, dear Pierre,' says Dora, much annoyed. 'You think it earns a ride on top.. But no! You lope and twitch and stagger on – you are the jester, Pierre, the merry beggar, on your string, a lurcher quite mispatched...'

'Yes, Dora,' says Pierre. 'Let's hear it all – your spite! Your feelings – come right out, a sticky web that catches you, bundles you up – from lady spider into sexless fly. The point is – we're expelled. Perfection – you can't set its terms. It's not an act...'

'What is it then, Pierre?' asks Julie. 'It's what you wanted. You made the definition.'

'No, Julie,' Pierre says. 'I didn't know how the rope would end – just that I'd be there ... the summit, and the view. Applause – but you're too high to hear. Maybe it's waves, maybe the swish of planets on their gyre, of stars folding in to mush...'

'That stew of limbs,' says Masha, picking over them. 'Maybe it isn't pussy's pieces – but ... Pierre! That trick, the rope trick – the boy sent up, comes down into the basket, quartered, maybe reconstituted, maybe not...'

'Oh, that's not one of mine,' says Pierre. '*I* went up the rope – no boy! Colonial legend, nothing more.'

'This flesh,' says Masha, 'it's quite perfect. Maybe from a statue. The head – they say it's singing in the stream. But – these arms – who needs more, to see perfection?'

'No, Masha,' Julie says. 'Statues aren't made of living flesh.'

'Of course – the difference is minimal,' says Masha. 'The form is all.'

'Oh no,' says Dora. 'It's Egypt that's the apex – expression, interpretation. Besides – these are monkey legs.'

'They're still perfection,' Masha says. 'Don't be provincial, Dora.'

'You're wrong,' says Pierre. 'It's the faith. Not the form – it's always the afflatus – it's the breath that stirs, it may be arsenic green and papier-mâché – but if it saves your soul – that is eternity.'

'Exactly what's wrong,' Julie says. 'It may sound vulgar to you – but what's missing is motion. Movement. That's what we must do – move. We'll be a clan, with our own laws, and goods and bads – we'll nestle where the money is, but a clan isn't about money, though if there's none, it disappears...'

'We've always been a clan,' says Dora. 'Just now it's tiny. Only us. Like a mafia, like Scots, or bandits.'

'What'll we do?' Julie asks.

'You mean accomplish?' Dora asks. 'We'll pass the time. you'll see, it slips away. That's all it knows how to do. Round the corner – it's gone. So shall we be.'

'We'll join the fight,' says Julie. 'In a modest way. Homeland. That sounds cosy.'

'Off we go, stealing the minimum,' says Masha, fearing for her horse, its fate on straight roads, no whooping, and no rearing up.

'Find a cart for Pierre,' says Dora. 'In the back there's chariots and unicycles, bathchairs and palanquins.'

'Lying on my back,' says Pierre, 'I'll only see the sky...'

'How we shall envy you,' says Dora, spooning porridge into him.

'Dora, you're so brusque,' says Julie, hiding her elephant gun beside him in his rugs. 'Maybe we should dump him, they'll take him in. He's pitiful, and they'll be full of pity...'

'No,' says Dora. 'We stay together till we die. Pierre – stretched out, seeing the blue, the clouds – we know he'll be the first. Horizontal so – he loved the vertical, now he'll be replete with paradise before he's even gotten there.'

She pulls Pierre's litter, Julie pretends to push behind. 'What is this thing?' asks Pierre, bound horizontal, seeing only blue and clouds, sometimes the rain – invisible and colourless – comes tidal in.

'It's a tricycle,' says Dora, taking command – 'You pedal on your back, it's for a trick.'

'It's diabolical,' says Pierre, 'a travesty of higher things. I can't pedal, as you know...'

'Mouth shut, Pierre,' shouts Dora. 'Overhead are cranes...'

'When I am really dead,' says Pierre. 'Lie me down, face down, in whatever earth you find.'

Masha scouts, runs round and round. 'You've planned the order for our deaths,' she says. 'It's clear, it's first Pierre. What do our special gifts admit? More time? More joy? Or just more graft... Tell us, dear Dora...'

'Long lives? Is that what you expect? Reward? Masha, you have it wrong,' says Dora, tugging at the cycle's rope. 'Survival and your gift – whatever that might be – have no connection. Life is partly logic, mostly accident – and I've the gift to understand how this all interacts.'

'Dora pulls hardest,' Masha says to Julie. 'But when Pierre's gone – maybe one of us two is next.'

'I've my gun,' says Julie. 'I'm not bothered. We're not a metaphor, nor an allegory. When Pierre's dead, we'll go our way. If not before. The thing is – to avoid mountains. They make you work still harder.'

Masha insists, 'We two, we're progressives. Dora's dance is quite reactionary – burying the hero. Don't get involved, Julie. She'll make you use your gun.'

'I'm progressive, Masha, naturally,' says Julie. 'Even though I don't know about progress... I think I might not believe in that too much.'

'We could be close in other ways,' says Masha, taking Julie's hand.

'Oh, there's far too much to worry about, Masha,' Julie says, pulling away. 'I can't engage with that.'

'Of course, Julie,' Masha says, 'you're bourgeois – nothing wrong with that. It comes down through your parents. Not that they were fascists, I'm quite sure – it's just you see the map a certain colour, you're used to having your own way.'

'No, Masha,' Julie says. 'My parents were a humble pair – and when they separated, both became quite poor. That is the law. It protects us all, Masha, even if you think it's crap and try to get around it when you can.'

They plod on in silence. Dora is trained, she strides ahead, pulling Pierre as if the rig is weightless.

'We might just sneak away,' says Masha. 'But those arms and legs – we must hypothesise – there was a death somehow...'

'There is no evidence,' says Julie. 'Dora cooked them up, and put them in our rolls. I couldn't stand the hairs...'

'Oh, I can take some hairiness in legs,' says Masha. 'My horse was covered in it.'

'It's quite a different thing,' says Julie. 'A meal is sitting round and pondering. A ride's just holding on.'

On the ascents – Dora is strong – but the descent... Whoa! and 'there he goes'. This is a desert sort of place, with caves and tumuli, huts with corrugated roofs, and far away the tricycle, come to rest, Pierre too, in his rest, his *pax eterna*... The quest – his – confronted, interrupted, then abbreviated. Nothing to be done. The accidents proliferate when you have only purloined circus stuff, pressed into service, improvised, nothing to grip, no pal to catch you, shout 'olé' in case you slip and smash.

'Now what?' asks Dora. 'Our purpose, our incentive – gone to pulp against a rock.' Too soon to weep – 'You fucking useless chatterers,' she shouts at Julie, Masha – who're quite indifferent, except – 'Oh no!' says Julie. 'See – my gun is bent.'

'Oh, that will do for frightening,' says Dora, losing patience. 'No bullets and no aim – you couldn't have held off hordes of guys like we have here, drunk or stoned as they may be, watching their television in their shacks...'

'You're caustic,' Masha says. 'Now is survivor time. Think of us!'

'Pierre is broken,' Dora says. 'Twice, and now for good. We leave him here. That is what you do. No one leaves much – it all should fit into a nut shell,' and she points down to the tricycle – 'His nut, his nut shell – it's quite pulped. You two should prepare to leave your little trace – just like Pierre did.'

'I feel I've seen the world. The stars, too, I think,' says Masha. 'And there's nothing I can leave. I've had nothing, nothing is what's left.'

'Well, Dora, what's the bundle you're bequeathing?' Julie asks, 'in case you have a fall.'

'Of course,' says Dora, 'I miss Pierre – that's all you can ever do for what has disappeared. But, my friends – let's bunk down here. Night falls fast in these latitudes, the bulbuls tune their string, the fauna wake or sleep, wherever we've arrived. I miss the frontiers, too – they told you where you were, what the people might be like. I think we're in Slovakia – or Poland. Even Austria. You see – it's indeterminate. Croatia? Slovenia even?'

'I can't sleep on earth,' says Julie. 'I need to say a prayer. I always have a pillow, and a scarf to wind around. I don't believe, of course, but every night I make a list of who is good or bad, and who's been on my side, and who I'd never miss... It's a prayer that makes each day a history – and I'm the judge and archivist...'

'You're an obsessive, Julie,' Masha says, pulling away. 'Cracking your knuckles, making snail whorls with your locks... You're just a little creature...'

'Yes,' says Julie, 'and I'm proud. To go to sleep, I have this gravelly road to travel down, the houses all have hollyhocks and poppies in their yards, a dog with spots, black brown and white...'

They're all asleep. They wake. 'This is the life,' shouts Masha, quite restored.

*

'I'll go and fight,' says Julie. 'Maybe not quite in combat. But I'll choose a side, a cause, and then enrol. No one does better than that. Defend the huddled masses, values, your integrity. Like the old guy said – "it lives on in the spirit – in the flesh, it putrefies".'

'Just imagine, Julie,' Masha says, 'those hairy people, paid to fight beside you. If you win – they won't want you along with them, and if you're dead ... well, that's your integrity!'

'Oh Masha,' Julie says, 'there's many consequences, not just tombs and tears.'

'Well, Julie,' Masha says, 'when you have found them – tell me. Tell me who's paying for your show. It all connects – I have a mind to seek some splashy guy, with mills for slaves, and foundries where the foundlings work, and refuges for refugees – the whole panoply... It's like a river, suddenly it sees the sand, and runs to irrigate: Cash, Julie! And then there's grass grows, and horses. Maybe an eland, and a goose...'

'Masha,' says Dora, 'the goose is you. You'll carry rich men's bags, and then they dump you, scuffed, unlabelled. Or they hitch with you, some Bluebeard finds a niche and bricks you in.'

'Of course,' says Masha, undeterred, 'you need to know the rules, and how to cheat. You, Dora? Do you pick up Pierre's flag, jump on his steed?'

'I plan to take a lot of paths,' says Dora, 'so's not to end like him. Training: that's my key. I'll work in therapy –

there's lots to learn, and then discard. I'll find out every secret, every knot and split in upright timbers, like the ones you want to bed with, Masha dear. Then – there's intelligence: it all links up. The guys who frighten you with terrorism: – you see, the mind's like polished wood. Imagine in your head, there is a shuffleboard: you have your rocks well placed – a winning pattern. All hang so delicate. Then – here comes another spinning piece – off to the gutter go the winning rocks – those that were poor Julie's values, say – and here's another certainty, hanging in. Poised, vulnerable. Cock of the board. It's polished wood, my friends. Nothing sticks, if all's prepared with wax and sand. And then there's cash, the river Masha sees, comes snaking in. Just think of tiny termites, humble coins, all scurrying round – and then a heap of masticated shit erects – an anthill fifty metres high, with soldiers, mothers, heirs and heiresses, and priests of every faith and none, and generals... And I'm the one to suss them out and keep the score...'

'I see all that,' says Julie. 'Maybe everything that's ever been can work like that. But once you know – it's all banal. The vision, Dora – up you go, you slip, you fall. The vision is still there – even further up and more inviting. You can't climb back, and up – you're lame – but in your head...'

'I know, I know,' says Dora. 'In the end, I'll go to scientific mysticism – runes, advice, expertise and commentary. Fame, or anonymity – I'll have known everything. Success, and failure – it all cancels out. I'll settle for extensive wisdom; being a sage.'

'Are you on my side, Dora – I wonder?' Julie says.

'Who's on mine?' asks Masha.

'I expect we've something that we share,' says Dora. 'Not much – but you two didn't work on that. And Pierre has gone. What might bind us?'

'The past,' says Masha, 'you forget that, Dora. The circus family – we all grew up in it, or wish we had, and that it had been more kindly. On the trapeze at four years old! Remember!'

'See what it's done to Julie,' Dora says. 'The past, mistaken for the present.'

'I love it,' Julie says, 'I read it with my passion – they did so much so quick, so strange, and left their portraits before there was the camera ... bigger than life.'

'I eat the mushroom,' Dora says, 'not the horse-crap that it grows in.'

'You leave so much out,' says Julie. 'Passion – that hits you like a war, unsuspected – fight, suffer, run or cheer. And our virtues – humanism, imposed on others, planted like it was an empire flag.'

'Very neat,' says Dora. 'You know, Julie, leaving things out – it guarantees continuity. It all comes round again, it must. It's all dying always, Julie, what we know, it's all yesterdays, opera: the circus won't go on – it's bits and pieces, odds and sods, you have to work at it and grunt and sweat. Grunting and sweating – those aren't for us, not our stuff at all – we got out well. Leave it to other guys with nothing but their bodies to exploit...'

'Is this your being sage?' Masha asks Dora.

'It will do for now, Masha,' Dora says. 'We'll trudge out of this barren place, our hero waiting, crashed, down there, waiting for the legends and the songs to gather round... We'll separate, and in a while, meet up and see where each has reached, and who was right, and who has failed.'

★

'Or else,' says Masha, 'we could cut it short. We know now where we want to go. So – where we are now – this will be our past. We'll eat our future – tonight's dinner.'

'If it takes ten years to be where we want to be, and where we really were, there, us, ourselves, in the future somewhere – I might not even be alive,' says Julie.

'Then it can be your short eternity,' says Dora. 'It's true – I'm as wise as I shall ever be. Why go through it all – the trials, the booze, the people, leaving their smell on us...? Right now – we can go there and back. Tell how it will be, without the fuss of living through.'

'How would it be for you?' Julie asks Masha.

'If I didn't want to run a man, I could run an office, I suppose,' says Masha. 'But youth – no; less and less of that's available. The young ones take it all – the drugs, emotion, people beating up on you, the tests for everything – the accidents, the awful men waiting like hunters with their little guns a-cock... No – it's turned out not to be me at all.'

'Julie – you'd be dead – so there's no point. Maybe you'd leave a diary,' Dora says. 'Not many are much fun. You could go anywhere, everybody wants a homeland, where it's just them and friends, and military cemeteries.'

Julie says, 'Forget the massacres, the rights, the wrongs, the guys backstage who hold the ropes and spread the net or let it drop. Causes are just – forget the rest. And yet – even the homelands can be bleak. Your friends are maybe not your friends. At night you hear the cop cars and the shouts. Well, you go on – you can't be Ottomans and just go on and on... And then – well, home's a complicated thing ... there's always people who can't wait to leave...'

'A true reactionary, Julie – that's what comes from carrying a gun and hassling guys,' says Dora. 'My public may be different – and I don't ask.'

'So, we're all sceptics?' Masha asks. 'Is that to be the sum of what we'll do? Now what? We all had brilliant futures, now we're back here without them. I suppose I could weave a tent... There's no one round about to come and be enveigled.'

'Art is art, even if it isn't seen. That's what they tell the spiders and the snowflakes,' Dora says.

'Maybe you hadn't thought,' says Julie. 'People falling down – they make no noise. Hardly. Asking for food – they don't shout. Breaking stones – they don't sing. If I must, I'd have a drum, and sound it for the silent ones.'

'That's your conclusion, Julie? That's your gift? It amounts to stick and skin and air,' says Masha. 'Conjuring each living thing to stick up out its burrow.'

'It's a parade, Masha, a march,' says Julie. 'That's why you need a drum. It's not the species, Masha, just the end of some – you see them – the elephants that trek, and lost their way. You can tell – you watch the birds, their spiralling. We'd be like that – birds in the tent, from perch to twig... except there'd be no cadavers there, not one...'

'This way, we've avoided lots of bad,' says Dora. 'Of good too, no doubt, but – why do I feel not doing all that bad ends up in the good account, although you've not done anything at all? Most people are like you, Julie – they use the animals as metaphor – the blue bird good, and unattainable, the rat – pedalling in your sleeping-bag and in your gut ... all the stuff that's hard to live with, the remorse, regret and loss – the thing itself you did. We know all about the animals, the loving care we lent them, making them do what they didn't want and never thought. Our will, our

cash, our culture – the fleas, made to prance in livery and
pull the coach, wear small fur coats and high-heeled shoes,
a golden watch and push-up bras... Nothing escapes, dear
Julie, no one runs, crosses the barrier, jumps the ditch,
finds the safe refuge, the medic or the armourer – no, hear
the shot? From Julie's gun, or else it's Masha's whip...'

'It was my first thing,' says Masha, 'cracking the whip.
Before the alphabet and sex. Besides, Dora – I have fleas. I
don't think they do tricks. I'm certain they're not clothed.'

'You're their savannah, Masha,' Dora says. 'You're just
right for them. That figure on your body – the golden angel
... site for pilgrimage, I guess. Against your skin – almost
invisible. You should have told us, though, you were
imprinted. It's for the high wire, I expect, we're all certain
to be up there too, our bodies working together, wards on a
lock – a handstand on a chair above the chasm, it's nothing
if you're fit. I don't know if they can be happy, fleas: they're
busy. That's the best. Cohabitation. It's like Julie – all those
guys she shot at – the right side? Who cares now, all
anybody wants is finding people they can get along with.
Allies. In it together. Being in the same squad, regiment,
whatever you're called upon to do. This insight – I didn't
invent it, I distilled it. Maybe I saw it written somewhere.'

'You don't think so much about morality,' says Julie.
'Hiding behind a wall. Knocking it down.'

'Well, of course not, dear,' says Dora.

'They give you packets of some stuff,' says Julie. 'When
you're in a spot. It's called "shampoo" – you mustn't put in
on your hair, it turns it white.'

'I know my wisdom is banal,' says Dora, wearily. 'It has
to be that way so I am understood. But for us three – it has
no grip, I know. Maybe – we should stand upon each
others' heads, and gain some trust – Julie on top, she's

lightest, least experienced. If we crumble, she's been trained, she learnt survival when she's dropped from 'planes. Now, Julie – raise your arms, embrace the sun!'

'What should I say?' asks Julie, perched on top.

'Oh, anything,' says Masha, wavering with strain. 'The motto of the sun is *carpe diem*, but of course, she does not hear.'

'Oh Sun,' Julie shouts out, 'lead us to the evening lands, and ever on, to where you sleep ... hear the sound of bulbuls calling us to prayer, give us our daily light ... up, up you go, so slow, reluctantly you rise ... to work, or else it is oblivion...'

'Hopplà!' shouts Masha. 'Well put, Julie, and now jump down.'

'There, Julie,' Dora says. 'You can read a map. You know this is the centre of the world.'

'Yes,' Julie says, 'I know. But not what it might involve.'

'It involves *you*, Julie,' Dora says.

'We don't like each other, but we have to trust. We don't know the rules, the laws, that function here, nor who may come up the hill, over the crest behind us,' Julie says, hurrying on, not listening.

'We've something precious,' Dora says. 'It's worth defending, even if you don't know what it is.'

'Oh,' says Masha. '*I* know. It's the training, and the trust.'

*

'Ours is the kind of organisation that attracts speculation,' Dora says. 'There's a whiff of originality, and of money. It's lean, it rests on the closest personal ties. It's professional, it's always near to making records...'

'Over that hill,' Masha says, 'there's a little store: they sell everything we need.'

'You know,' Dora goes on, 'in this area, there's bands of guys – not looking for trouble, but for money. Not *our* money. The continent is full of them, they used to be called "enchanted wanderers" – they're not enchanted any more. Some are so pissed off, they don't wander now, except for up and down the corridors. Treat them with respect – we're foreigners here too, and want to be treated likewise, with respect. Even more. No merit, none at all.'

'Here's pathos!' Masha shouts. 'A house – a sketch ... a shell ideal for crabby runaways. Some guy gone to work in Germany, never coming back. It'll suit us fine.'

'It's the place where you wait for Wozzeck,' Julie says, and shudders. 'There's even the pond. I have the knife, the reputation too.'

'Come on!' says Dora. 'I managed to shorten your existences, cutting out the tedium, the blur and blot. That's wisdom – not the knife. I won't have you selling sex, Julie – it isn't worth it. It has no price, at all events, they say. Masha – you'll play the horses. There's lots round here – they're sure to run them off against the book. Julie can help you get your winnings... It's only temporary for us...'

'Lying here,' says Masha. 'We see only some of the stars, none of the clouds, that Pierre saw. We're adrift. Even the sky – the lovely blue is dirt. If it were clean, we'd see it black.'

'Masha,' Dora says. 'We'll fix a roof – although ... enclosure... You may need it, I sure don't. I'll protect you. Some have the Prophet that protects – at least, consoles. Religion promises a gentle death, relax, sometimes – recreation. I promise nothing – day by day, you'll keep watch, and I'll assess the risks. Remember – we tumblers,

we contain the globe... Siam and China, bending into
pyramids, Japan and actors pretending to be animals,
unusual monkeys ... the shamans and their sleight of hand –
the rope that executes, but also exits you from jail.'

'It's only temporary,' Julie says. 'I'm glad. I like to hear
the tick and tock of someone measuring out my time – but
then – there's also standing down, and cleaning kit, and
polishing your gun.'

'There's no chimney,' Masha says.

'That's right,' says Dora, 'in my house, nothing is
consumed.'

'Building a house,' says Masha, 'you start with the
chimney.'

'That's not how I see it,' Dora says, impatiently. 'There's
no bell either – but listen!'

'A flower!' says Julie. 'Harebell? A cow. Or a train. A
church. A sleigh ... a book, a candle...'

'There!' says Dora. 'It's like the suitcase, under the bed,
with all the clothes for dressing-up, the passports and the
Luger. "Oh the chimneys" – you want that? lives short and
going up in smoke? The bell tolls – it doesn't tell! Pierre
failed. He died. Me – I don't want to leave a trace in
history. To do that, you have to die. It's a fact – Julie does
what she is told. Masha leaves it all to chance. I don't: I
have no past. I'm the naked figure in the light, twisting and
twisted, going nowhere, a idea white, eternal. You two –
you can be mine, no past, no history. No lies, no cover-up,
no malice, and no venom. I'd like to say – no house, no
passport. No treading on this ground, no blood upon your
precious feet. Forget about being human – cherish the
immortality you both have in you – you know what I'm
referring to. We'll see...'

★

'If you want to keep the rain off,' Julie says, 'we'll stretch some canvas over.'

'It'll seem less squalid so,' says Masha. 'Water's not my element – it's the clowns that throw it everywhere.'

'Dora doesn't notice,' Julie says. 'She's an acrobat. With that, you have to concentrate.'

'Up the hill, Julie – and we're away,' says Masha. 'Any time you want...'

It rains. The clouds sail high above – maybe it's Slovakia. The bands of rootless men swarm all around, not finding what they want. Nor what anybody wants.

'Dora,' Masha shouts. 'Julie's been hurt, kicked in. She went behind my horse, singing a song...'

'Stove in,' says Dora. 'On her golden angel too. She's quite flat – those ribs – she's an umbrella inside out.'

'She's a hedgehog,' Masha says, 'turned outside in. Can she be saved?'

'It's not my beat,' says Dora. 'Mine is the talk.'

'Maybe the men ... they're doctors, probably,' Masha says.

'My angel...' Julie sobs. 'Concave.'

'Don't cry, Julie,' Dora says, taking command. 'Even if you die, as probably you will, now or after – you have the spirit. Or, better, you have had it. You have understood...'

'Fuck the spirit,' Julie shouts. 'I am broken up.'

'The horse? The song?' asks Dora.

'No mark on either,' Masha says. 'It was the Song of Destiny – "water dripping from rock unto rock..."'

'That was a hazard,' Dora says, 'The Brahms – so far from home. "Blindly, we all pass away..." It was unfair to the horse too. We all get scared by that music.'

'Inflate me,' Julie begs. 'Pump me up, guys!'

'You may have the words wrong, Julie,' Dora says, 'though we can't check. There are some high notes – you should teach the children.'

'There's no children, Dora,' Masha says. 'Those men are too young. There's no way there'll be children.'

'You two,' says Dora. 'You know I don't watch over you. Maybe I should, and keep you safe. Safer. I don't keep you here. There's nothing to make you stay, I know. Nothing special. Probably it's not secure – people roam around. There's no doctors available, or not enough. In the old regime, people had long lives, and wished they hadn't. It had arrived where it was going. If you want to leave – tell me. I'd probably come with you. Masha – you'd have more chances somewhere else. Julie – more stimulus, love, money, somewhere to work from.'

'My golden angel,' Julie sobs, 'distorted.'

'It protected you,' says Masha. 'There's a guy I know – he'll do the restoration.'

'I shouldn't let him touch you, Julie,' Dora says.

'Oh, he was famous everywhere,' says Masha. 'Tattoos and body paint retouched – he was the best. Not everyone there, in that land, could have tattoos – that did for him. He ran. He'll touch up Julie's angel. She won't feel it, hardly anything. He was a hero too, saving people, all that... He's lucky that's all over now – he can start it all from scratch, skins, friends, people, everything.'

'The important thing,' says Dora, 'is keep on breathing. Concentrate on that, poor Julie.'

The guy bends over Julie, tries not to look at her breasts. 'Those wings – it's like Aya Sofya,' says the guy – 'except there's nipples tucked away in there, half hidden in the feathers. Holy Wisdom – hmmm, I'm not convinced that's what they hold. This here's my sternum hook – I pull you out, and you're cylindrical again. The horse – was not so tall, or it would be your head.'

'No,' says Masha, 'but it would have seated two. I'm used to that – and others standing on, or underneath.'

'I'll stay here,' Julie says. 'It's aimless, but the ride to Germany is worse. We'll call on you, Khalil, if we get kicked again.'

'It's quite specialised, what I do,' he says. 'Just doing that – I'd starve.'

'Oh, we can't pay you,' Dora says. 'It would cost a fortune, what you do.'

'Icons!' says Masha. 'They are big round here. You could attempt – it's formulaic, and you can't go wrong.'

'Easy to say!' Khalil says.

'My angel isn't religious,' Julie says. 'Not at all! It's my own talisman.'

'You're fortunate,' Khalil says, 'to have one of your own, even though it didn't work.'

'There, Julie,' Dora says, 'you're our golden girl again. Don't go near the horses. You know why I brought you here...'

'You went on,' Masha says. '"Forward" you said it was, where we were going to. Pulling your perfect Pierre, brought low and useless.'

'Well, Masha,' Dora says, 'you can speak to people here. Maybe you know how it was. Not so good, I'd say – but trying hard. Being things not seen for centuries, that I'd not want to see again. And now, we can't go further on. It's all destroyed. And going back? You haven't got the granite in you – you run like chickens, here and there. Prepare, you two! Heresy is in your hearts, and fear as well – the worst subjects to resist a siege... Imagine – suppose it were all to end? Short lives – can you enjoy what you might have had?

The little that you did? That all happened in a tent, it's true: it couldn't last. An awkward landing, a leg placed wrong ... the little that's enough...'

'It was just a show,' says Julie. 'I was on guard, in case it all got out of hand – stronger than a safety net, my gun. I never needed it – those lions were too afraid...'

'It's no one's fault,' says Masha. 'No one's responsible, so nothing can be changed.'

'I was there for fun,' says Julie. 'I would not have fired. I was on their side.'

'Oh the poor horses, round and round they go,' says Masha. 'I couldn't bear it. And my showng off ... bad cheese!'

'You were right,' says Dora. 'To do it, and after, to despise yourself. I was the same, waiting for Pierre, reaching the top, apotheosis. It couldn't be. The clown – down he went! The clumsiness – in him, his common fault, right from the start.'

'It could be done no other way,' says Julie. 'The management were right – it was the only way to get some fans, book the best acts. Masha – what a delight you were!'

'Listen,' Dora says. 'You're slow, you two, you slow me down. I showed you idiots the short cut. Discard the lives that can't be lived without accidie. But no! You bog down. You're nondescript, and mediocre. I'm off! I can't stand you, or this place. Death would be an indulgence... Here, there's nothing left to steal.'

★

She runs up the hill, away from the unfinished house. She's right – she's given Julie, Masha, nothing; worse, they haven't understood that they should give her life, invention, lots of love. Julie, Masha, they're like all the others, roaming, stopping, growing roots, blooming, fading, rotting. All you can do – is leave them – there's bands of hungry guys'll take them up...

'You circus animals,' says the guy, the Gaukler – juggler, conjurer. 'You run and run – it's all part of your act. Look, Dora – what you do is this: you rent a room, an office, for a day. Have interviews and make a squad. Then, you've a month before you need to pay, you've time to think of what you all can do.'

'That's what *you* do,' says Dora. 'Fortunes, Gaukler. I can't concentrate enough. I had a team, but they went round and round.'

'Then,' he says, 'change your face. Go into movies. Hire good guitarists, steal their riffs – write songs. Do rehab, change your sex. Book stadiums ... die by your own hand beneath the lights.'

'There!' says Dora. 'Said it like I do. What's the point, doing it all, in what they call real time?'

'Ah well,' the Gaukler says. 'You want immortality. I'm looking hard, and when I find it, it'll only be for me! You're tough, Dora, but not enough – or rather, you're indifferent. You won't survive. What you have – won't do at all – the world's still round, but all *en craquelature*, an old pot quite unmendable.'

He picks up the round pot, grey-white, small blurs of red, and black, gold, blue, but crazed, the glazing worn, the cracks like wrinkles all around. He throws it up, and up, and spins it round, and keeps it spinning, while he adds some other globes – some like water-filled balloons, and some grey pebbles – puts them all into a circle, catching, despatching, swearing, not dropping one – 'You see,' he pants, 'the different size and weight – that is the bugger of it all...'

'It's wonderful, dear Glauker, dear Uwe,' Dora says. 'You shouldn't give it up. It is your art.'

'Oh,' says the juggler, 'I am the sun. I'm the last one who retires: even if a few get dropped – it's just "Olé" and on – all in the act.'

'Where I was, we didn't mix, of course,' says Dora, 'but there were too many accidents. Not a place where anything gets done – it's Babylon without the tower. No common language, lots of claggy mud.'

'You could have stayed and built it up,' says the juggler. 'The Tower. Halfway to space.'

'People will come – they come to see most things. It's out of time, the contracts too – but it would have brought you fame... To do it well, you'd need communism – maybe they didn't think of it.'

'Before starting something new, I should come clean about myself. It's true – I let Pierre go,' says Dora. 'He'd have let me slip, so's he could climb the height – but didn't have the chance. So, he alone's responsible. Then, I cured poor Julie – Masha was to blame. The horse – I didn't frighten it – it must have been the fault of Masha, she didn't want to ride away with Julie on the pillion... Oh dear, that German music... And tell me, Gaukler: myself – have I let myself go, slip, slide?'

'It's true,' the Gaukler says, juggling still, 'you're rather straggly. The mud, the straw... The German music didn't play a part.'

'Guilt, blame,' Dora says, 'what do those mean? I've hardly started changing things – and already I feel no remorse.'

'Of course,' the Gaukler, Uwe, says, 'our profession –
our calling, our striving – takes the colour out of us. We're
angels, soldiers – of course, you don't look in us for
personality, emotions...'

'Julie had an angel, and a gun,' says Dora, trying to find
colours appropriate – 'She was blonde – and Masha, dark.'

'If you feel you have to suffer, Dora,' Uwe says, 'you
could join up...'

'That's not it,' says Dora, 'you've just said so.'

Uwe knows she's right. He eliminates one globe on each
circuit, until only the shabby off-white pot is circling.

'See,' says Uwe. 'It's all Galileo, the falling bodies –
falling, accelerating, with no effort. Then, try throwing
them up! But once you do the sum – juggling starts from,
and arrives at, what is true. It's dull. There is nothing more
– no deities, no finer thoughts, no project, no other
loveliness, no other reasoning, no spreading of the wings to
cuddle huddled masses. All you have's the truth, sculpted
in your head...'

'That's what Masha said,' says Dora, 'round and round.
There are regrets – on the trapeze, you miss your tail. It's a
great absence. You're unstable, everything requires a
compensating...'

'You learn all this too late,' says Uwe. 'When you want
to leave, have already left, the tent.'

'I can't do fortunes,' Dora says. 'What they want to
know – it isn't death tonight.'

'Remember, Dora,' Uwe says. 'It's fortune that they
want, not truth. I told you – chance is the key to all belief.
The truth is stony. No one thanks you for it.'

'I talk to you, Uwe, I watch your balls, you juggling with
them, like Mister Galaxy, and I think: "What others do,
what you're supposed – it's all ridiculous. The prize. The

acclaim. It's all receding, it all slips away. Masha – she just went round and round. Talking to others, drawing them out. She was a void, herself. Julie – she'd the gun, the angel too – neither sufficed. Pierre ... tripped and trundled off.'"

'Maybe there is no prize, Dora,' Uwe says.

'There must be,' Dora says. 'Even if it's one I make myself and give to me. It requires no unanimity – there's thousands awarded every year. I have a spell to cast, I'm sure – and yet it's me who runs from crone to *mago*, seeking a clue...'

'Your hair's not bad,' says Uwe, puzzled: 'Now you're not on the rope, it's true, your breasts are covered up. Your brain is fair. Experience – you'd say exotic, if you weren't a circus type... Your character – unfeeling, and quite frantic ... forceful, though... Your birth – it gives no clout to us, we are a caste...'

'That's not it at all,' says Dora, turning away. Maybe she weeps.

'We aren't sisters, brothers, Dora,' Uwe says. 'We do everything so they should be strange to us, because we know we'll need to slay them – this one, that, who strays into our camp.'

'I'm quite prepared for this,' says Dora. 'But – there they all are! The water-sellers, camel-drivers, guys who fix your telephone...'

'It's all transformed,' Uwe says. 'We all pretend to be animals now, do ballet with our clubs and rings.'

'No, no,' says Dora. 'I must look for something else. It's always Araby, or somewhere hot – the tent, the sand, the smell of camels – that will never change.'

'The novelty's all taking off,' says Uwe. 'Higher and higher it goes. Your stuff, Dora – it's the dead past. If the new project all falls down – you'll just be standing underneath, shaking your head and staring up.'

'I want to scream, Uwe, and tear my clothes,' says Dora.

'They're already torn,' he says.

*

'I'll call the doctors,' Dora says. 'All I have's my pain.'

Masha rides off, Julie leaves – neither seen again.

*

'Self-inflicted. The dark side,' says Jonathan, the expert.

'Kicked in the head,' says Charmian. 'How can you do it to yourself? Even if you kick your height?'

'It might have been a horse,' says Dora. 'A brick fallen from a tall building. Me – falling from a tower. A punishment...'

'Quiet, Dora!' Jonathan shouts. 'Maybe they couldn't see your face. If you were veiled. Or you crossed into someone's territory.'

'We come here by 'plane at the weekends,' Charmian says, 'to diagnose.'

'I'm an artist,' Dora says. 'I'm used to tumbles.'

'There's unhappy people all around,' says Jonathan. 'Try not to cross with them, Dora. It could end much worse.'

'You could wear body armour,' Charmian says. 'Like my friends do.'

'It wouldn't be me,' says Dora.

'Avoid the joyless streets,' says Jonathan, 'or accept the cultural divides, and take it as it comes. There's murderers amongst us – keep your watch.'

'I'm used to a tent,' Dora says. 'You know who's in there – it's from the Mughals. They lived within the pointed roof, the flowery panels, hunted from them, brought back the animals; and to save their lives, the beasts – they sang and danced, and played with tassels, biffed each other ... were dressed in brocades and muslin shawls... All long ago – the memory does linger, though...'

'That could be the link,' says Jonathan: 'With your unfortunate ... in some way, your provocation. The Mughals aren't respected here.'

'Leave me,' Dora says. 'The people who could help are dead. I'm not looking for a place, just an address. Bind me up, straighten my hands.'

'We're doctors,' Jonathan says, 'we don't do cures. We fit you in a cultural group, and then we do a diagnosis. We come by plane, helping out, in these religious cities, where there's so much pain. How long do you expect to live, dear Dora? There's some who live till they can't remember if they are alive, others – they're mayfly. You started bad, by being beaten up.'

'I know,' says Dora, 'though – I might have fallen in the sand. Short lives, that's full of meat and movement – that is what I hope. The city's full of bachelors – does that make it a religious place?'

'Don't do philosophy on us,' says Charmian. 'They tried in Paris, and it didn't spread. Those guys – they read a book, and chattered on, saw a movie or a massacre – and wrote it down. They said in slow time what everybody knew. Don't try that on us. You are a victim, but you're feisty too – they cancel out.'

'Let me alone,' says Dora. 'I'm not crazed nor destitute – nor pious either. I have held on to perfection's legs, as they were arching upwards – we fell, of course; I trudged with the broken dead, then reached the marches, a hill between the nomads and the devils. And afterwards abandoned ship, my crew – hungry in the grass, besieged around.'

'Your nose will lengthen out,' says Charmian. 'Just now, it's lodged back in the bone a prevision of how you'll look, a bone-spud on the shelf, your body gone to dogs. Chickens too, I think.'

'It's been the missing episode,' says Dora. 'The kicking. Now, I know everything. Here, there's the war, love and rejection I have thought I knew. My comrades – betrayed, of course. A horse – perhaps that waits? Bucephalus? Pegasus? We're all the chosen one, of course, but I am trained ... even without a horse, the wings ... the beat...'

*

'No holy foolishness,' says Uwe. 'You're grounded, and in need. Those bandages – they give a sacred look. Maybe it gives significance to the pain you feel... I'll give you cash, my friend, if you assist me in the act...'

'No, no significance at all,' says Dora. 'And Uwe – you've no tent. Besides – I don't go backwards. No revisiting. I'm a climber, not a catcher of dropped stuff.. No tent, no circus – it's definitive. I don't perform outside and in the cold.'

'The street is where you start, and mostly end,' says Uwe. 'Your millions – come somewhere in between. What do you expect? When I do magic, out come those homing doves – do you think they come from nothing? You think it's heresy? A false creation? Or a parody?'

'No one believes you made the doves,' says Dora. 'We watch you – some of us are rich, the rest are loitering. There is no message, Uwe – just a trick.'

'My conversion earned me paradise,' says Uwe. 'Down here, for now, it's not so good. Alas, my engine, motor – it is breaking up. Starting from the head – I lose my count, how many clubs, how many swords I've tossed. There are advantages in my brand-new beliefs – although it's still the one big egg, monokrator, snug in the single basket, that you trust. Monotheism simplifies, and – if you do what's right – there is no blame for anything you do. That is the common theme – but I find the greatest comfort where I have arrived, with all my comrades, doing what is right...'

'But Uwe,' Dora says, 'you juggle and do tricks – how can blame arise from that?'

'You had your doctors, Dora? Right?' says Uwe. 'Jonathan and Charmian? Who came by plane... Well, I have doctors too, some learned ones. Ask them.'

'I'm sure you're right,' says Dora, anxious to dismiss the talk, 'I'm an athlete, Uwe: when the body goes – I'm rubbish. I'm the flower that blooms at dusk and dies at dawn, ready for the early bin.'

'Short lives,' says Uwe. 'Maybe those are best. The sinless children... Doing right – you do it once, what profit is there in a repetition?'

'No old-time religion, thanks,' Dora says: she might weep. 'Where is my good life, Uwe? When does it start?'

'You're trivial, Dora,' Uwe says. 'You're a vessel dead in dirty water.'

★

'Their intelligent eyes!' says Dora. They stand before a huge peaceful tank of fish, she and the lady, expert in fish lives. 'That's a *rascasse* for sure.'

It's red and yellow, pointed, bony crests and billows – it's a fire.

Troops of grey sprats, seized by a single inspiration, toss themselves – now, they're silver dollars, they flip their tails and scales – a score of rhythms pulsing in the mucous and the cartilege, a silence rigorous – some gambol and some lurk.

'And where is it all going?' Dora asks. 'Some are super-powerful and haughty, then there's flocks, the ones in gangs, all with identical tattoos, pacific, vegans...'

'Oh,' says the expert, 'they don't go anywhere.'

'Well, all right,' says Dora. 'Let's go inside. It's like swimming in the mercury behind the mirrorglass...'

'Oh no,' says the expert, 'we're not food. And we can't eat them.'

'I don't see your point,' says Dora.

'They've arrived where you acrobats aspired,' the lady expert says. 'They don't touch the ground. They've all your moves, they're every shape and twist.'

'And they eat so cleanly!' Dora says. 'Not like lions – that blood and scumble! Down go the little ones, swallowed smooth, the pink and purple delicacies – no struggle, no chomping at the gristle. No cry. And – you're right – they tumble and they double round – and yet the medium is thick and sticky treacle, slows it all down, those human pyramids – they'd fall so slow, no hollering, those mouths like sphynxes', always pronouncing distant languages, never a sound...'

'You must have seen fish before, Dora,' says the lady expert. 'They all do that. When you catch them – then it's Saint Lawrence! They roast in air – ah! the torment ... but you've seen the suffering...'

'You can't have too much of it, Pierre said,' says Dora. 'But – yes, you can!'

'They have nothing, nothing at all,' says the expert. 'Nothing is theirs. They scrounge. Not a pebble, not a briefcase, a pair of pants, a watch. They're like you – a body. Gladiators. Mouth, belly, anus – but you forget those when you see the movement. The perfection of the whole.'

'There's parasites,' says Dora. 'And parasites to clean the parasites.'

The pair stare, they make their sense of all the lives, concentrated – like they were involved in ceremony – a deposition, recessional, clan at a wake...

'Yes,' Dora says, 'you've made it perfect. It could be – one of our hells. The unclothed bodies circling round, waiting for ignoble deaths.'

'That's quite perverse,' the expert says. 'It's a system. That is the life, it's not the individuals' existences.'

'Oh,' Dora says, 'don't get me wrong – I'm not attached to individuals, all the big things expected of each one. The creatures here – what's their emotion? They say it's excitement for the sex, the food, – and anger. I think I'd feel the anger too, desperation muted, the little ones pretending they'll escape. All the rest, the shades of feeling – maybe they're around, under the rocks, inside the fleshy flowers... And might we talk of love, beneath the wave?'

*

'You're wrong, Dora, my dear,' says Uwe. 'Don't tell me all this crap. The water's not our medium. It's true – all kinds of crazy thing grows there – purple worms like feather boas, fish with umbrella necks and ostrich plumes – but... Dora, it is Bethlehem, or Charenton! We watch, tap on the glass.

They – the inmates – are dining on one another! We stand and marvel as the colours change, the flesh engorges, purples – to us, it's sunrise, and to them – sunset. The lady expert tips them in – each day, another bucketful. And those, instead, the huge disposing ones, their long long sharky lives, enormous journeys – pole to pole – what's it all for? What do they see? It's dodging nets and hooks – is that the good life that you seek, Dora? Or is it prettiness? A special shape?'

'It's all a point of view,' says Dora. 'Maybe next time – it's birds! If you believe – a swarm of flying dragons, waddling toads... Use your imagination, Uwe. Clues for us – they're all around! What will happen to us next, our limbs, our heads...'

'I'm firmly in the sand,' says Uwe. 'My piste. We all live there by the extraordinary, or by illusion. We leap, we climb, we make things disappear – but in the end, the mystery's revealed. Quite unmysterious. We're trained, like the seals, the poodles. We're earthy stuff. The clowns – they bring us down. Theirs is the order, theirs the trump. Ice water down the trousers – that is life, dear Dora – not the pretentious anti-gravity, the flying feather stuff.' He holds Dora tight: 'Remember Julie? Well – a troupe went out, went East. She disappeared. It seems poor Julie, with her useless gun, was welcoming the caravans... Security out there, you understand – they saw her brandishing, and took it for intent – aggression, terror, who could think there was a place of innocence, of welcome... Her angel – that will bear her up, no doubt, her passport to the stars... But think – a life that's scissored off without a second's thought...'

'And Masha?' Dora asks, clinging to Uwe, ignoring her dislike... Not taking in the death...

'It's the horses,' Uwe says. 'The Huns, the Mongols –
then the artillery, the Turks. All mounted. See those horses
occupying the Hungarian plain...! Masha's a nomad.
They're not seen kindly, though everybody started so ...
and many carry on, and end... It's not a title much
respected...'

On he talks, and Dora asks, 'Does she live, and did she
bury Julie? Did she sing the song...'

'It could happen so,' says Uwe, exercising his wrists, and
throwing up some plates, 'that someone dies, but it appears
that those who're living on, are much, much smaller... They
dwindle, distances increase. Round there, in the unfinished
house, where you all lived, without a roof, we see no happy
place. Maybe she had a horse, they scent the river, symbol
of long life, and purposeful, it quietly flows down and
disappears, into indifferent seas... She could have gone
East, further, further back, back to the start...'

'Swallowed up?' Dora asks.

'A little fish,' Uwe says. 'You could look for her. Fits
your epic tasks.'

'In the end, you'd need to sell the horse,' says Dora. 'It
can leap borders, even the fences. Smell out the mines. But
can't bake you bread.'

'It's a going home,' Uwe says. 'Alive or dead. You can't
paint a decent picture now, not one that would do justice to
Masha's ride: remember "The Bogatyrs", "The barge-
haulers" – those were artists who put their finger in your
life. Remember – "the picture is a form of bourgeois
aesthetics which is not required by our form of life" – so
everywhere it's just scribbles now. Floor tiles. A swirl of
snow. In China too. People who weren't even communists.
Pictures that aren't pictures. Communists – all gone. Too
simple, and too hard, they were. If there's no camera –

there's no record, no imagination – just generalities, wind in the dust...'

'She mightn't need a picture, Uwe, if she isn't dead,' says Dora.

'Oh yes,' says Uwe, 'she and the pictures – they're dead for sure. Fascism was ended, then there was hope, then hope deferred, then none at all.'

'The scribbles came from America,' Dora says.

'Exactly so,' says Uwe. 'So Masha has no one, no champion. Riding, leaping, dodging. You can imagine... The steppe, the taiga, on and on ... joined by the other bags of bones...'

'It's no use ranting, Uwe,' Dora says. 'Nothing will come back, nothing will be found. Ruins falling into ruins. Nothing is to do with anything – it's all inventions and luck.'

'Well,' Uwe says, 'I'll juggle on. Politics – it's never been for me. And you, Dora – you don't bring good fortune.'

'I always moved,' says Dora. 'You have to change the scene.'

'You should have stayed. The circus. You find nothing, and abandon people,' Uwe says.

'You can't abandon people who don't want you,' Dora says.

'We have no nation,' Uwe says. 'We live in a tent. And so, there is no war. You flee because you're vulnerable, not because there is a threat.'

'I have nothing,' Dora says. 'Why should they be after me? I'm an apostate, where there is no orthodoxy. Perfection. That's my goal. That's why you're not in view, Uwe.'

'You've two chances, Dora – the dance, or space,' says Uwe. 'In dance, there's movement and the flesh – but yours

is weak, your insides – they are on the outside now. Veins
popped. Muscles – hanks of twine. Then – there's space. If
there is spirit, for sure it prowls out there. Still, the universe
is not a happy place. The monsters are invisible, it's true,
but huge, like floating coal pits, and they overpower the
rest. The rocketeers – they send up army officers, in case
there's battles they can win. They come back down, their
eyes are white. Maybe they've been replaced out there –
some zombie woven from intestines creeps inside their
shell... We're sitting in a Bengal flare in full display, dear
Dora. There is no happy end.' He weeps, but not for Julie.
'Julie's angel – rots with Julie, underground. Poor Masha –
in her wooden hut, in some abandoned village, eating wild
garlic bulbs – even the vampires leave and go to town... My
parents sang about "the last, decisive battle", when
mankind stands tall. I sing the song – but juggling's my
game, and it must see me through.'

'Oh Uwe,' Dora scolds him – 'I don't want career advice.
Nor yet a history of the world. I have this chance – to start
again! The wake is done – on, on – alone and clean as
dawn!'

'You need a man, Dora,' Uwe says.

'For sex?' asks Dora. 'I poke my finger in my eye because
I'm blind. That's a cure, Uwe?'

'For protection,' Uwe says, not convinced.

'I went on a journey with a dead man, Uwe,' Dora says.
'And now my friends are dead.'

'Before the war,' says Uwe. 'It was all green. Then – it
was red. And now, there's been so many wars – you can't
even hear the noise they make – it's traffic, throwing up the
grit.'

'I know all that,' says Dora. 'It isn't history. You're
talking poetry, poor Uwe. It gratifies, I guess.'

'It's a boys' world, Dora,' Uwe says, juggling away, turning to ignore her.

★

'All this – you could pack it all away in boxes, in an hour be on the road,' says Dora. 'Now, there's this wheel.' It spreads out. There's a little tent, but mostly guys are wandering round the stalls – there's shooting, screaming, strong persons, rockets and the rest. A row of animals who know no tricks.

'I've tried the rest, now, I want to try all this,' says Flavia, grinning at Dora, waving her hands. 'There's people moving everywhere – see – there's acts that come from where there's wars, they think this is a haven, they don't see that miniature world wars are just the prologue to a roundabout, a ring of accidents and overtures that will do for us ... or maybe we shall last them out.'

'We'd be the dross left when they'd made the steel,' says Dora. 'Our brains must go to make more muscles. Everything that's real will change into a mind enormous – we shan't reflect a thing... No morning walks, no playing with the cat – reality will be transformed so quick, so utterly – our heads unable to reflect the change. We'll be the illusion, chased up and down, the landscapes jiggered, twisted like the clouds, the smoke and cinders in our eyes...'

'Oh come, Dora,' Flavia says. 'There's far too many of us that we'll disappear – besides, if we're not there, nothing will exist at all. I read the book. It's like the Martians – when they'd had their fight – they all went into caves and starved...'

'I read that too,' says Dora. 'But – Flavia, I hope you aren't an expert in such things... Do you know all about the fish – the proliferation of cuisines, exclusive diets, everything that wriggles taken as it flees...?'

'Oh, screw the fish,' says Flavia. 'And, Dora – don't go near that cage!'

'They respond to love,' says Dora, jumping back.

'That is their difficulty,' Flavia says. 'But don't tell me your problems, Dora – if you know them. They're all in the past. The dead don't haunt – they have enough to stomach those metamorphoses that invade their shells, the dreams left on the bone... Let's go in here. I know about these things.'

The booth says 'speculum speculorum', there's mirrors all around. Dora's upper body swells like an inner tube: her head's a white and wizened ball set up for the strike. Her legs a-dangle like two candle wicks.

Flavia has elephant legs, a face tumescent, two tiny and unequal breasts like nipples on a rubber thimble... 'See!' she says. 'We make a pair. Our bodies are derisory, but the true reflection's of our minds...'

'I don't spot that at all,' Dora's minnow mouth squeaks out. 'And how'd they pack the glass for travel on those roads?'

'It's foil,' says Flavia's froglike craw, 'like what you'd bake your sailfish in.'

'Oh Flavia,' Dora says, 'how I wish I was away from all that! The show, the people! You with that blonde hair, your dark face – you could almost be my Julie, dark as she is now, underground, in the black soil, her angel cracked and peeled. Or Masha – yes, she was dark too...'

'In an ashram? You?' asks Flavia. 'It's not you. Besides – you're a freak.' And she waggles her fat hands, fingers like courgettes.

'No,' says Dora. 'It's to leave body: and the sideshows. You see the guys... How their spines arch back to smack the hammer down, cannons up the clapper to the bell, they're bending to the bow, shooting the straight arrows at the twisty targets... is it possible they don't know, the braggarts ... the soldiering ... the scavenging ... the tight grottoes where they'll live and try to breed ... the scuts fleeting in the underbrush...? The finish...! If you do the training, you must know the goal. We're the only ones who stand before the mirrors, Flavia, here in the cave, and see our minds: smaller and smaller: or swollen more and more...'

'You must take it in, Dora,' Flavia says. 'And then it's yours. Just – don't try to step inside, to try it out. Don't go near the black water, Dora – it doesn't feel a thing, it sucks you in, you're plankton, Dora, don't forget.'

'When we go outside,' says Dora, 'our thoughts will settle back, into the banal. In here – I have amazing thoughts – the states, and their economies... stand them here and see them change their shapes...'

'Don't exaggerate, my dear,' says Flavia, moving around, changing from length of whitened tripe to bloater. 'Some large things have blocked and frozen, there is no defence, and no attack. In any case – you're not the type to be a nurse, a doctor, militant or pamphleteer – Uwe's the juggler, you – you are potential, only that...'

'Flavia – I was for perfection,' Dora says. 'Julie – maybe she was hunting for the spirit – that old guy...! And Pierre's fall was just an accident, and Masha's horse – it ran and ran, just as she wished...'

'Exactly, Dora,' Flavia says. 'Don't whine. All of you did the right things. It could all turn out the best...'

'Thanks, Flavia,' Dora says.

'It's your vision, Dora,' Flavia says. 'There's no one looks for gain.'

'It hasn't been enough, Flavia,' Dora says. 'Parts have been murderous.'

'Say it, Dora: how to live, where to go,' Flavia presses on – 'I think you're more a Buddha than a Christ – you're not the family sort.'

'Flavia! I don't want that at all! I'm a new kind. I don't want to read and write and sit cross-legged,' says Dora, pulling away from Flavia, 'no Uwe, watching the missiles marching past. No audience, no mike.'

'Well,' says Flavia. 'You need new clothes, for sure.'

'You seek the best of us, I'm sure,' says Dora. 'Well... It wasn't goodness I was after – just to reach the top, be last one of that line that took a million years to stand erect and lose its tail – or else ... the first of something... And yet – I wonder if I care that much about the species after all...'

'Oh, nobly put!' says Flavia. 'And what we need is clean straw now, to rest us till the dawn. I'll not be missed at home, for sure, and Dora – you need someone to cherish you, and promote...'

'It isn't straw you want, it's hay,' says Dora. 'And I am not so sure that you can see me as I'd want to be...'

'That's friendship, Dora,' Flavia says. 'Maybe I'm the first you've had.'

In the morning, Flavia says, 'See, Dora – take this pashmina shawl. I have yak too, but this will suit as well.'

'But Flavia,' Dora says, 'it's not cold at all, and stuff around my neck...'

'Don't let it catch up in the whirligig,' says Flavia. 'It'll choke you, like the dancer... I was a dancer too, until I stopped.'

'I guess the spirit counts,' says Dora. 'There's lots around. All kinds. You never know which one will come to flesh and up and bite you.'

'Up here on the wheel,' says Flavia. 'You see how it's all connected. All those lines diverging... And you at last – up at the top.'

'It isn't that,' says Dora. 'If we were in Italy, the roads would come from Rome – but all clogged and knotted. In France – you can choose a country road, that's only linked to villages. In Moscow – they're all slow, from top to bottom. Only in Germany is everything linked up...'

'That's cute, Dora,' Flavia says. 'It doesn't help at all. I don't mean countries – I mean continents.'

'See the birds,' says Dora. 'We're up high – but not at all to them. It's just a place to sing, look down upon, and there's the dabs of colour, the rust and cinders, the grass, the geese moving to and fro... It doesn't mean a thing to me.'

'It's to set your scene, Dora,' Flavia says. 'I brought you here. They don't have freak shows now – the freaks are us, we walk among them. Remember – the ninnies, the hyenas... But if there was a parade like that – you'd need to ask what side you're on: the ordinary – or the sports: the oyster's painful pearl, the yellow diamond, green rubies, the albino wolf...'

'Oh Flavia,' says Dora, 'how you confuse the landscape! It must be your Mediterranean genius... Taking sides? I'm a well-made freak, that's all. See that pavilion?'

'There's a scent of desperation over there,' says Flavia, 'and growling.'

'They had to be set free, the animals, by law,' says Dora, 'and so they put them in a cage.'

'Those lions,' says Flavia. 'Look! They know they lost. They snap at us, play the hard guy – but never made it to the top. The birds fly higher, the horses – get taken to the races. No one wins for keeps. You, Dora – I need for you to strive. You can get there, somehow, to the top.'

'I'd like that too,' says Dora. 'But from up there – you see the crowd – but is it you they see?'

'Oh faddle,' Flavia says. 'That's quite reactionary, Dora. You make your own identity, you rise above whatever holds you down. You haven't got the knack. I am your friend – I'll push you up...'

'Those lions,' says Dora, 'they had their day. Now, they're just a metaphor. King of the nothing. Then – there's the camels ... look where they carried the poor Tuaregs. The desert galleons...! The poodles in the boudoir, fleas in your crotch, the matriarchal elephants – every kind has its strategy, every strategy was taken on by us. The fall – that was the theory: either it happened at the start, the first reproving splat! – or always underneath us, the constant challenge of the void... Oil and nitro, Flavia – they were the crutches we used to stagger to the peak ... what now? The flight? Up to the stars?'

'Don't disappoint me, Dora,' Flavia says, quite disappointed. 'Don't get all wise on me. Wisdom can shorten all our lives – it's only knowledge after it's gone wrong...'

'I would have left showtime behind,' says Dora. 'But, Flavia, you do insist! Every resource is here, I know, all history within the tent and on the stalls. Our life in nature, warning and reward – protecting, cautioning – those nuts

bewigged like advocates, sugar cocoons that rot your jaws –
the howitzer, its blackened finger pointing to the sun...'

'Nonsense, Dora: at the most, it's aiming to the moon,'
says Flavia. 'Yours is the vision, my beloved – you're a true
climber, you have the faith, you'll spin up there, a silken
knot between your teeth – a classic. Forget the prancing
dancers, rolling their rings around the floor...'

The pair of them – can't see how to go forward, how to
retreat. Maybe the upward's all that's left.

Dora says, 'It's not my scene at all. How can I escape?'

'We'll find a path...' says Flavia.

Then she shouts, 'Hey! Dora – take care – your
pashmina! – I told you, don't go near the whirling cogs...!'

II

WHERE THE PHILOSOPHERS GO

'You can't imagine the poverty here,' she says.
'Having no money, however much you've had – until more arrives – that's it!' he says. 'Poverty!' Everybody knows it.'

'No, that isn't it at all, you fool,' she says, and there is silence.

'See!' he says. 'The gangs have marked the houses. This road were on's between the l8s and the 8s.'

'Back to the hotel,' she says, 'I hate this place.'

'You needn't be frightened,' he says: 'We're not part of this scene.'

★

'I liked you better when you were an alcoholic,' she says. 'There was transition. Like putting a glass plate in the camera. It might come out black all over, or a silverpoint, or crackled, treetops drawn by spiders. Now, you're just a you.'

'You thought you had the cure for booze,' he says. 'And you could stand up all the little soldiers, all over the world. With acid – after a while, you can reach down into the hole without it. The angels fluttering there... The drink – it's always different for a while, but there's no depth, no sea,

67

just new surfaces, until you've tried them all. Then, if you can, you leave those rooms.'

They watch the cars below driving very fast, the guy pulling a cart with two empty barrels slow, very very slow.

'This is a good war,' she, Bianca, says. 'It's not like with drones and jointing knives, our guys and theirs, the clean and the dirty, our sort and who knows whose sort... Here, there's criminals, with no history.'

'They're winning,' he says. 'They'll go on winning till they're all gunned down. Then, goodness can come.'

'I'm not looking for goodness,' she says. 'I'm dodging.'

'Our good guys have built a wall to keep the fugitives out,' he says. 'Our country's full of fat old guys who steal. And – those bodies here, tumbled down. They've fingerprints, but don't have names. How do you live with that? And on the other side, any other side – there must be guys who think like me. We all have countries, we all carry some other primal things ... it's like the song says – "No, I don't love you, I just wanna be held when I'm scared"...'

'I'm leaving you,' she says. 'Don't get emotional. You, and the children. It's inevitable. When we've done the report, I'll have the ticket changed.'

'Do we have children too?' he asks.

'These beans,' she says. 'They explode in my stomach. I'm going down to get some stuff.'

She walks across the road. Nothing hits her.

She's never seen again.

That can't be true. Someone always sees you – even if you're dead, and this place, you have to watch them all the time, everybody.

He never sees her again.

That's what she said – she left.

★

'Rodney Hawkett', says the label on his door. The guy, Rodney, says, 'Should we look for her? Bianca? Quite a mystery there.'

'No, no,' he says: 'We can't put our finger on her. No secret, no mystery. Not knowing, not worrying: that's us. She's gone where millions go, and we don't know.'

'If we look,' Rodney starts to ask. 'Where to begin?'

'There'd be a procedure. But – no end's envisaged to it. And if we want to find her, there's no procedure for ends, solving it all and starting off again. And – why the search? What should we do with her? If she's in a hole? We'd know where she is, who's got her – can't do anything about it...'

'Right,' says Rodney. 'She'll be someone who's dropped off. Missing in inaction.'

Rodney's been to school, had some education too. There's my report for him to read. How friendly is the place we were in? Why would you want to go? Who can get out? What do those numbers mean – 8, 18? A study to be done on that – maybe a movie too?

★

The kidnap? 'The trouble was,' Bianca – the woman he was with and went missing – says to her friend, 'No one came looking. They tried to sell me, but...'

'So you were kept for sex?'

'Oh no. For fear. Mine was so great it seemed to be a value to them. They keep you if you are a saint: it takes time to flower from what you were. You mature before they martyr you. They weren't afraid at all. I made up for that. My fear – I showed them they still had the power. When I reached the end, they'd get rid of me ... down the escarpment, like a dog, like the book says.'

'I can't believe,' says Bianca's friend, 'no one looked for you.'

'Oh, maybe they were right,' she says. 'I'd no idea where I was.'

'Why did those evil guys, the bad guys – why did they want power? Without money. Not much enjoyment even if they'd sex on you. It seems hollow.'

'The power was to make sense, give a meaning, so's not to feel afraid,' Bianca says. Her friend, she thinks, is rather stupid – but her own explanation doesn't seem so bright. 'It was part of their job,' she says. Those months – she was sweaty clay put in the fire, an unworked shape coming out a cooked lump, a gruesome thing, in its core a squirming pulse, a worm macabre and blind.

'Well,' says her friend, 'now, you know where other people are. Your partner. Your report. Your escape – a liberation, surely ...'

'They went away,' Bianca says. 'Those people. No escape. I was just left, worthless. What's the point of starting things again?'

*

Bianca's friend says to another friend – 'Do you think they took her? She doesn't look like. Maybe she just went off.'

'She's finished,' says the friend's friend. 'Not her fault. Someone else's will, being under that – it shows up the whole performance, from crowns to clogs. You can't make a case for anything, after that.'

*

Bianca's former partner, Vince – he's waiting for something. Meantime, he sits next to a clerical guy on the big wheel. It's to waste time, though he'd prefer to be alone, at ease.

The guy says, 'I'm just a lay therapist. I don't tell the stories, do the songs.'

'You're a priest,' says Vince. 'Spoiled all by yourself.'

There's a cool between them. 'I don't pretend you'll all be gone to paradise, immortal there. I suggest – there is some choice – ground-level, limited. The devil took God up and offered him the view,' says the priest. 'Up here we see everything. None of it will ever belong to us. I offer it to you just the same.'

'I accept,' Vince says, 'I've nothing. It's another con – first God made it all, so he was being offered just what he had made. Like he was a proletarian. Now – the con is new – you can't give, I can't take.'

'But all the rest is good – identity, rights, sex,' says the priest. 'Guilt and repentance. All up to you. That stuff – I can't give or take away.'

The wheel wavers at the bottom of its round. The weight of the two of them holds it there. The machinery would lift them, but they only paid for one circle, one up and up, and down. There's no fear – aeroplanes are far more dangerous, the view is less. You'd not fall here – you'd stick, like monkeys in physics or mechanics.

★

Vince wants this job. A job. The employer guy says, 'Ha! Recommended by Hawkett. That old shit. I'd trample on his flayed skin, a rug before the hearth, a spitty fire – yes, pocked by birdshot from the anthracite. I'd stand on him and warm my bum. Never too little of him, if you can't make him suffer!'

Vince, the postulant, says, 'We were in that sad country – a report: fancy visiting, putting money in, tossing off a little article half-read, by someone impermanent: in State, maybe...?'

'You were on the wheel,' says the interviewer. 'Hmmmm.'

'I should have been with people at the top of life. Like the ball in the pin machine, but starting with the lowest scores, going counter – right to the top. Instead of guttering out.' He doesn't say this: waits for the next question, the next card. He's only rubbish in his hand...

'You lost your partner,' says the boss, the guy who's dealing, interviewing.

Vince, who was on the wheel, the top, lets his mind, his memories, go soft, fall off the spindle, spool out on the floor. Is this all there is, before what's next? – this room, the questions that come, don't come. He keeps the mantra going silently, 'Jack of diamonds, oh jack of diamonds ... that's a hard card to find...'

Vince says – 'I'll look at anything, and remember it.'

That's all you need, to get the job, any job. Get kicked out too, of any job.

His new boss says, 'Your work would be: do anything I tell you. Remember your profoundly wretched, compromised and cowardly soul. Keep in your sight the people lost, the challenges not faced. Me? I want to reach the top, to mix, even talk, with the talented, creative, and the rich. Be one of them, earn my biographers; their adulation, their respect. Your job's to push me up.'

'It's more important, then, for me than it is for you,' Vince, the new hired hand, imagines. He'd be the new assistant – kingmaker, master of the prince's bedchamber. You need to know how it all works, the society, and reach the top for someone else, without a pole, a spring, a ladder – from nearly scratch.

'Remember,' says the boss, 'your fault. The woman you deserted, having unwanted sex, short and jagged, with bony brown boys, their faiths and death inked on their unloved skins... And don't fuck with me. You're broken and in need. Send me to glory – then kneel before me: your creation. Pay tax on what I give you, and may your food cling to your purple gums like dry raw oatmeal. Sleep floundering in your sweat, and run the streets, cold and crabfooted. Obey my orders and invent your own: don't tell me the secrets you discover. Make me a whole, a hallowed man.'

Vince, the new employee – now he has a contract, some cash, he is 'I'. Vince is 'I'. I'm to operate the social elevator. Bellhops ... they're gone too. Do it yourself, arsehole. Press the button, wait.

Here's a modest guy, scrubbing the marble floor. Singing the song – the awful song, his terrible country...

'You know,' I say, when he has stopped his tale of gangs, corruption – all the rest that brings him here, and can't imagine going back – 'The answer is,' – and I sing: '"My name it is Sam Hall / And – you've got to kill 'em all." There's no other way. You can't do it here, we're modern in this civilisation. But you guys can. No alternatives, no priests, no choices. And no self-doubt: that's a rabbit's tail someone pinned on, to make an easy target. Historians, philosophers – in the jail they go, if they won't run. Sculptors and potters – they can't waver, make mistakes. They're safe. They know how to make the choice. The rest ... is jelly in a bucket. Wield your bloody ladle. Forget the roots – cut them deep, and pour in quicklime. Yours is day one. This is the way, the only way...'

He's laughing now. Maybe – oh no! – maybe he's an 8, an 18. For sure he'll have a cousin or a cop who is...

'You're an illegal, friend,' I say. 'You should be a refugee. The thing is – you refugees are messengers of war. It's always so. You let them come, you turn your back – it's just the same. You think – all the guys within the Pale of Settlement – if they'd all come here ... there'd still have been a war, for sure – a big one, no one spared. Civil wars, uncivil ones...' I stare at him, as if he's the commanding one. Where, exactly, how – would they have gone? It's a hard one, that. Not worth pursuing.

★

Drinks. My boss – there's ten to twenty million like him – if they were on a scroll, in China, perching on those sugarloaf mountains – it would be gross. A termite hill. Not worth an artist's title, those numbers – an affront to modesty. Then, there's Africa and India. Millions of rich guys, looking down on him, the boss: indifferent, scornful, superficial. In their grounds – plinths, organic forms in bronze... Behind the glass – incunabula, narwhal prods: take you two lifetimes to appreciate, to amass. Then – death, dispersal. Vanity, all vanity: oblivion. A family of heirs – spring up through the trap from hell, to fritter everything away.

'I've been observing you,' the guy who's staring, sat beside me, up here in the cloud, pulls at my sleeve. 'If it's ok,' he says, 'I'll run my tab upon your tab. It brings a saving, in the end.'

'These bars – up so high, there is no view,' I say. 'Cold blue, the sky; or porridge.'

'You can't be spied upon,' he says.

'No,' I say, 'and I'll not pick up your tab, entwined with mine.'

'Wrong!' he shouts: so loud, his hat falls off. Inside there's inked 'Andy'. Maybe it's not his... 'If you're a general, you sacrifice your soldiers. Otherwise – you are a fake. To have your victory – there must be skeletons dancing round your bed.'

'If I'm a general,' I say, 'I'd not be pushing someone else to end above me.'

'That's the spirit,' Andy says. 'You know it's vanity. And – better that it's yours. We all pick up those tabs, and pass them on. If you can't pay – you'll need to run down thirty flights of stairs. That's why they put these bars up high. They're up high so you can't get out without paying – unless you run real quick... They block the elevator. So much for machines ... wheels without wheels.'

I settle up our tabs. Andy's been there for a week, it seems. He grasps my arm. 'Now, you should see my friend, the flight instructor. I call him Icarus, though it's not quite right. This time, this incarnation, it's Icaro. The higher up you go, the colder. So, those wings lost traction – you shouldn't blame the glue. What you need, my friend is – go right to the top: all by yourself. Forget about your boss. That's squalor. We can trick you out, with what you need. Money – we'd give old stuff – venerable, venerated. And then – you add the new. Invention. A perfect wedlock...'

The drink's at work. Andy, pulling me along – to me, he seems a cat on X, ecstasy, a flying Hirschfield rug, through the pubs, out the windows, not paying now: over the walls, spikes in our pants, discussing destiny, cabbage and beans, bourbon and pills, until 'Another friend, dear Icaro,' says

Andy, losing his fur, his pace, becoming almost human, a reel of speeding pictures... 'Try him out, Icaro,' he says.

They fit me with the helmet: it's all green and grey below, blue up top, if I can skew my head right round: 'The sacred book,' Andy confides, 'says in the realm of God, that starts ten metres up – it's all divinity. Angels, suchlike. That's why they build those towers, skyscrapers some call them, and put bars on the top. No longer law that men must live by – you're in paradise there. I guess the angels like a tipple too – and if they fall, there's wings.'

'Fuck you,' says Icaro. 'Anyone can knit a pair of wings. They do not always bear you up.'

Andy says, 'In the desert, there's no mountains, everything's nine metres high. It's obvious they thought God's realm, the angels, if you're in that mode or heresy – lived just above your head.'

'Now,' says Icaro, 'forget the virtuous world, the simulacrum. Try the real thing, and fly. No helmet. Watch for sacrilege. You must expect some tumbles... Try your strength.'

It should be easier, without the fakery, the helmet and the pictures. 'You need to take the right philosophy,' says Andy, 'that moves along. Let concepts bear you up. Experience without them – would be just the simulation of a flight. No aeroplane around, no tail, no feet, no horns to warn the rest. Sensation without context. A drag, and frightening too.'

They're chuckling as they try to fit me with a grubby pair of wings. 'He's better off without,' laughs Icaro. 'The worst part is the launch.'

I'm on the edge. Nine metres – or ten? It's worth your life, and heaven too. 'There's a slope and grass,' says Icaro. 'All green – like the poet says.'

'It seems to me this is a roof,' I say. 'A drop. To earth.'

'There's trees up there, sprouting from the tiles,' says Andy. 'Olives, a passion plant. Jump and glide.'

I live. It's like the first flight, on the beach: you land quite bad, but you're in history. Icaro and Andy laugh.

'History? That's not the point,' says Icaro. 'You can end there as a flop. Usually – you're dead. The thing to do's to grasp some wing, angelic maybe, that yanks you up, and gives you shine.'

'The point is different,' says Andy. 'You think one law trumps all the rest – the law of gravity, of *gravitas*. But – we're so ephemeral – where does our gravity end? Hole in the ground? An urn, a mausoleum – or in dust, anonymous, that clogs your brother's lungs – and so it all goes on, until another law breaks in. A law we all ignore – when we leap up. Yet – there's heaven for us all, or most: where there's no gravity. We laugh – there is no dawn nor dusk, nor *gravitas,*

so – laughter unceasing. Icaro – his namesake didn't drown from gravity – but, the tale goes – from disrespect, or hubris, ignoring some advice about the altitude that's clearly wrong or else there wouldn't be PanAm, TWA, and all the rest.'

'My bruises hurt,' I say. 'The law is punishment.'

They laugh the harder, 'Why,' says Icaro. 'This guy's a wit, a genius, a most ingenious faller.'

'No, be serious,' says Andy, and to me, 'You flew. Next time we'll find a taller house. Guys did it all the time, before the Revolutions, in France, and science too. You're merely lacking in the philosophy, the confidence that leaders have. Night flyers, they were called. Maybe it's easier in the dark.'

'I must explain,' I say. 'My boss will ask why I've not launched him, his ambition.'

'You're walking on those sticks,' says Andy. 'Tell him you learned a lesson for him. "Choose bedmates that don't push you down the stairs."'

'Why do you care so much for me?' I ask.

'Appearances, and time – that's where my interest lies,' says Andy. 'The sticks, the crutches – they seem resulting from an accident. We know – they come from your success. And time: the world, its time, is folded like a fan. Those pubs, the hostelries we drank in, flying over walls and hedges – arriving in the painting, five hundred years ago, when my friend Icaro went down... It's folding timescapes.'

'Hold it, Andy. It's all a fable, about Icaro, both then and now. Everything we know and do – it happens all at once, then it is gone. The painting's made today: the pubs, the walls with bottle glass atop – they happened once, and disappeared. We're only consequences. There's no success, no failure – we are blots of liquid ink, we dry. There is no fold that brings us near the past, our faces pressed on some Aegean pioneer's... Time is a scroll,' I say. 'That's wrapped so tight – it never is unwound. Your hat. Andy – it must be yours, it can't be Warhol's. He never wore a hat. Time and appearance – that was him. Not you.'

'Who's to say?' says Andy. 'Someone else has found a head to fit his hat. What interests me – us – is handing your ambition, your achievement, back to you.'

'What do you gain?' I ask.

'Percentages,' says Icaro. 'That's all there ever is, you shouldn't ask for more.'

'I couldn't bear to see you,' Andy says, bending down to look up at me, the angles full of shade. 'Shovelling beauties random in your boss's boudoir. When we could have them for ourselves... Since he chose you, I knew he couldn't ever make it, wherever he might want to go, to be. So you must see that's the case. I shan't be a cat again, I promise you – no caterwauls, no jumping over gates and walls. Those pills we took – they eliminate our worms. The universe – it's made of wormholes – the living creatures end up inside us. Don't you feel cleaner, purer now?' he asks. He pulls me close. 'You are my poem. Lines from you – they'll come to me at night, or if we have to take the road again – "Yes!" I'll think. "That caught the pulse; there the thought lay down and curled up on the picture, and they were one."'

'That's opportunism,' I say.

'Oh no,' he says. 'That's wedlock.'

★

Rodney Hawkett tells me, 'You got the job. There's an end to it. You go on. Success, failure – you'll find, for you – they're much the same. Your boss – that shit – he thinks those clouds are full of lovely people. He's an idiot: they're full of odd tennis shoes and plastic bottles. You find them on the beach, all washed up. Bodies, too. Watch out!'

Rodney Hawkett's bones – he keeps them in their sack of skin – you wonder how. The shoulder blades – two china bowls cast down and cracked ... the belly, mottled like old books, the organs wizened like old plums, purple, nearly draining out, down the filament of sex.

'What should I tell the boss?' I ask.

'Keep away from the truth,' says Rodney Hawkett. 'That holds good for me, too. I want lots of things, some you plug in, some you put in the bank – truth isn't one of them. There's no socket.'

'Maybe,' I persist, 'the arts. The talk about them. That knocks off the lugs, the roughness: then you file the sharp bits down.'

Rodney Hawkett nods. He wanders round. His bedsheet leaves a black grape nipple bare: a monk's scraggy shoulder. It's good to get out of bed sometimes, but he should dress: a stretch, a shout – that's what you need.

★

'My models,' Andy says, 'have nothing to do with those ambitious guys, the depressives. I think a lot about the fables – the self-sacrifice. The hare who leaps into the fire to be food for the sage. It all seems whimsy – the contemplation, the lives you'd like to live – but really, it's quite physical. Making a bridge with your body so your monkey subjects can get across the flood; getting eaten so's to help someone.'

'Andy wanted to find an evil guy,' says Icaro. 'Not one of the wholesale types that's into politics, money, mustering camp-followers. Those are the multipliers, they turn one killing into millions. No: a guy like you, Vince. Faithless, insensitive. Not evil "bad" – just evil good and bad.'

'I don't feel the tug,' I say. 'There's no appeal. Who'd want to be his object?'

'Oh, you just want rewards, and you fear the punishment,' says Icaro. 'Try to keep your face a blank for a while. Think how many shapes there are in it.'

'No whimsy, Icaro,' I say. 'No magnificent promises that end up as a bowl of milk, a pocketful of dust. I don't need educating into nothing, I know it well.'

'That's not it at all,' says Andy. 'I'm sure you know real killers. Machismo, money, fear and dirty trades – that's of no interest.'

'I'm not jumping in the fire,' I say. 'I'm no dinner! Andy – you are my dearest friend, but: no!'

'He means – why this, not something else,' says Icaro. 'Or nothing else at all?'

'I know exactly what I mean,' says Andy. 'And this guy – he is a candidate. He looks, he seeks: I find.'

*

I tell the boss: 'You know, to send you up the stairs – it's right I need to try things first. Like tasting for the poison. It's a dice: enjoy the juiciest bits, they may be strychnine. And so I get the fun, the chance, the risk.'

'Yes,' says the boss. 'I quite see that. But – you could end up getting all the fizz.'

'I'm not the mountaineering type,' I say. 'Ascents are dangerous. and when you reach the top – there's nothing there. Remember the song, '*maledetta noia*' – bloody boredom. That's what faces me.'

'We could call everything off,' says the boss. He pushes back his rolling chair. Some muscle tone, a hint he's used those pedalling machines, bolted to their spot. He plays 'the eager son', sniggering within. Rodney Hawkett is his mentor, would be his grand old father – that's the generation, before they invented doctors, dentists... Those old guys, quavering, determined, doctrinaire – there they go, see! the flames behind the door, it's a cat flap for old tigers, up they go, like straw...

'Advise me,' says my boss. 'Gain your pay.'

'Exactly,' I say. 'You speak of "gaining the summit".
Nothing's gained. It's like the pay – a week goes by, you're
poor again... Unless you have the itch: you have to take the
last train, and the first, the first station and the last, the last
biscuit or the biggest. It's an obsession. Where does it
drive?'

'I don't know,' says the boss. 'I'm an obsessive. I do
those things you mention, and many many more.'

'It's maybe seeking a perfection,' I say. 'But it's not
perfection. It's something to do and then relax.'

'You must tell me about perfection,' says the boss. 'That
is your job. And – does it involve me in calligraphy?'

He holds out a broken hand, steel-pinned in the middle
like a hinge. 'My friend – she shut it in the door,' he says.
'Some   question   defining   about   sex.   That   isn't
mountaineering, nor can it lead to some perfection...' I
nod, but he's not satisfied. 'She wasn't satisfied,' he says.
'Is it perfection when you're satisfied? Is it the feeling, the
act – or the state itself, a platform? Exercises? Winning at
blackjack, over and over? That would give me satisfaction,
that's for sure.'

'Your hand,' I say. 'It has something of the perfect...'

He waves it, it flaps – 'My body – is a circus,' says my
boss. 'Can you have a perfect pratfall? A cure – that turns a
hand from something that can grasp – into a clown, an
acrobat, you leap, you make a pyramid of men... In the real
world, they don't exist, don't function. Yet – there they are.
Six guys stood on each other's heads – what does that
mean? To paint the ceiling, pick your apricots? No,
naturally not. A perfect human? Just perfect, as humans
aren't *for* anything, but they can *be* ... no more than
themselves, no more, transformed from being less than
what they are...? Growth, progress – those are finished.

Maybe that means perfection can be attained. But – and here, my friend, arrives the paradox: is this perfection the *best* thing there can be? Well, clearly not. Or not in an exclusive sense – it's good for humans, possibly, but perfect crabs have what is best for them, and viruses, and elephants.'

'That's where the first lesson ends,' I tell the boss. I can't go on.

'No, no,' he says. 'The last word's always mine. Perfection of oneself, your species: isn't *good*, you see. The guys who link the two, the one, the all – they've always held the stage. It isn't so. The perfect man – kills all the rest and crams them in his perfect mouth and grinds them with his perfect teeth. You get my point, examples take shape in your head?'

I'm silent. It's the only way to halt the flood.

*

'He's a casuist,' says Andy. 'Those are easy games for him and his, if all he wants is friends. We have more serious adventuring to do. He's worse than Hawkett, and they're both too late to be a nazi with the uniform.'

'You must be a volunteer,' says Icaro. 'The fire service. Yes – you must be a fireman.'

'H is for happiness,' Andy explains. 'And it's the name of a bomb. See how we want both. The biggest bomb, the nearest to a perfect one. "Noooo," they say. "We want one, not to use – just decoration and for frightening. We're compassionate." And there it is: the cookie jar – you steal a cookie even if you know you'll be found out. You swallow it right down, you drop your bomb. So as to *be* found out; the naughty one, who's badness must be forgiven. That is the path to love. Authority, veneration too – of course, there is a pantheon. There's death and war – and mediators, whom we respect, of course...'

'I've heard all that,' I say. 'I know – when the music stops, your big ears hear the wisdom, the enlightenment. But why should I be a fireman?'

'People want money,' Andy says. 'But when they see the guy who has a pile of it – they laugh. She's vulgar. Maybe she's not even happy. You think you will respect what you want. It isn't so. You respect the poverty that you don't want. You deride the wealth you wrestle for.'

'Bombs, Andy. Happiness,' I say. 'Where does the fire come in? Look at my round head. There is no third eye, no tranquillity. My empty hands ... no attributes, no power: no sword, no justice, no forgiving. Fire is a pepper up your arse. It makes you jump and run.'

'That's what firemen do,' says Icaro, annoyed. 'You should know. They put out fires. Now, you work to make your boss a hero, respected. Everybody does, who delves and spins. It's to puff up some guy who gives you bread. Stale, too. Look at the fires the bosses make – fireworks. It works! The fire works – so do you. You work to set the flames and see them leaping up, exploding, making the pattern. Forget it. Take your pitcher. Pour it on the flame...'

'Icaro,' I say. 'This is banal. It never works, to set the fire, extinguish it. We build what others have designed. Whatever you knock down – the blueprint stays, immortal, fecund.'

But – the fire: we live by it. If – when – it dies, we die. The three – we look up at the sun, cover our heads, submitting.

★

I'm a fireman. Oh – how we hate the common run – cats in the trees. Forcing the locks to empty rooms. Water, smoke, minerals clagged with earth, the poisons... Not our elements, no, not at all. We are people of the flames: those tall palaces, those glassy spikes – it's not our element, they're made of sand, they splinter and implode. Icaro was wrong: the fire – it makes itself: it's not a toy, a simulacrum... You don't risk it by miscalculating. You earn it, seek it. It's creation, blooming from destruction, it's revelation from the wood, the straw, the skins. To die in the fire – it's a gift, a blessing. Icaro deserved his punishment – to rise up to the sun in arrogance, not in love, surrender ... just to flap his wings. If – if only – with longing, he'd flown up to perish in the fire, as though he'd never been. That's perfect love.

That's what they say.

We need the flames, their dance, their shout. Us firemen – they try to damp us down, to drown.

We're tied in to diving suits, a travesty: our heads in brazen bells to stop us looking up to where the flames aspire... 'No, no!' the captain cries – 'Whatever else – do not go naked in the flames! – no sacrifice, and no delight, fulfilment, can be required of you. Nothing in your heads except the song – "burn, burn", the babies and the pigs – a hecatomb – someone up there lives on the scent, their incense...'

It does no good. We need to see the flames ... the colours – sapphire blue, the yellow melon flowers, our blood – red as coxcombs. Our passion... With what regret we put them out, put them away, our flames, waiting for another show.

'That's Hawkett's ancient house,' I hear a colleague shout... At last! A pyre that ends in orange, springing to the sun; a misty grey of ash is left, and not a trace of black, of death...

Old Hawkett too – consumed to his last, an offering, spiralled up – the tender tongue, the roasted beak, the runny sheep eyes – a slender cuisine for sure, but all gone, eaten up.

Yes, I think, as we squirt our final drops on silent embers – he made a show... Not a witness, just someone curious and questioning. I'm glad he got burned up.

'I saw the whole station, the firemen – dancing round, all skin and hair,' says Andy, reproaching. 'But you resisted. You didn't jump right in...'

'No,' I say, 'but – it's hard for me now... My work. I can't go on, I don't believe in it. I've seen the fire, the little flickers we have now, and how it ends – all, everyone, the rocks, sea monsters – all eaten by the sun. Or doing it ourselves, the ending. It's a temptation ... better than sex or water when you're thirsty...'

'Yes,' says Andy. 'Temptation is to be resisted too. The more you can resist, the better is the end, surrender, the falling... No, you can't work for your chief. He's ignoble, his ambition – it's unreal...'

*

I tell the boss I can't go on. He can get thousands like me...

'Yes, of course I can,' he says. 'But you're my rabbit on the stick. You've fallen in the fire. I've lost: I cannot lose. I'll ride your spirit till the end of days...'

'Oh no,' I think. 'I never thought. The guy's a maniac. Of course...'

I say, 'I'm not your good communist, boss – I know the situation, and what needs doing in it. And I don't do it. Not a bit of it. Quite the contrary.'

He's not listening. Or he doesn't understand.

'This form,' he says, waving it. 'It follows you from job to job. The way I've fixed it, though – you'll never work again. The fire, the end ... abandonment. No one will pay a guy like you, who takes it all to bits, and sees the stalks and stems, the ladders and the synthesis, the little greenish blobs of life that waver mindless up and down...'

'That isn't fire,' I say. 'It's flowers. You do it in the schools...'

'So,' he says, 'you betray, deny. You'll wander round the world, quite unappeased, anonymous. They'll mock you when you come to beg.'

'I believe all that,' I say. 'But you'll just sit here, vindictive, on your own, unloved...'

'Yes,' he says, 'I know all that. It's good. It's me. I'll be the boss, clandestine, murderous. I'll give my orders. The booze – I'll have it all myself – no partying. No courting. Whores. No conversation, no collecting stuff, no friends and so no enemies – just introspection and enjoyment. It's where it's always been – inside: just as the humanists believed – the divinity of myself, impregnable, unique.'

*

'It seems, Andy, there's a form,' I say. 'You fill it when you're born, it follows you around, precedes – and if some guy puts down a – what? A query? Doubt? Dissatisfaction? – you never work again.'

'Oh yes,' says Andy. 'It happened with poor Icaro. Out of a cloudless sky... And in a while – you learn to live without. The work you never get – you learn you didn't want it anyway...'

'Farewell, then, Andy,' I say: 'Friends for ever.'

'It's a sad day,' says Andy. 'I hoped to hone and burnish you. Push you up, through the trap, and on the stage. Profit from your activity, better still – your inactivity. What they call big crime – it's what is left for you, though it's of no interest. Disasters come from heaven, or from teams of guys who are too big to tumble down. Governments, not gangs – they rule. Crime just suckles on their hindmost tit, I fear. It's petty. You'd be a bug in someone's ear, or someone's telephone.'

I wait. Andy says, 'Sit back. There's no roundups here, not now. You're not of fighting age – or you'd have faked your birthdate, so you're too young, too old. That's what the Syrians did, who wouldn't fight for France. You're not a surgeon, so there's nothing useful you can do. These are liquid days, my friend. On the radio, there are always songs – touching, tender, hard. Listen to some words, don't be ashamed when they make you cry – you're in your elastic garden now. Forget Icaro, forget things dropping from the sky – no one can come down on you...'

'There's always "next", Andy – that's what the radio's for,' I say.

'Come on, Vince,' he says. 'There's people doing things that fifty years ago would have been a miracle. Dancing on Mars. Calculating when we all will fry. "Up to the ceiling, down to the floor" – remember? your rough relatives used to swing you up and down. Now, there's machines for that. There's lessons to make you a good father even if you've got no kids...'

'There's movement, Andy,' I say. 'But nothing deep. Or still.'

'Lessons, Vince,' says Andy. 'If you're really helpless.'

'It's the nomads, Andy,' I say. 'They're underneath my eyelids.'

'I have no truck with them,' says Andy, laughing. 'Those little terracotta carts they made – then the bronze; twisted and crude. As though they'd only seen them far away. The wry reward for travelling and never getting there – it's an ice tomb on the steppe. Everybody knew – it was the usual failure. Down to the frost. Dress warm and well. Too bad.'

'You're stuck, poor Andy. The customary parasite,' I say. 'You sit inside your city, listening to the horsemen circling round. If everything becomes a city – then you'd be safe. No trading off your daughters to the chiefs. Those kids'll serve you in your senile days, as you lie gaga on your litter, laughing up at towers and ramparts. It's no use. There's quests, and voyages. Same endings, but what you look for's different. Icaro was on his quest. It did for him. And yet – the quest was over, a success. We all can fly. He thought it was a voyage. Voyaging – you're not seeking one big thing, a goal – but several, all familiar, all with a tariff on the door. Night flights, and one night stands. On, on – vibrating beds and porno for a quarter. You say you're seeking something – it's the same thing, over and over. Wandering – pushed and pulled. Taxis at dawn: the frontier. A document – will it protect, against the dogs and guns...? You're right to doubt. Pack your bundle – or you dump it there, beneath the hedge. Maybe you'll be back for it – there's no one cares. The quest is something else. You find a fig tree, lie back – the quest can start from there... Those blue birds – come and shake the branches – down will come the fruit. There's figtrees everywhere – you might lie under every one – there's blue birds plentiful... They migrate. They're souls. For sure, they're not monogamous,

they don't bear you back each year until you croak: *they*
croak, a requiem. No – everything's renewed, for ever it's
the same. The form – it doesn't change, it waxes, wanes,
sometimes the tiles are blue and sometimes green – the
heaven and the faith – they're much alike...'

I could go on, but Andy says: 'That's crap. The voyage
has no end. The quest – no start. The voyage – it begins in
nowhere in particular. The quest – is stasis. An itch where
you can't scratch. Real nomads – they have beasts, each
year they do the up, the down. It's agriculture, Vince.
Without the shit to burn – you'd freeze. Their economics –
based on crap. Not voyaging, no quest. Invent the spade –
you dig a trench – and with the earth – you've made a
rampart. There you are! Mechanical. A conurbation.'

'Icaro...' I begin.

'No, no,' shouts Andy. 'Forget Icarus. Our Icaro – works
in insurance. He thinks he's a crude beast who wants out
the door. It isn't so. He isn't trapped. He's salaried. A
bureaucrat who weeps because he has no feathers on his
arms, no compass in his brain. Pitiful. Don't read his
poems, Vince. Try sipping at reality. Remember, I'm you're
life-coach: if you don't earn, I don't eat steak.'

'I'll be your crude beast, Andy,' I tell him. 'So long as
there is action. I'll climb up on the stool, I'll chase the
clowns, I'll catch the flyers as they miss the net... I'll do
what it takes to get your ten per cent...'

'It's much, much more than that,' says Andy. 'Start
thinking thirty.'

'If you've no job, you think of joining 8s and 18s,' I tell
him. 'Short lives. That's the new thing. When I hear
"Amur" – my hair roots tense. The river – shrivelled by the
drought; the snow – it stings like salt. How can we live? The

beauty's gone extinct. Those plodding songs. We lie down in the cold. We die. What else can we do?'

'Ah yes, the Gobi,' Andy says. I see the tears prick in his eyes.

This is our passion. Roaming with no beasts, no destination. Whatever you are looking for – you'll find it there, in plenty or in desolation. Anything at all, whatever. Or nothing.

'Well, I can't go,' says Andy. 'I renounce. I'll find some other things to do. You can't, you won't. You won't give up. You won't invent.'

'Of course,' I say, needling. 'The animals see us. They scout us all the time. They know – those we don't kill, will starve. They'll go before us, just. You need them, you need new collectivities. The buildings – they see us too, in a lesser way, as we see them, quite likewise. Don't say it, though, they'll think you're mad. Say "architecture". "Dance", not dancers. Besides, the dancers never look at you. You're not on their horizon – it belongs to them alone.'

'Collectives,' Andy says, 'those are what you overlook: the guys in joyous lockstep, like the geese. I fought the class war for many years – till I got tired of losing and repeating...'

'Crap, Andy!' I say. 'You've never had a home. Never enrolled in anything.'

'Do you want a woman?' Andy asks. 'Not that I pimp. Or know your tastes. But – it's always easier to find a woman for a friend than for yourself. They say they still work miracles – even though we don't believe in them...'

'Andy, my record's worse than most,' I say. 'I'm sure you know what woman's best for me – hunting's

interminable. The dates! Think of China – the quantity!
Then – there's the documents...'

'A dog, then? A cat?' Andy asks. 'A crow? Raven?'

'That's the track,' I say. 'A voice.'

'Try these,' says Andy, opening his sack. 'There's discs.'

We listen to them all – the women – in cathedrals. 'Too
electric,' Andy says. 'In that huge space, it resonates with
the expanse – why roof it over, then? It must be fake.'

The baroque, and the impertinent: singing with lips sewn
up, in boxes for the dead – in urns: in winds... There's
males, a trilling in the head: and musky mezzi, a tenor
cuddled in their breasts.

Andy's eyes are closed, the lids are a bruised blue, with
baby streams of red. The mouth droops, a pure drool runs
down inside his shirt. He's in the melody.

There's playful, tearful, trills, purrs and growls. O
seasons, o betrayals, o pyres for lovers on the shore... Lilacs
and millstreams. Sentiment engraved on plastic. Voices.
They're solid forms, laid down on nothing, unfleshed,
breezes on the silver dishes – some, in life, as thick as
trunks of olive plants; some brass, some zinc, some – iris
stems.

'They're all traduced,' I say. 'You can't see the face – all
could come up from the same throat...'

'You choose a moment, then,' he says. 'It's all the same,
and all the same to me. A voice has left behind its body
anyway – and on a disc – well, nothing on to something, as
they say, is nothing, only what you want to hear.'

'That one!' I point. 'It drives along, that voice. Where is
the source?'

'I've no idea,' he says. 'I'll not desert you – but ... who
the voice belongs to, I don't know. It could be pure
electrics. You would have to search.'

'And finding – would be happiness?' I ask.

'Happiness is moving on to something else,' he says. 'All music is farewells.'

'I know about farewells,' I say. 'You pushed Icaro in his chair – down the hill he went, into the water. He can't wheel back up the slope.'

'That was drastic, I admit,' says Andy. 'It's hard to call it bad. Not good – just filing patterns. Much of everything is that – designs. For instance – you could start a reservation. Not Indians – animals. Nature. They have the instinct so they won't all die. That's helpful for you. And – Icaro got on my nerves – that dreary tale...'

'I don't feel at ease with good people, Andy,' I tell him.

He acts surprised: 'Your priest must have told you – in animals, there isn't good or bad.'

'I don't know which side that guy was on,' I say.

'Lion and lamb,' says Andy. 'We disobeyed, like Icarus. It kept on going bad, after him. Disobeying is the game. Now – we're flying everywhere, sometimes by night.'

'It seems too easy, put like that,' I say.

'That woman, Bianca – you could keep your animals near where she disappeared. Go look for her,' says Andy.

'It's your obsession, Andy,' I tell him. 'She's dead, or she's alive. Looking won't change a thing. There's no badness in any of it. Besides, she wasn't tender with her family... And – I'd forgot – those animals. They all have families – every sort. Monogamy and orgies, regurgitating for your kids and eating them... Socially, Andy, it's a jungle.'

I stare at his pale eyes, his dusty hair, the skin laid on like flakes or scales. Everyone's a priest, their own ideas on end days, how to live a long and useless life, and have the rest work on to cover you when you are old...

'Hey, Vince,' shouts Andy. 'Wake up to the plan. You rent a plot of forest, fence it round...'

'The animals?' I ask. 'And knowing about the trees, the snakes...?'

'You haven't understood, my friend. The fence is there to keep the crawlers out,' Andy says, 'The scratchers and the roarers too. You're stockaded, so's you can dig in peace. Gold and sapphires in the mud. What d'you want with animals, a-falling in the holes? A space – no animals at all! If the moviemakers come – you hire some creatures from a zoo. You find the treasure. Then comes your launch – success, flamboyant backcloth – a cityscape, your bride – you have to be a couple, but you have a document to keep your wealth secure.'

I meditate: 'It sounds like greed, dear Andy. And there'll be competitors... The gangs... The taxes...'

'It isn't greed, dear Vince,' he says. 'I'll skim and skin, and so will all the rest. It's finding what is hidden. All religions have a mystery ... what's underground – that's the best kind.'

'It's not about religion, Andy,' I say. 'I sat next to a guy on the wheel, is all.'

'Rodney Hawkett – he was into conservation. Not of himself – that clearly didn't work. Of unknown things. A loving paedo. Like your boss – up to the ceiling, down to the ground. You see the world at boot level, then up with the flying things – you think they're owls. No – they're cameras and bombs. It's all the same strategy, what they have,' says Andy.

'I won't dig in those guys' empty holes,' I say. 'I want big gestures, laughter with a paint moustache, hands on my knee, hands soft and pale as butter, under the table...'

'Get used to brown hands,' says Andy sharply. 'Do you hold the quiddity of all you've seen? No, naturally not. It all moved on in spirals, it spun away like sugar. Holes in the ground – hold on to them – they're solid, silent and still.'

'It's all negative. I see the whole scenario,' I say. 'Me, the indigenous lover, the extended family, some in the 8s, some the 18s. Betrayals, shootouts. Riches found. Guys hired – some steal and some defer. The bugs you eat, the clawmarks round your ears – those begin to weigh, your gut degenerates. There's more riches, less work more luck, and it's paper that you buy and sell, and more slick guys who cheat and flatter, more ceremonies, old guys who have dull funerals far far away, and guys that hate you smarming up...'

'You don't want to be a loser, though,' says Andy.

'It all comes from rubbing up,' I say, irritated, then annoyed. 'Things, people. Caroming off: your balls against the others.' Like toads in mating mode, you clamber up, over the viscid backs. You're quite anonymous, you've the same blunt nose and wriggling paws as all the rest. But for the pile, you'd just be croaking solitary in the slime. Friends: do they hoist you up? You hope they're nonces, strangenesses, out of the game... They pall. You the albino, Andy; Icaro with bleached hair and peeling scalp, the eyebrows blackened like moustaches...'

'That's from his trip,' says Andy, backing off.

'I'll do it all myself,' I say. 'I don't need animals, hungry and peering in, and gangs that prowl. Paying percentages! I know where I am making for. Imagine, if you can – the crowd, some in rags and some in ermine tails, they cry, '*Slava, slava*' – the bells are going mad, the clappers glow a revolutionary red. It's Stalin! Stalin! Here he comes, pushing through the crowd, alone, the stiff green cape, pen in one hand, the other holds a paperweight. He's here before us, and the crowd moves back. Then – what?'

I pause, although I know what's coming next. 'He sings,' I say. 'It is his moment, and he knows. It is the summit, and he sings. Solo, of course.'

'What does he sing?' asks Andy, 'And what about those guys behind him?'

'The chorus? That's what they are, that's what they do. Acclaim. They don't sing so well. You need to do things by yourself, know when exactly is the time. What does he sing? It doesn't matter much: there's something of the "Song of the Forests", I should say.'

'There's an audience,' Andy says, 'soaking in or spitting out.'

'No, Andy, that's not it,' I say. 'You're solo, or your chorus. There is nothing else. No audience, no booking, tickets, and no money back.'

'OK,' he says, 'saving from extinction. Striking it rich – neither attracts?'

'Those are normal. Extinction always happens – delaying it... that too. It's imperceptible. Wealth – exactly similar.'

'There's a new kind of gathering,' Andy says. 'You should go. There's no agenda. Now, there's no marriages, people live too long. Death is bland and dull, you long for it – perfunctory the funeral... Someone nominates a festa every day – each creed, a celebration, there's commemoration constant, no rejoicing.. the glorying days – they sail above, like swans, the honking breaks your sleep. So – don't count the rites. Get together – maybe something happens, maybe not.'

It's a variation. A potlatch with nothing – maybe no one – in the pot. Old guys, in a clump, standing on a platform, drooping like tallow candles. Each one full of wisdom, each wisdom is the same and incommunicable. No train's expected on the platform.

'I had a partner once,' I say. 'I invented dialogue for her – that she was kidnapped and released, or killed. I never heard from her.' I'm making party talk, jollying up someone who says:

'These gatherings are useful for confessions. Once it was deciding if to go to war. Now – that just happens. That's much easier.'

'Oh,' I say, 'don't give any weight to anything. You always meet up with people you could travel with, and then they disappear as well. You never know their names. It's to show you're in a species,' I tell her.

'My name's Aisha,' Aisha says. 'And yours is Vince, a chain around your leg.'

'All these feckless people here – they could decide to rampage out and burn some houses, Aisha,' I say. The thought excites, the possibility – it rouses me.

'People pair off,' she says, 'because they see the animals. especially the birds. But really... If you live close to a desert, you lose a lot of people there. Forests too. And railway lines, cities.'

Then – there's gangs, armies, occupiers. There's no problem losing what's encumbering.

'All the excitement, then the boredom – it distracts,' says Aisha. 'It's better doing what you have to do, not exchanging names.'

'What I have to do,' I say, 'I do it, eyes shut. Humming something else.'

'That's wrong,' says Aisha. 'All lives are tragedies, of course – and that's banal. The thing is – your life's your story. You can give it structure, decide who are the characters, the plot. You step on that boat, punch out that guy. How does it hang? Control's the thing. Beware the horses, Vince – they eat your cash like hay. Sex? You're not a master: best leave it out.'

'Who's the story for?' I ask, though I know quite well...

'Oh, the story's yours,' she says. 'No one is interested in any tale except their own.'

'You might give a hand,' I say. 'Be good, be generous. A joke?'

'All that is up to you,' says Aisha. 'If you do an epic, be sure there's someone literate at hand, to write or chisel.'

'But...' I say.

'I know,' says Aisha. 'My grandfather used to sing the song – "Arise, ye prisoners of starvation, arise, ye wretched of the earth..." The thing is to give your story a shape, so you can go back over – have a laugh, an honest tear, a frisson of regret. Then...'

★

'You're right, Andy,' I say. 'Those gatherings are old style. Romantic, like the té dansant. She stole my jacket.'

'A good one?' he asks.

'I should say so,' I say.

'Some people want to drive a Merc and live in a hut. They call it culture, but it's just a choice,' he says. 'A coat – you can't get far in that.'

'All this talk – it doesn't fit my coat. It was padded, for a lineman.'

We're both annoyed. 'What annoys me most,' I say. 'Apart from the cold – is the trick itself, the oldest. Someone confides, proposes a long voyage that may resolve everything, or give details and prospects you live with the rest of your life ... and it's about something else. The story that you hear comes louder than the story that is really just to lift your jacket.'

'Yes,' says Andy. 'That you fell for that – of course, it's chance, not choice, so you suppose – it makes me wonder if I'm doing right to keep on bearing with you, putting up with closeness?'

'Fuck you, Andy,' I say. 'The jacket didn't want to get liberated, passed on to someone's lover.'

'Maybe she thought it was owed to her – the scam, having to tell the story, use the language, sticking with all those people – all waiting for some synergy,' he says.

'I'll take the mischance as a message, Andy,' I say. 'If you've no coat – it means 'get nearer to the sun'. Not climbing hills: going down south, where there's faith and poverty.'

'You're slick,' says Andy, not approving. 'Like an empty pan. But – if there's still some warmth inside...'

'Yes, Andy,' I say, breaking off with him. 'Maybe you can cook your egg. Aisha told me how we struggle up the hill, the crest is mist, and up and up – the view will be superb, our legs grow weak, our lungs dry up, two apricots, we lie down with the rest – the air is thin, we fight for it, there's knives and baseball bats brought out That's it, the mystery. White light ahead.'

'What mystery?' he asks.

'How we all got on the hill, and thought there was another side, a view, our legs would take us up – seeing the bones stacked up, we might have guessed. That is the mystery, my dear old stupid friend,' I say.

'Well,' says Andy, 'out you go!' He opens the door, like to let a cat out, nothing in.

'It's snowing,' I say.

'It could be rice,' he says. 'Hold out your hands, thumb and forefinger together.'

★

Soon, there's sixteen of us, in the snow. Striding along, of every sex, thinking about it, us and ours – sex, our faces first white with the frost, then black, mincing, floundering as if we're on the catwalk in our fashion heels. On our heads, like mushroom caps, straw hats woven tight, you see stoneturners wear them, in Japan.

We're dressed for sharper worlds than this. Ahead of me – a guy bearing a long pole, a shorter hook, shiny, collectable – the long stick jigs the trolley back on the wires, the hook's for shifting points so the tram can follow its true destiny. We're all thrown out of somewhere, a useless trade encysted in our hands – gluers and tackers, makers of jet jewellery, solderers, stuffers of fine sailfish...

'Don't just tramp,' shouts Steve beside me – 'Sing! Sing every song, they'll come out to feed us, like we were the birds...' and so we do. Everything is possible.

We lose some mates – we stride along, our long white bodies, black faces. 'We are the best,' we shout, we who are left. The snow falls like a curtain – you could only see our heads, the snow our bed, our sea. We swim, we paddle.

'You must believe,' shouts Steve. 'This is how we evolve. In equations, in the earth, the sun, the twist divine – that little extra turn you give the key – the lock is free, the extra twiddle's for some divinity. Or – it invokes the spirit in a metal... salutes a privacy, an ingenuity... For sure – on every planet God has left not sons alone, but twins... And off they've gone, our comrades, looking for the lost twin daughter, ancient as the seas, bearing up our luminescent skiffs, our fishing ferries plunging down, our slaves, our contraband, our oils, our motors–'

'Steve,' I shout. 'We must avoid the drift. If we go down, we'll need to wait for spring...' But on he talks, '...our motors ... evolution...'

'We should have been four,' I say. 'But we're just two, our best two frozen out, or stumbled off, consumed by the beasts I love – who can keep track? Or – gone underneath the ice. Black shrimp-eyes fixed and sideways...'

'Ours are the tropics, Vince,' says Steve. 'Everybody knows they're sad – between the cancer and the goat with pointy horns. What do you expect? Everybody lives in huts and tents...'

'I don't know you, Steve,' I say. We're in the melt – a pink, anonymous. The black, the white – gone somewhere, invisible. This was our highest moment. What were we going to do, we sixteen? Maybe the other twelve – maybe they managed whatever it was, and became famous without belonging to a club, ranged in a totem. Maybe Steve has the rich interior life I don't have time for in myself, being so occupied with dealing with him, and Andy, getting a job, not wanting it.

'I work for your boss,' he says. 'To find new things, you need laboratories. Just sitting here amid the mud – you don't discover anything. You need a guy who leads, with cash...'

'No, no,' I say. 'I'd quit.'

'The boss is like the ancient guy who burnt,' says Steve. 'Dry crusts against the flames. One side's philanthropy, the other – well, he makes us skip. You'll see.'

'No one has two sides,' I say. 'We're one-dimensional – or else we wouldn't stick, we'd tumble on the floor.'

'We have come through,' says Steve. 'People invented what we've just experienced, made it a metaphor, an epic. See – there was no need. It's real. We're pink again, no ash, no clinker. Here's your payoff – your boss's conscience,' and he puts a thin envelope inside my shirt. 'I'm a scientist,' he says. 'My job with you is done. Find a tower of the winds, and listen to them. Pay the rent. Snuff in the air. Suppose you were up there, looking down on roofs, gliding, spiralling up and down, waiting for the dead to be laid out for you... Aren't you better off? Just as you are. You'll only need an oil lamp, yellow light to match that old French paper, those yellow mysteries. They're piled up on the stalls. You can't understand the words ... but there are murders constantly, then justice. In not too many pages. Go to bed, dream of pink dawns.'

Steve's another genius. I admire him – there's nothing else to say. I say,

'All the people here – they come, like us, from somewhere else. You forget, or else you cry all day. Driven out – by friends – for sure, no one cares about that tale. Armies, heretics, the drought – that makes news, but no one cares that much. The moving on. That's normal. Do you wander, do you stick? They say that's the crucial point ... the species, sedentary or nomad. It doesn't work that way, of course. Everybody wanders, from Summer palace to the Winter one, Paris–Moscow and then back, and nomads build their cities, start collecting tax. Then, there's thinking about abstracts. Humans, they say, are the only ones that think of things not there... and yet – humans are artisans, making things that animals have never thought of, can't handle with their paws and scales – that's why the bigger beasts lie around: they muse all day, on things that aren't...'

Steve bustles off, into the market. Red hot peppers, purges, stuff that makes you sneeze. 'I have to find a thing...' he says. He's never seen again – it's not a kidnap, I'm quite sure.

*

In the room I rented, there's a woman, fingering my stuff. 'Othmar's gone to mosque,' she says, 'I'm sure he will be back.'

'He's not from here,' I say.

'He converted when he found me. He teaches German – that's where they all want to go. Then he gives their names to the police,' she says.

'I don't know any German,' I tell her.

There's little for me here. I don't wait for Othmar to return.

They all drive fast here in this town.

In the market, there's some very rich. They'll likely lose their cash. The very poor – where will they land? Do they hope to pick it up, the cash, as it goes falling from above?

They're from here, and not. I don't believe in that, travelling and staying still. I don't believe in mystic painting, nor the holy wall where one day it might appear to me, nor in sages, nor in studying and coming up with vacant skins. Once it was here, now it's utterly gone, gone utterly. I don't believe it, not at all, but it's missing. Even if it never was, it can still be missed.

The little guys – they started all the trouble here, wanting a looser life. Poor little guys? Who beleves that. Poor guys never did anything here. So – the little ones began it all, and the big guys stopped it. If you want to believe something really bad – you can believe that. Everything's belief, all made up – epics, revelations, and equations – we forget what the blind poet said last night, tonight we sit around the fire and hear it all again.

It's hard to know ... where's best: maybe a small country, three or four people, abstemious. I could be a soldier there, irregular. The best kind, keeping out of trouble, with no penalties for skiving off. A tailor or a sailor? – there's periods of beggardom, and you need to sew the canvas bags. Rich man, poor man – as you walk along, you're neither. Nothing here to steal – just clothes dumped by the track, never a whole person left inside, curved bones, too twisted to be arms or legs.

Ahead, there's a couple, stumbling along.

Gennaro and Maya Reza: 'We make up names so's when we arrive,' Gennaro says. 'We'll fit right in.' We walk along together.

'When we're somewhere else,' says Maya, 'we'll think back to this awful place, everything will glow, there'll be eternal festa. Cousins and aunts, our children, making honey all together, dancing before the hive.'

'Why are you leaving?' Gennaro asks me. 'The war? The poverty?'

'It's because I don't speak German,' I say. They stare. 'And all the rest. Everything you wouldn't want to know firsthand.'

'With us,' Gennaro says, 'it is the fear.'

'Oh,' I say, 'I don't listen to what they say. I don't watch what they do – don't look up, or down. Those curved bones – I'm sure they never have been straight.'

'Ah,' Maya says, 'it's the fear that makes them curve.'

'The fear,' I say. 'Is why no one wants you in, when you have got there. The fear's a plague.'

'Families should help,' Gennaro says. 'But – they make it worse.'

'You should avoid those people who have ghosts,' I say, thinking of Rodney Hawkett, burnt to toast. Exalting, we all danced around... My boss – full of rancour, his eyes – two pills dissolving: storing the anger in his gut, elbows asplay that can burst a gate, set you running down the street, screams stream out of every hole in you, you're kicking in the doors, what's compressed is red and yellow, foamed in spate, a fountain over everything. Out it roars like writers' crap on walls – 'Blast' 'Magic wood', 'Frack'. Not knowing where he wants to finish up – despising the rich, the guys like him. How to spend his cash? Founding museums, collecting stuff like it was bets on greyhounds. Buy stuff, buy titles – hating it all, all's a mantra, quite beyond you... Maybe dead, he plans, he'll enter in your arse and eat you up and leave the shell...

'It's the fear,' Gennaro says. 'You may think it's something else. It's in you like a vine, a white blind eel. It makes your legs go pippety-pop. You have it worse than us – from friends and enemies – all the crusading axmen, all the holy warriors, the jailers, the warders in intelligence, wearing their gowns and pointy hats.'

'Don't be afraid of me,' says Maya, holding on to me, letting me inside her eyes: 'I'll keep you company, and I won't keep you safe.'

'I trust you, Maya,' I lie to her. 'We're nearly where we want to be. No one is interested in us. We're just poor guys – can't fight or work, valueless, along this track...'

'There'll be a border. Everyone comes here – to occupy. I guess there's money in it. There's no way you can escape,' Gennaro says, pushing us along. 'There's always aeroplanes scouting. I guess they see us. We'll go to where they come from – that way, we'll be safe.'

He whispers to me, 'I don't trust Maya. Going somewhere else – it's the first step away from me.'

'Do you care, Gennaro?' I ask.

'It's a little thing, like they keep on happening to everyone,' he says. 'It's when they pick you out. You're standing in the crowd – and then the finger points, you've to be the hangman, or the corporal, or the guy with his eye in a sling,' and he laughs – we both do. It's an old expression.

Up ahead, there's a low bar: The Edge, it says. 'If you know it's a low bar,' Maya says, 'you'll never get on in your life.'

Gennaro says, 'That's true – if you've ever gone in one – you're ashes. Floating dregs.'

'If it's for the border guards,' I say, 'they'll for sure be heretics, and there's alcohol.'

We three go in. There is alcohol. Maybe some of our twelve are sat there, in the shadows, back from their poles … on theirs, there's dancers, there's an angry stripper too, I hope she doesn't fake her rage – this stew needs peppering up.

'Hey!' I say, 'I ought not to be here. It's trivial – but if I drink – short life to come. You must choose to have one: there's *Vita* in that bottle, you can drink it long or short. A short – like if you want to live – a mayfly: devoted to good or bad. Which – good or bad – it's quite indifferent. Long lives – there isn't one between us here. That's all about the flow to a conclusion – always a disappointment.'

The guards keep people in. Other guards – they keep them out.

This guard's called Rocco – like his mates, he's chosen a brief life he thinks is good for him, for everyone.

'Your friends,' he says to me, 'they have no hope.'

'I had suspected that,' I say. 'But – all they want's to walk on, ahead. Hope's abandoned. Movement is the thing...'

'You seem a gent,' says Rocco, feeling for the cash tucked in my shirt, quite playfully. 'You could be a no-man, your own land ahead. Your friends – they have the fear. Not wanted here or there – it's the infection, terror, that we're told not to let in. Or out.'

'Gennaro's too old to be a soldier, Rocco,' I say.

'That's exactly what we need,' says Rocco, 'old soldiers. They can occupy before they die. There's cities going empty – others that's too full. Shift people round. Equality, that's what we need. When that comes, we'll take Maya too.'

'Oh, come,' I say. 'It's not just soldiers live in towns. Besides, you do control from far away, intelligence, in quantity. Then there's the baking, butchery...'

'You remember butchery from Rodney Hawkett time,' Rocco laughs. 'No, Gennaro's useful. You're useful too – in quite a different way. You draw the maps, you choose the presidents, talk to your foreign friends, ally with them. You and your boss decide the lot. Ration the water. Then – there's the sun. You keep us worshipping indoors, going to vote, all that – but – we should prefer to start again, take off our clothes, run in the burning sun, take back our rightful colors, charcoal twiglets running through the midday heat... You, you keep us in the modern way. Work. Flying all enclosed as if you're on the ground...'

There's drumming now – a guy from Senegal: the stripper's stripped – she dances on, puts back her clothes

the wrong way up. We drink our *Vita,* and we slap our
knees and click our heels – don't feel the pain. We kick out
with our legs, the arms fly round – those, we can't feel.
Love. Ah! Love. How we would make it, feel it in the
blood, make it hum and wheeze, if only brain would
animate our genitals...

'Come, come with me,' I whisper to Maya. 'We'll live in
no man's land... Pass the fence, the ditch...'

'You're a zero to me,' Maya says. 'But, of course.'

'See the city, where we'd live, down there,' I say, 'where
you can hear the donkeys bray. Gennaro could go round in
the evenings, light every soft yellow lamp that hangs there
like a lemon, ripe and sweet...'

'Yes, yes,' Maya says. 'Lying on the roof, the stars
clustered up there like flocks,' and maybe she weeps. 'It
could be Gennaro's home. But – it's not my city. I'm not
welcome there. They'd know me from my name.'

I drink more *Vita.* 'It's banal, Maya,' I say. 'Talking of
no man's land, of whole cities there... Cities are all like that
– there is no welcome, and we love them for it...'

'No, no,' Maya says, 'Take me away with you, far far
away, and you – turn into someone else.'

'I'll reason with Rocco,' I say. 'Shunt me towards him.'

'There is no universal reason, clean, without vibrato,'
Rocco says. 'There is nothing universal except the universe.
Gas and stones. Lots of nothing. To reason, there is a
ceiling, quite impenetrable – call it God, or happenstance,
your pot on the fire, bribe in your pants... That serves to
get you through the day and round the corner. The rest – is
dreams of luxury. My weapon is your ceiling...'

And it's true – I've fallen and I'm wedged here beneath
the bench, my ceiling – most hems are dirty, mostly guys
aren't wearing socks. 'Oh help me up,' I try to shout – but

if I'm up, I might fall down again, I need a peg, a glue, more hands, a shanty or a prayer.

'Leave him be,' Gennaro says. 'He's overdone the *Vita*. We'll find another crossing, climb the fence.'

'No,' Rocco says, 'It's too late for that. You can't just live in places, without a history, a past, a future.'

'You can't keep tabs on everyone,' I say.

'Of course we can,' says Rocco. 'That's what your money's for. Who'll pay our tab? You! And where've you been? You blabbed about Rodney Hawkett – that's a decease. And all the rest? Are you responsible? Friends disappeared... Now – here comes the tab...'

'You took my cash already, friend,' I say. 'Before you ask – it was a present from my boss. For showing him his aspirations were all vanity.'

'Ha!' Rocco shouts. 'You're out to be the clever sort – that we don't want. We live by vanity – we don't like folks that's cleverer than us... They put themselves on wrong sides, and won't be argued with...'

He kisses me on the top of my head. They bring the tab. *Vita* – even when it's cut to make it *Aquavit,* is costly here.

'The more we keep you simmering, the more you think of crime,' says Rocco. 'Yours, ours. You're angry now...'

'No, Rocco,' I say. 'I'm still trekking to my happy place.'

They laugh. Maya says, 'Gennaro, of course I love you. Giving you up, going with someone else – would add a poignancy, make it a broader theme...'

'It isn't in the contract,' Gennaro says.

'Did I hear "the dance before the hive"?' shouts Rocco: 'I'm the gatekeeper! Mine's the transition – place to place, not time to time. Who'll push up that ceiling with a show? Berlin in the Eighties? Kick 'em up – higher and higher, up the ceiling goes, into the blue ... ignorance or innocence? Let's lose them both. Up on the stage...'

★

'Can't you walk now?' Maya asks. 'This box is heavy, and the wheels have fallen off.'

'I'm terminally ill,' I say: I'm lying here, spilled from my cart. 'That *Vita* – it's killing me. But... I can't walk. My shoes? Oh no...'

'You didn't do a perfect strip,' Gennaro says. 'You started with your boots – it stopped the show – your ignorance and innocence had stashed your savings there...'

'My cash reserve!' I say. 'It fluttered out like doves, I bet.'

'Some thought you had a belt of gold,' says Maya. 'Your nudity made us dread – we didn't pry. A belt of chastity, your boss had maybe had it forged and fastened on. It takes the fire to get it off, then you are rightly done – and roasted too.'

'It's true,' I say. 'My boss had them made for loyalty. But – I betrayed. I never even saw the smith, the hammer and the fire. Of course, that Hawkett was a platinum man, you'd need to melt him in the fire to judge his worth. They're all like that, the real big guys... As good as gold and twice as valuable...' I prattle on. Gennaro says, 'Hey! We're off, through this fence, Maya and me. You'll find some boots, if you survive. The army has them – you could join...'

They're gone. My box is wedged between the here and there. Maya and Gennaro scuttle through the maize, their rich inner lives, unexplored, tiny white flags like rabbits' scuts, undulating as they run. I'm unsure – do I want the here or there? What did I say when I took off my shoes? I hear Maya, shouting back:

'A discourse worthy of the best. You're truly Vince the prince! If you had subjects, you'd be loved – but you spoke of the objects – the nebulae, the universe – then what? When it ends? Will the purpose be revealed? And – should we add some goodness to our bad, or are we just ephemeral, sad beasts who've lost our tail and claws and found some awful substitutes? Faith in science, worshipping the sun, cherishing the beetles, remembering the dance – all was brought out, dear Vince. And then – the denouement. The golden wave! Your shoes, your clogs – the bills you sprinkled out like amber rain, soaking the lot of us – and you, a poor man, drunk and poisoned with the *Aquavit* – your inner life, turned inside out like dirty pants to make them look like clean... You never said you loved me, Vince, but I'll remember...'

And she's gone. I didn't love her, though that's the story that resounds. And now I'm stuck, abandoned... At least I kept on my socks, in them a further stash of cash convertible – the stuff of dreams, that buys you tickets for the wheel...

'You were Silenus...' she shouts back, fading out.

*

'We want people who can garrison,' says the sergeant, the recruiter – Rocco or his brother. 'When you occupy a place, first you must cut out the doubtful ones. It's about right people in the right space.'

'That's obvious,' I say. 'Who wouldn't want that?'

Sure I want that, and I want a pair of boots. 'I was in the fire service,' I say.

'That reference to Silenus,' says the soldier. 'That marks her. Where she was – that's silly talk. Where she's going – they'll see she's different. She'll thieve. You mustn't do that.'

'I don't believe in Silenus,' I say. 'There's a trace of hedonism about me, that is all. And I'm suffering for it.'

'That's good,' says the sergeant. 'We're not beasts. We're not shod,' he laughs. 'Not by smiths. Your boots are over there.'

He kisses me on the top of my head: 'We'll cover you,' he says. 'Your fears, doubts, anger. But don't desert, we'll shoot you.'

'Must I take an oath?' I ask.

'If you like,' he says. 'But it sounds like last century. Just put on your boots and try to save your pay.'

I musn't desert, I tell myself. 'I'll go and pick some mushrooms in the forest,' I tell him, Rocco, or his brother – 'For our lads' soup. There's a mystery in a mushroom... It'll help them decide who they want in and out.'

The sergeant winks. 'A good stew,' he says. 'Proof's you against stones getting thrown. Better than *Vita* – that makes you feel bad.'

The friendly forest, the faces on the trunks that wink, the branches sweeping down, shading me as I run – these wonderful boots: sleek as a fox – I run. There's a hole in the fence. Maybe they'll keep putting cash on my paybook, maybe I'll get medals. A band for my funeral.

As I run, I grab some mushrooms – down they go! I might join the Chinese army, with my skills acquired – go see the shamans – and I fly! Like Icarus! Over the ditch, the minefield – a noble arc – I flap my wings – no, it's not feathers, it's my mushroom power. Imagine – an army with battalions of naked men in flight!

But – do I want to spread the story round? The mystery becomes banal... There'd soon be millions in the air, like dragonflies, in armed and unarmed combat – the fields strewn with the throbbing bodies tumbled down – a new dimension... Migrating populations – flailing off to warmer winters, blacking out the midnight suns, building their nest on Notre Dame, an evening oratorio as flocks fly back to bed from picking fruit and berrying in the woods... Angel cities, everywhere.

You come down – it's not the sun melts you, not your presumption: your body's used up all the mushroom juice. Icarus – poor unlucky soul – a stall! the blue above, the blue beneath. There's no way out. He should have fallen up, upward in the sky. The sky that should be black. Dirt makes it blue. Make a splash – you might be saved...

I land quite gently in a tree. This place: it feels like a small country. I've met the leaders leading everywhere. Power over one person – you feel it all, intense. Power over a million – there is no kick, no fun, no prick. The people groan and cheer, suffer and hate – you don't. You needn't. Others will do it all and live with it – the struggle. Power over twenty guys – just strife and ridicule: think of it – sex over twenty guys – what would that mean? It wouldn't, surely, be the sex you'd pant or pay for... Or – you might ingratiate yourself, win their vows, their interest. 'Service before everything' – you, under everybody else. Power – hallucination, panic, strut and reticence: whatever helps to make it work.

There's a castle, and beside – a bigger building, no crenellations; that shows you've conquered, don't need the castle now. Dishonoured people at their desks.

Inside the curious big building, there's guys like Rocco in the corridors, stopping their chatter when they stare at me.

'Maya Reza,' I ask. 'Just to see how she is. She was independent – couldn't afford a trafficking.'

'Oh,' says the guy, 'we don't take names. Those change – it's kinder not to write them down. It's better that the folks just disappear. It's natural: some – because you didn't care. Some want to disappear. Some, most, perhaps, just aren't there any more. It's better, that she can't be found.'

'I know,' I say. 'It happens all around me. People come and go. There's not so much that you can do. It goes on so.'

'We're perishable,' says the guy. He takes a shine to me. Not to Maya, he's no idea about her. We laugh: me – because a 'shine' – that's an old expression. I don't know what's funny in his mind.

'You know – if you've no address – they'll have gone thieving. There's nothing else, unless you're handy,' says the guy. There's another expression, makes you laugh. Cry, if you're the nostalgic type.

'If you've an interest of a general kind, in people and what happens to them,' the guy goes on. 'You could make it a career. All the people – who knows what they did, where they've gone ... you could look for them. Publish your search. We – don't keep a record.'

That's the end.

He says, 'You seem an important guy. Made yourself a soldier too – you're a weapon! That was noble.'

'Oh yes,' I say. 'I work too with a big boss,' and I give the name. 'I deputise for him. I'm his philosopher. And – I'm a protégé of Rodney Hawkett, tragically melted down.'

The guy says, 'And Maya? A lover? Terrorist, maybe.'

'Of course I loved her, like we ought,' I say. 'She could be angry. Docile too. I never went inside her inner life.'

'The cops will take a note,' he says. 'Of her. Your snitching on her – that makes sense, if you're quite prominent, the type who sticks around, and gives particulars. We'll find her – and you too...'

I leave him an address – the park where there's the wheel. 'Some fifty hectares, where you can amuse yourself, at any time,' I say. 'I'll welcome you.'

'Thanks for the invite,' says the guy. 'It's a commitment. Both of us...'

He takes a book, a gilded cover: in his other hand – an orb, a globe. 'If you should let me down,' he says, 'here's an agreement, signed by everyone. It's good for all the planet, here in my hand, in miniature. We'll chase you round it, if you fall short and wanting. Now – gaze at this wall!'

It's light and dark: a childish scrawl of blob and blur. 'The universe,' he says. 'Dawn and night. You fly, you spread your wings, you take a ship – anywhere and everywhere. We'll hunt you down, wherever you hide out and raise your shabby flag.'

'I understand,' I say. 'But – that address I gave – it does exist. You good – your best – time awaits you there.'

He puts away his orb, his book in every tongue... He switches off the wall. He waves me to the door.

The flying, my fall – mushrooms don't come in.

I've done a foolish thing.

*

'Oh no,' says Andy. 'You're back. No – a life's not lived like this. "Decisive interventions", that was to be the aim. Besides, there's people looking for you. You gave that name they say it can't exist: "Maya". Can't be found, not on a list.'

'Maybe she's gone underground,' I say.

'Then it's murder – not mass murder', Andy says. He's much relieved.

'Maybe I got things wrong,' I say. 'It's always possible.'

'There's the Hawkett legacy,' says Andy. 'Yours, since you were on the scene, the fire. It's treasure trove.'

'I was getting short,' I say, pulling myself up.

'No, no,' says Andy. 'Not cash. People. "Decisive intervention" – so, you decide. Maybe – have a dream that's realer than the real again – transform it all. Hawkett – he's left you people who're in debt to him, or that he owed. Ready for anything.'

*

'I can free you from Andy,' says the lady. 'Him and Icaro, two leaches, living off each other's blood.'

'And my team?' I ask. 'Jazz dancers, monocyclists, poodle trainers. Renderers, web-makers...'

'All of that and much much more,' she says. 'Too bad there's no bikers. I do love a thuggy type...'

I'm amazed, I gaze... 'Yes, dear,' says the lady. 'It's a shift. The best ladies wore them once. And – watch this pin.' It seems to hold her knickers to a belly-band. Her body's very bony-thin and very round, in parts. That aspect's not worth considering...

'You didn't do too well in tests of action, nor humanity,' she says. 'Right down the middle. Norm: should be your name, though Vince is bad enough... Maybe your forte should be politics. But your teeth are grey. Go see the dinosaurs – they had a smile that dentists couldn't chip away. You need a grin, but not when you inspect your troops – there's always someone making history, a bullet in the chamber, then in you...'

'You've thought it out,' I say.

'Oh yes,' she rushes in, 'it's all about the paintings, dear.'

'Yes,' I say, 'I've seen the movies – the Duce, in the chapel, finishing off the sketch. Oh dear – the colours! Stalin in the monastery, the frescoes ... and poor Eisenstein, the criticism ... did him no good. So, they say, Stalin rubbed it all out, the painting, the building – a perfectionist – his good side...' We pause, maybe in awe.

'I thought it was the style,' I say, 'not the execution. Romanticism, writing it all down, thinking there would be a future. All that stuff.'

'Look,' she says, 'I've thought it out, I don't need commentary. Come home with me, on the way you'll think about having sex, when we arrive, we'll toss for it. Remember – once you've had it with another – it's hard to fantasise. Hope's better deferred, you know.'

'The guys I knew – Andy, Steve – what were they? What becomes of them?'

'Just call me Lady Bea. That's short for everything that starts with "B" – the lady means I'm not a queen,' and she laughs. 'Andy loved your emptiness. He thought he could fill you up. Steve – you lost the other pilgrims. Then the snow – it melted off your boots – the boots you lost, with all your cash, being ungirdled in the pub...'

'Yes, yes,' I say. 'I know all that. But *them*. The people I've been with, who ran with me across the fields, looked back with tearful eyes – "Save me, save me" they seemed to cry...'

'Yes, that was what they cried,' she says.

There's a youth in her room. 'He's not my son,' says Lady Bea.

'Round me,' I say, 'people seem not to last so long.'

'All the culture Stalin had, his handwriting, so well-formed – all came from the church, you see,' says Lady Bea. I think she ignores my questions. 'Maybe that's the case,' she says, 'But I don't ignore *you*, not at all. Most of the best, the documented ones,' and she unpins her hat. 'Are dead. And – you are right – pins are important in my life. They serve to fix what is not you to all the rest. There is no theory that accounts for it, except in abstract terms, quite tentative.'

The youth tells me, 'Beatrice clings to the lady title. It isn't pinned, so she can do without. If you have sex, the rate is half and half. If not, you get the discount, forty-five per cent.'

'I'm sure you are related to her,' I tell the youth. 'And the pictures. On the walls and lying on the floor. Grass. Beautifully done – even the colour's right. It could be real.'

'They *are* real,' says the youth. 'If you're a soldier, you recognise it at once. It's cover. For hiding behind.'

'This Beatrice,' I say, 'she must be a recruiter. That's why she's good at categories.'

'All those people in your legacy,' says the youth, 'they must have preferences. It's like a country – people knowing where they want to go. They'll all get kitted up, and take an oath. Beatrice is special – she puts them on a catwalk. That way, you can see where they'd best fit in.'

It's oppressive in the room. There's too much muslin and velvet here, it's Bloomsbury but there is no cat.

The youth, waiting to age so he can be recruited, moons around, listens to Cobain...

'Usually recruiting's done at school,' he says, 'But if you don't attend – it's soldiering direct.'

Beatrice, filling in paybooks, hums Delibes. 'Don't goggle, dear,' she says. 'It's me that has the eye. I sort you out. The struggle, yes, it does avail, for that is all there is.'

'I've heard that, Beatrice,' I say. 'It always seemed a metaphor.'

'There is demand,' she says. 'The old, the young, prospectors, spies – the guys who run it all and watch the screens...'

'Struggle's quite vague,' I say.

'I got you prised away from Andy,' Beatrice says. 'And – I know what you're getting at as well. I'm full of it. Culture, cooperation – taking another turn. Africa's long behind us, naturally – the first long march. Those fossils, covering the globe! I'm more into rats – how they'll suffer, the poor things, when the air, the water disappear...'

'Andy was a lazy type,' I say. 'He hoped to push me where he wouldn't go.'

'That's the devil's work, my dear,' and Beatrice and the youth leap up, arms in the air, their fingers locked. They gyre.

'Andy's gone!' the youth cries out. 'That sponge! The labours, the heavy lifting – those remain. That's what Andy groomed you for.'

'You realise,' says Beatrice. 'When your troop files in – they're not the past, they're not your slaves – they're not your friends.'

'Hide behind the curtain,' says the youth. 'You never know what they have done, and where they want to go with you.'

The curtain's gauze: the faces of my legacy – they look alike, soft focussed. Beatrice questions them – where they've been, all that. She gives each one an envelope. The youth has joined me, stands too close, he smells of acetone, of glue that sticks the aeroplanes. His twiggy hands – too close to mine... 'See, Beatrice has assigned them all,' he says.

'That's no advantage I can see,' I say. 'Not for them, and not for me.'

'Oh yes,' he says. 'It must be done. She places them – it's a new thing...'

'And me?' I ask. 'What's to become of me?'

'Well,' says the youth, 'we have no cat. Maybe she plans to keep you here.' He shows his teeth to show he's made a joke.

Outside I watch the guys assigned, opening their envelopes. Some have drawn blank, but everyone strides off – towards the poles, the sun, the snow that's done for people that I hardly knew. Off they went, those messengers – they don't come back. Those messages – a one-way show, the destination gone away, just as they arrive.

'I'm quite confused,' I say to Bea: 'I don't know where I stand. Nor where you – nor Hawkett, dancing in the flames...'

'Oh – just see him as a portent, dear,' says Lady Bea. 'Our instinct tells us all has changed. We're global now, and if it all falls down... Look at this marquetry...' and she shows me two long boxes, one cloudlike, billowing, with roots and leaves of cherrywood set in, the other tiny one, of chipboard, and inset 'Nachlass', 'the unnamed'.

'That's for the boy,' she says. 'I picked him out to boil my eggs. Quite useless... But, we are prepared. We just need someone who will nail us in.'

'You're quite unlikely, Lady Bea...' I start.

'The eggs we thought would hatch – but we must be content, and boil them, like an eye,' she says. 'Eyes must be hardboiled. Maybe you are the one that's left, your last labour the last screw – that's for the boxes, if I don't reach immortality...'

'What's going to happen, Beatrice?' I ask. 'And why is everything I thought gone rancid, the people that you see – all spun away... you hope for this, or that, it all turns round...'

'Well,' she says. 'You nearly learned to fly. And nearly tried to tell your truth. See – how unavailing that all was!'

'What is your destiny?' I ask. 'Maybe you've reached the end before, or several times...'

'Oh no,' she says. 'I fight my fights. Last woman standing, that's my role. Of course, there's devastation – but the fig's a mighty tree, resourceful, generous. There's me beneath, big birds that shake the branches, so...'

'And then the angels come,' joins in the youth, 'to end it all, and start it off again.'

'Yes, yes,' says Bea. 'Though you will not be there.' She turns to me:

'He oughtn't to be here. But when it's time, I'll send him back to where he was before...'

'I shan't take my envelope, even if you've one prepared,' I say.

'You're unreliable,' she says. 'You get nothing. And remember – the earth turns, spins your friends into oblivion... the morning star comes round again – see – now it is the evening star! But once a star...!' She smoothes the antimacassars. 'Reaction always wins. That's how we've survived so far. Evolution is as slow as worms who build big wheels. It still is more secure than constitutions and the cops.'

'All ends in death,' I say, 'except for Lady Bea.'

'That is the halfway, where we've reached so far,' she says. 'First, there'd be your labours: then will come – modifications to our genes – the fins and tails, the scorching breath, ungainly smells, the loss of speech – all's to change, the adaptations ... everything transmogrified. Useless to criticise my underwear, my decor – all will be mutated, back to the slime and claws. Enjoy your beauty now, mine too – you'll seem grotesque when the rest have seven arms and eyes and live in ceiling cracks and sing like toads.'

'I'm sure you're right,' I say. 'But – those guys that Hawkett dumped. Where did they go?'

'Oh,' she says, 'converting, Vince. Some make believe in distant worlds, some float in the ships that get you there... knowledge of everything, friends with all, the true religion, each has their expertise – life must go on...'

'Not necessarily so,' I say. 'If you are right...'

'Oh, don't lose hope,' she says, kissing the youth on his brilliantined crest. 'Some sell motors, some patch you up, some give you therapy ... look out the window, Vince: human life – it's all there.'

She's right, it is. 'We shall have tea,' says Beatrice. 'Before you go?'

'Where am I going?' I ask.

'I'm brilliant,' says Bea. 'But I don't predict.'

'Does anybody know a grace?' asks the youth.

Into my head comes a phrase – maybe the absent Steve invented it – 'Certain strategic salients of bourgeois power remain...' Should that be a grace? Is this a salient? Who's taken over now?

'You're right,' says Bea. 'Culturally, this is a dump – the trunk where they keep clothes for dressing up. Good music – where's it gone? Now – eat your egg.'

'Be sure to dip your soldier in,' says the youth.

'There's feather stuff in mine,' I say.

'Now, aren't you the lucky one – it's for absent friends, but those wings won't take you far,' says Beatrice. 'I'm always sad about the grace. It can't be hard to make one up. We all have hope.'

'I only hope for what may come about,' I say. It sounds prim.

They both look shocked. 'Haven't you been listening?' asks Lady Bea. 'All my lads are mercenaries – they don't hope for anything – and nor do we.'

'I can't wait,' the youth says, beating with his spoon. 'Mobilisation! I hate just being kept.'

'After everyone else is poor because of you, you and your mates will be in poverty as well,' says Bea. 'You're a plague.'

'You took my heritage,' I say. 'Someone earned from that – not me.'

'It's an accident of birth,' says Lady Bea. 'The wheel turns, is never still.'

'Sex – it's the same,' the youth complains.

'I tell you stories, dear: you take them to your cot, enjoy yourself – in the big world, you'd have to share,' says Beatrice – 'I guide *you*. I don't guide your hand.'

'Before I leave,' I say, 'Give me your largest thought.'

'Drink what you can of your tea,' she says. 'And – this could be your grace: "Poverty brings conflict. Riches bring conflict, but the weapons are much bigger." That should help you, dear.'

As I leave, another squad swirls up, pushes me aside: I say, 'There's love in that ménage,' but they don't seem to hear.

*

'Now I'll do Kutah-Qamat,' says the singer in the underground. 'It means "You are short, my beloved – perhaps because you are my life, and my life is going to be short."'

The less indifferent of us, maybe the more aimless ones – we laugh. For sure, that's what it says, the song... We laugh away – the singer – she's not fazed.

She's done: she isn't paid. 'It must be the translation. I did a course – I'm not one of them. I'm poor, is all,' she says.

'You're right,' I say. 'It isn't funny. It's true – but what's it worth? Who can tell?'

'I could have studied equality,' says the singer. 'Saving human lives by calculation: saving wolves. Instead, it had to be Farsi, for the time.'

'Not many do it,' I say. 'Not here, in this place that looks like Copenhagen. Even if they don't finish...'

'How'd you finish a language?' she asks, getting angry. 'Besides, I don't like healthy digging ... all those worms ... And there's lots I don't want to be equal with.'

'No,' I say, 'I mean with a language, there's a point where you try to speak, and they don't laugh at you. You could try memory, rocking to and fro.'

I peek at her licence, that you need to sing in this flat grey town: 'Melissa'. 'That's a name slips sweetly off the tongue,' I say. 'I guess it's sexual, all those words. Of course, she's even angrier.

'I don't mean anything,' I say. 'Not about anyone, not me or you. Just words, slipping off...'

My tongue.

'The song was so beautiful,' Melissa says. 'I wanted to pursue it, turn into it, like a sylph. Of course, that leaves most of life outside. Even more, if you're successful, have to repeat.'

'That outside's the part of life I live in,' I say. 'And beauty – it's so contested – what its value is, where it lives, what languages it speaks. What's left without, where we all live, mostly.'

I give offence, continually. Speaking has intimacy, even if you haven't meant it, as if you stuck a finger in a nose, a stranger's ear. 'It's all in the past,' I say. 'Beauty in the future – it makes no sense. No – it's all gone by.'

'The past – wasn't at all beautiful,' she says. 'And you're right about the future. Beauty's the unicorn, hidden behind the tree.'

We've reached to terminus. We stand, each ready for a conclusion, on the platform: 'Beauty teaches renunciation,' Melissa says, 'and we desert it for reality.'

'That's crap,' I say. 'You don't need teaching to renounce, desert – absolutely anything and anyone. And often deserting's the best way – whether you do it, or it's done to you.'

It's been a charming interlude – it's good it's ending. And Melissa – certainly she's short. She wears a pair of cavalry boots, long and creased – a mistake, if you're so short; not small and harmonious, just not long enough, disproportionate to everyone.

'Goodbye again,' I say. 'I shan't pester you. I'm off – the trip is over.'

She doesn't set off for somewhere. 'I ride this train,' she says, 'It's work.'

Of course! She's always on the same train, up and down the line – impossible to leave her – she's always where you know she is. Better than picking rubbish – it's still work for an untouchable.

*

I find Gino's apartment. I start to say Bea sent me. 'No, no,' he shouts, 'I don't want to know all that. Most everything of what we know is over. It's experience, dead – what you had in mind to do with it – whoa! there it goes, it slips away.'

'Right!' I say. 'What's your news?'

'For me,' he says, 'if you go through it numb – existence – I wouldn't care, I wouldn't know. It isn't even up to you. You falls asleep – are you dead? You wouldn't know, or care, and nor would I.'

'Not archaeology,' I say, 'not war, nor precious metals. I won't follow you or anyone for those. Not a secret, nor a mystery. I've done all those. Not a second best – the blossom – peaches? cherries? Old guys whittling? Trying those fried beetles – how delicious! No, not any of those trips, not by a stick's length.'

'Oh, dear Vince', he cries, 'how you are one of me!'

The artwork, stacked against the walls – it's Fifties, bold and sentimental. Papers too – travelling the Berlin underground, orphans playing spoons – but aren't those bones? one stop further and it's socialism – trying atom bombs on South Sea islanders...

'Those were my father's,' Gino says. 'I haven't bought a thing since he went off. If he is memory, removing them might do it harm...'

He laughs. He's a great joker, you can see.

'What then?' I ask. 'I've travelled in a pack. We crossed a frontier by both ways... It taxed our legs. And the people! –

with their stories, being counted and then disappearing. Guardian types – stepping out the frame of bad movies, their names thumbed cards filched from ruined tenements ... unpunished, unrepentant.'

'Numbers!' shouts Gino. 'Don't give me numbers. They're for counting, and for games of cards. Useless for mathematics – they're ignoble, from the unit dump. And religion's hooked on them – it's all an invite to a massacre. Sixteen of you, are there? Come to explore the world, convert? Right – your heads go rolling down the steps, bleached skins tacked to the sacred oak, eyeballs on skewers for the temple monkeys, testicles rolling in the hoochie koochie dancers' game of marbles... You're crazy – advertising numbers – it's betting your mother on a pair of threes...'

'Tell me, Gino,' I say. 'Everything. And leave your father out.'

'Energy,' he says. 'It transforms everything. Makes bronze, makes lime. Keeps things standing – release it and they fall ... the tree, the fire, the carbuncle and the kiss, the dragonfly and the haiku...'

'I get all that,' I say. 'I met a woman on the metro...'

'Oh,' he says, stretching up a thin finger to touch the clay parrot suspended from the ceiling, 'negative energy is good too. Routine stores it in your battery. Stretching like a cat two metres tall and elastic like a picture or a choir singing ... It's like voices – they're not concerned with harmony – just the reach, throwing nets on an empty sea, up like a seahawk, empty spirals in dry air ... then down, caught nothing, ready for the climbing wall, the puzzle tree...'

'We're the new charge,' I say, as Gino hustles me along, 'We plug in ... and then...'

'Wait!' says Gino. 'The talk – it must be right. Look at those guys – bound to their wheels – wheels for prayer, then every day – repeat, repeat – a tick, a tock of every clock, the climate's fucked, and yet it's springtime clothes, and fall, and candles lit, here come the three, the wizards orientalist – out go the twelve, the miracle's of numbers once again – now, here come the lambs, we'll cut their throats, and here's the ass... this time – who is the ass, who's to be flogged with beams, and who is resurrected, who's nailed down, who's taken up, who's for the pit...? Numbers and repetitions – dead is dead, you fools, the end's the end, spring won't return, you shot the bears, poisoned the fox – they're gone, into the storybooks...'

'Yes, Gino,' I say. 'Pray every day and worship calendars – it's finished – if it ever was. Now, it's food and capital – and that repeats as well – the seasons that there aren't, the fire that eats the manioc, the numbers don't add up, someone has filched those bags of gold, is in the counting house and fondling his queen – there aren't that many blackbirds left ... yes, Gino, you are right! we're chanting those old counting songs, eleven jonquils on the grave and four black horses for the hearse, four angels round my bed, three spirits lift me to the golden dome – aaah! down I go, they're demons made of fog, that's thirty fingers let me slip, down to the crypt – swift as the hypothetic ape, thirty-two the feet each second whizzing down the invisible rope ... and down, we're winding down ... how many millions of years to go? a blink, a hohum in the universe, it's heating up, it's freezing down...'

'Yes, Vince,' says Gino. 'That's the scene.'

The moment – it resolves. He says: 'You need to put a wire deep into the brain – if the universe possesses one, or it might have just one big toe – we'll charge that up as well.

Off with the old, the drift, decline, the mended shoe, the button strangled on its dwindling thread... Of course – there could be disadvantages. We'll never know how long the charge holds up. And – it could mean, for us, a shorter life...'

'Oh, so long as we don't know,' I say. 'I have in mind a person, already halfway to the revelation, a prisoner of habit, to and fro, entrapped, ensnared and begging uselessly...'

'Exactly so,' says Gino. 'You think you do the guy who has no cash, no food, a service if they get a sack of flour... You know – she doesn't – that the cash is stacked up in the bank. What will sort her out is revolution! The sages – they can't point that out, and nor can you – you'll go inside. Life over! The revolution, this time done right, that's what you need...'

Gino lays out the benefits – it's energy you need to stand upright, throw down your spade...

'Of course,' he says, 'you can't enjoy your life unless you think it's over soon. Your sin, the guilt, betrayal – is not original: it's just a sin. Live with it – it's yours, no one can steal it off you. Without it, life is less enjoyable – the punishment will come, and let you measure up. Try heroic: the heroic mode! I'm not thinking of the thugs and oafs, of course,' and he bends to kiss my head. 'Without your bad deeds – what would the good ones be? You must break out, dear Vince. It's perverse, this shackling to your past, your slithery recall of what and why you might have done... I've long passed that...'

'When do we set off?' I ask.

'Where?' asks Gino, laughing. 'Who said a bunch of friends would go, open the prisons, stop a war, write lampoons for the mags? That's old-time fantasy, my friend, you can smell it, stinking on the page. That's not a foundation myth, dear Vince – it's folly, pure. The charge, the juice – can come from anywhere. Leave aside the persecuted, the innocent – they all have their day. A page is left for them in every Book of Kings. The worst: they already have it, it's their pillow, and their plate. All must change, so that the smallest thing can change. A jolt, a volt, dear Vince, is not a plaster or a splint – your teeth will itch, your hair fly out, the rabbits shoot out of their holes – and every egg will hatch, maybe we'll turn to silver gilt ... this project, Vince, it has no nurse; no holy water drips, no mumble reels up on your screen, no prayer and no excuse...'

'Just let me see the machine, Gino,' I say. There's scepticism somewhere in me, like a cyst.

'Oh dear,' he says, 'you're a gadget freak! I expected better. You must start from the need, and then the answer. The unanswer, if you have the question wrong. Any guy on the corner can run you up an apparatus. Listen,' and he pulls me beside him on a pile of news – 'communist spies will rule the world,' says a headline – there are two laws. One should be repealed: the second law of thermodynamics, that says we're winding down. The distances grow far and bleak, there's frosting on the telescope, it cools and slows, the gas burns all the pans you left on stupidly... The other law says no! Nothing is ever lost, the energy rolls out, an everlasting sea, with whales of infinite fecundity and heft, over the horizon are the dinosaurs and all your ancestors – no one thinks of you, nor you, I bet, of them. Less and less – or on and on: that is the choice. You see, dear Vince – it's bloody laws! Who made them? Who enforces them – how can we repeal, and have our world fired up, all hugger-mugger with our friends, and Mahler when we wake and Fauré as we sleep...?'

'Oh Gino – this is what I feared,' I say. 'The promise is a joke, a spoof.'

'It was a test,' he says solemnly. 'To see how far you trusted me. Keep in your sights the physics and their laws. That is what matters. If you prefer silence as you sleep and wake – you're philistine, but nothing worse.'

'I trust you, Gino: but you seem extravagant – even rococo, in your scheme,' I say.

'Forget the scheme. Let's say – there is no plan. Things change, wind down – and they should simplify – their end is nigh. What do they have to lose, by sticking to the rules as if it's still day one? Take cash. Once, you dug and sluiced, assayed and lit the fire, and made a lump and held it in the die and struck, and struck again, and had it weighed, and maybe clipped, or copied even – then to the treasury, the market, the legionnaire... the solid mass goes in your shoe or in a hoard – and on and on – the bearded despot on the front – he dies, the goddess on the back – she never shows, but still there's blood and fisticuffs to have that disc! Now, all you need do for cash, is put the paper in and turn the wheel.'

I take my leave. Gino's a genius, no doubt, there's little history and happenstance that can resist his analytic mind. But – what if he's a charlatan? He says his words are free, and I don't pay. Can this be all?

*

I must take the same train back. I tell Melissa, 'Gino has the big idea – so big, it isn't viable.'

'You could try,' she says. 'If you've not got one of your own.'

'I don't know what's involved,' I say. 'He's lots of space, if I can't share with you.'

'Oh,' she says, 'I share already. You know – hotels. They make you pay while you're asleep. As if a corpse paid in the graveyard. If you don't move around, it's all quite clean.'

I laugh. 'The payment's for the dreams. The more you pay, the more the dreams reveal. A cash reward for nightmares.'

The only money I have left is in my sock – how much there is, from here, I can't imagine. I say, 'Gino's not recruiting. All the others are. I can't think why some of them have turned me down.'

'It's probably the height,' Melissa says.

'No, Melissa, it's not that,' I say. 'I have ambitions, and they see I'm capable of running bosses, interviewers, and all the show. It's envy, or it's my disillusionment, I'm sure: I'm bigger than the job – I take them for a run...'

'If Gino has a room,' Melissa says, 'I could share there. Not that anything would change – I'm sharing now. But I'd not go with you – you have no feel for words. You're just a mirror: those don't tell you anything. It's all already in the silver on the back. There can't be two of you: the one you are is there, behind the glass – there's nothing fresh, no warning.'

'We've been warned, Melissa, many times,' I say. 'More is pointless.'

'Look at the air,' she says. She fans it with the Book of Kings: 'There's particles and weapons, storms – just about everything. It's got too thick to breathe. We should have an expedition – lie on couches, drink the tea, in places where there's nothing but the sand, nothing to do at all, the boredom and the lack of faith ... maybe we could get tattooed. Kohl round our eyes.'

'Who do you share with, Melissa?' I ask her.

'There's my friend, Holly. A great capacity for love: on the side, there's tarting. That's an old expression – it's not supermarketing.'

'I know exactly how it goes,' I say. 'Maybe you should concentrate on that short life, Melissa. It could be a fad, seeing that it's necessary, and coming anyway. Last things you could do tomorrow. In a week. Me, paying the singing lady in the metro...'

Gino won't let us use his room. He hasn't said. It's what I'd do. The room is full, but not of life, or death – for that, it's valuable.

I ask the artisan on the corner – 'Energy for Gino. Has he ordered...'

'Oh,' says the guy, 'I made the boxes, like a coffin, only vertical. You sit in, and hope you don't end up in horizontal.'

'No, no,' I say. 'It's like charging up the universe – instead of trickling out, you renew the kick. It works like hay or electricity – awakes the pole that jogs it up again – the whole: desire, creation. Not going backwards – just...'

'I understand,' the old man says. 'But like so many, you have got it wrong. Electricity – it doesn't leak away when out of use. It's waiting in there, like a muse – a jaguar that leaps when you depress the switch. There is no power draining out, making the stars explode like cathode tubes, the distances increase as if the edge recedes, loses its reds and greens...'

'It's all technology,' I say. 'If it goes one way – it can be reversed. A woman says you're not the one – you're tossed away and sad. But – she is free! It's life for her, a bruise for you. In some rare case – you both are free, or even grafted on to one another... There's many ways of cheating the inevitable, the blur and blot, the poet said...'

'No,' says the craftsman. 'It's not on. It all decays, it tarnishes, it splits, it comes unglued, the solder cracks, earth turns to dust and wood to ash.'

'Gino wants a machine...' I say.

'No, he's wrong,' the old man, Beppe, says. 'Energy's quite outside the tin and nickel. It's in us.'

'He knows,' I say. 'He wants a box...'

'He'll end in one,' says Beppe, laughing. 'If not a vase. Come out the back.'

The shop is a *bottega* – a counter with a bottle and some flex, a shelf above where you can sleep or snoop – but out the back – it is a world. There's houris sleeping on divans, peacocks white and purple, tall yuccas where the shrews can nest and glide, a stand of pampas where a family of wolves returns my stare. There's green, brown and gold, living furs of grey and white.

'I observe the wolves,' says Beppe. 'We lost our top wolf – he got too smart, a neighbour shot him. The pack knows life more fully than we do. The big bright underwater beasts, their enviable brains – I have no room for them, alas.'

He shows me round. 'We keep our heads quite clean of what we can't observe,' he says. 'Here, no fetishes, no guards invisible, no guardian avatars in masks... No boxes.'

I laugh, 'Then, nothing dies, and nothing needs a charge?'

'That is the way,' he says. 'I don't make puppets. What I seek – it must exist, be present from the start. Maybe we should have stayed beneath the waves, and let intelligence take hold. Now it's too late – we thought we'd found the shore, that it led up... But no: there's empty shells and stranded weed.'

'The guy – the top gun?' I ask. 'Top wolf? Blasting the experiment.'

'Oh,' says Beppe, 'he wasn't top of anything – not even of the shooting class.' He makes the gesture, on his neck.

'Well, what's the core, the shape, the drive?' I ask.

'I thought of protohumans,' Beppe says. 'It's true our end is ugly, nigh – but at the start the energy was there, the evolution swift, the pace was fast, the destiny, alas – disaster.'

'You're breeding protohumans, Beppe? Prototypes?' I ask.

'Put it like that, it has a nazi sound,' he says, 'though everyone is toying in that way. There's counting too – you need it to be capitalists. It's tough to learn: – maybe some birds can help. They're numbering the eggs, you see, then having to regurgitate. You need to get your figuring right, no one wants to sick them up, the frogs and such, more than they need.'

There's the yucca leaves, and then the sky – without the incurious lofty trees, the town's too flat; they even put the trains under the ground.

'That wolf,' says Beppe. 'He had a grin. He carried off an ape I'd just brought in. Maybe it was best to send him on. I don't believe it, but it fits the story so.'

'I've no opinion, Beppe,' I say. 'Except – I guess I have. He should have ate the ape, and there's an end...'

'You underestimate my difficulties, friend,' he says. 'That's typical. When we got to sitting down all day, and calling up our friends if we forgot a word, a place – our brains started to get small. Things to solve – they got beyond us. In the pack, we had to know a lot of stuff – the beasts, the plants, the rain. All gone! We spend the evenings gawping at the stars, the distances, inventing dreams about them, fearing the drop.'

'The breeding aspect, Beppe. Maybe it's reserved for you,' I say. 'I see you have some beauties lounging on divans...'

'Oh,' he says. 'That's not the experiment.'

'Well,' I say, 'if you're not the patriarch, initial seed, the primal cell, eternal father...'

'The size of brain,' he says, 'that works, lights up all through... You find it in the people who've survived a war, maybe been tortured, run, begged for bread, asylum – they must know everything. Their brains – they are immense. You find those people on the underground, no one wants them up here in the light.'

'The question's still unanswered, Beppe,' I say.

He goes on: 'Short lives. You have to force it in: experience, the wisdom. We forget most of what little's been transmitted to us. We don't know how to survive,' he says.

'That's evident,' I say. 'You map it well – the starting place. Then, it's all problems that you cannot solve.'

'Yes,' he says. 'You're right. I see the problem. I've no clue how to resolve. I'm quite like Gino. What did he say about that room he has?'

'Oh,' I say. 'What I suspected – "No, you're not dossing in my private place. My ancestors – they may return and need the space..."'

There's room on those divans ... but I don't ask.

'Money, Beppe,' I say. 'I don't care about space – that's a nazi thing as well. Setting questions – that's wrong too – when you've no answer. Anyone can set up a world like yours. My need is – getting lots more cash...'

'Mend these stools,' he says, pulling some that limp, from a wood chest. He laughs, 'That way you'll have some guys become more sedentary; see their brains shrivel, the same song in their identical mouth.'

When I finish mending, he gives me cash – brick-sized. 'That's far too much,' I say. 'It tempts. I can spend that in an hour, have nothing left again.'

'Do what you want,' he says. 'It's not so much. You don't know how people live, all the cash they take, hoard up.'

'That's true, Beppe,' I say. 'But don't forget – it's not just us, the project. It's the universe! The whole shoot – to be put in reverse.'

*

I take the train – of course, there's Melissa. 'What's that sewage stink?' she asks.

I tell her all that Beppe does: those little chairs, like mounting blocks – maybe for horsemen; how he loves his animals... 'Oh,' Melissa says, 'those old guys – they all build stuff like that, stock up with all the women they will never screw, hope to be eaten up by something that has loved them once. What a hope!'

'The smell!' I say. 'It must be printers' ink. The parcel Beppe gave... I've suffered this before. Those virgin notes...'

'You better spend them all at once, or not at all,' she says. 'And run. Maybe buy an aeroplane, take off...'

I think of it – creation. Rolling back, a tidal boom along the shore – the reds spring up from every pocket where they've lurked – the snooker match starts off again, reds in their triangle, then place the reluctant pink and brown, the dawn and dusk. All ready for the break, the pristine frame...

'The cash!' shouts Melissa. 'I'll avoid you till it's spent.'

That's good – but then – the train is always waiting: and on it, the sound of wheels, the 'short life' song. That, you can't avoid.

'Vince,' she says. 'You're at the top. You're where your boss had paid to be. Your friends – Andy, Steve – pushing you. Now, Gino, Beppe – pulling you towards the peak.'

It's true. I'm favoured. I think of Maya, not of Gennaro.

Melissa goes on, 'Beppe – maybe he wants to be top wolf, now there's a vacancy. And – horsemen... not the apocalypse, that's all been done. They ride in from the desert...'

I'd like a wolf to fill me with their love – when once they say they love you, it's for life, they don't go cold. The same with cats – that way, you see that love and sex are separate...

I say, 'No, Melissa, you're quite wrong. The mounting blocks are there for starting from. No one is coming in – there's riders leaving, that's for sure...'

With Melissa, there's always a terminus. In fact, there's always two, one at each end. Most other things – there's no end, no point where you arrive, no credit for being on the way. That's true of things – thoughts, systems, images. People, though, they're a terminus, they decide their own and hand it over to you – some with a knife, most with indifference. 'The thing, Melissa,' I say, 'is that Beppe and Gino don't agree. I can't be with them both. Beppe's organic, Gino – is mechanical: the history, factitious. Beppe's is self-indulgence, totemism. He has the snide money, he can buy anything, and ride away – fast and faster.'

Next day, Melissa says, 'That's a fine shirt, Vince. Boats, sails and wings.'

'I told you I could fly,' I say. 'You wouldn't know – but I can be *sympa*. Fancy – wafted me, into the store.'

'Your smell has gone,' she says.

'I dumped those notes,' I say. 'I met a guy. A cop, I think.'

'What?' she shouts. 'You bought a shirt, and sold your friend – sold Beppe!'

'He must have known,' I say. 'Preparing to make a getaway...'

'He couldn't ride...' she says. 'And there's no horse.'

'You always ride,' I say, 'if you have nothing else. Black horses from the hearse, out of the traces – for him, and for the houris. Besides – it was my social responsibility: I didn't quite say "who" and point.'

'So, that cop paid you for the slush?' she asks.

'Remember,' I tell Melissa, 'I didn't sell old Beppe – I sold the money. And Gino paid me too – not to ask to stay with him. He's flush – his father built the atom bomb, and left us this advice – "don't look up, ever" – and now, everybody, black, white and brown is making one, down in the cellar, a bomb: it shows you have some faith, even if it's only that you'll win, or get away with it.'

'It isn't colour that's at stake,' Melissa says.

'That's just a metaphor, like flight,' I say. 'There's flight to get to a new place by air, and flight that's running anywhere at all as best you can.'

'They'll trash poor Beppe's compound,' says Melissa: 'And the animals... the trees...'

'Gino's machine is less impractical,' I say, hurrying it along. 'This shirt. Maybe it reminds you of the poem – "the cemetery beside the sea".'

'He got it wrong,' Melissa says. 'He talked of seals, grazing below, he should have said the sails, those dhows have sails that look like white doves' wings. But anyway, it's all about his muse...'

'Ah yes,' I say. 'The innocent. A moving picture, all the same.'

'Beppe's released his soul,' says Melissa. 'You don't need be religious to see that after death there comes the flight, the wing, the flame ... the seed – it flies, quite free... Those horses – what delight! To leave the hearse, gallop over the red sand to those red granite outcrops...'

She doesn't sing her song – we do the circuit, the train empties, fills, and empties. 'Don't go with Gino,' says Melissa. 'You've lost so many that you've not appreciated – I don't see you, fiddling with those tiny screws and stripping wires...'

I say, 'You're right, Melissa. What you say, is poetry. But nothing regenerates – only shamans think that way. The soul is evanescent, up it goes and out the chimney. It's a consolation – one that does not console at all.'

'Well,' Melissa says, 'I have to work the carriage up ahead. Decide what you want most to believe. You disgust me. It doesn't change a thing.'

'They say you have to work at it, belief,' I say. 'Like you sing your song, Melissa, and no one pays. One day, you're absent – then, they remember you, the shortness, your truncated life – stuck in the train, the up and down...'

'It's all a metaphor,' she says. 'I don't believe fuck all. Nothing that I'd tell you. It needs someone, to pull it all down.'

'So,' I say. 'You don't believe you're hungry? That's just fine. You can't go into politics, not if you're hungry. You can't take my money, not if you're going into politics, and I won't give it you, even if you're into politics. So – if you're hungry – I'm not buying food for you...'

If she's really hungry, she'll not think about politics, or doing much about it.

She's already long gone, up the train. She should learn more songs.

★

Gino says, 'I'll hand the work on to you. See...' and here's a pile of papers ... some have baby faces scribbled on. 'I'm nearly there,' he says, grabbing the graphics, scrumpling them – 'It's not a doodle, forget all that – here's the start... And it goes from here ... and so ... and then ... it follows that...' His breath is like marsh gas, and my eyes go grey, like mushrooms under oil...

'This much is right,' he says. 'It makes a bomb. That's physics from the marrow. We know how the fiddly bits are screwed together, what happens when they spring apart, collide, or just get jiggled...'

'I understand your terms,' I say. 'It's these equations... I missed some weeks of school, and so the principles – whatever discipline this is – were rusted when they were ladled in my head...' Gino rushes on,

'My father stopped halfway – of course, that experiment made a flash and wind. Too bad there were those guys just clocking in on that particular day. That was the path. But – you must be...' and he stands on tiptoes here – 'Very very careful as you go ahead, that everything just doesn't fall apart. It is a risk we scientists must boldly take – but watch it! When you make the sphere, before you pull the switch, I might suggest you check your caculations ... one last time, as they say.'

'So, Gino,' I say. 'It's all in the last page. Keep for your archives all this extra scrip... And tell me why you've given me the job, the last equation, that turns it all around – from expansion and decay to compression and new life...'

'It's the compression bothers me,' he says. 'It's not that we've got big, bigger, as everything streams out old style, expanding horizons, fading. If we contract to millimetres, certain tasks become quite tough. Like going up the stairs, drinking a pint of booze ... and there's the chance that all you'll get is one huge bomb... But – you're the expert, now it's up to you. I'll spend the next, the other, fifty years awaiting me – making a bower, like old Beppe did – the hearse parked round the back, the houris ... maybe a tank of dolphins...'

'It doesn't seem it goes like that,' I say. 'Not decisive. Short lives, dear Gino! You've already had a lot of years – the birthdays, and the festivals; – you know the drill, how each hour resembles each, how boredom tarnishes, the presents pall, the sacrificial beasts – they bleat, they struggle, they piss upon the ground with fear... Maybe that fear belongs to you, dear Gino ... maybe your doodles tell the tale equations don't...'

'Listen, my friend,' says Gino angrily. 'Just don't explode the universe. That's all I ask.'

*

I show the last page to Melissa: 'Those symbols,' she says wisely – 'In the next room to Farsi, they're doing Early Georgian. Those are *asomtavruli* characters, no doubt at all.'

'I don't think so, Melissa,' I say, quite gently. 'I need someone who can distinguish rejuvenation from a bomb. I must have missed that day at school again – so much went on there, but – away it goes, the wisdom, and gone for ever.'

'If it was worth,' Melissa says. 'He would not have passed it on. His father set off the worthy massacre – the money trickled down to Gino. Gino follows Beppe, and probably Beppe, or *his* father, in their turn set up another massacre... And so it goes. One generation slices ears – the children take the cash and shed the tears.'

'I fear,' I say, 'that's all a commonplace. In their bedroom, in the cellar – reviving the universe, blowing it all up – every student reaches Gino's point. Later in life – it's Beppe's.'

'It's true,' Melissa says. 'It's Epicurus and Democritus, – flow or particle, decline, eternity. Beppe and Gino. Your ancient golden egg, dear Vince – it looks and smells like all the rest...'

'Well, Melissa – not everyone has a cellar or a bedroom where they work things out,' I say.

'The rest is trying to make fortunes, some by writing songs, and some with dollar clichés, and the filigree,' she says. 'Vince – promise me, it's not just that you don't understand this sheet that you don't see what it means...' and she waves Gino's last page at me.

'This really is the key to the big door, you think?' I ask. 'It's poetry, Melissa. It doesn't say how we should live, nor how we can protect ourselves from states, or save the elephants. It strives – we respond, because we strive as well.'

'Is that your best attempt?' she asks. 'For you – it has no more significance?'

'Melissa,' I say. 'Hard times confront us. This paper–' and for effect, I scrumple it '–is myth, it's our re-foundation. Let's find a worthy place, and stash it there. If we can find some humble guy who'll work the next step out ... we'll play this last, this first card, then.'

She's not convinced. 'The dead?' she asks. 'Do they resurrect? Or just there'll be no more? Not giving birth to anyone would be a great relief.'

'It's metaphysics, all that stuff,' I say. 'Will there be night, will there be day, or light, or dark? That tangled way's aesthetics... Formalism, abstraction – do they do a dusk, a dawn? Come on! You're old hat, Melissa. Big sculptures stand out in the rain – they don't complain, and nor should we.'

The dark – it's all around me. Melissa recedes, as if I'm drunk or dead. Maybe my old partner – Bianca – maybe she'll hop out, from hiding in her urn, to give me hell.

'Melissa,' I say, 'I got away from Icaro – now, here's another chancer, Gino. Are they my destiny – their promises unfulfilled and unfulfillable? By me, at least.'

'If it's your destiny, it's mine as well, and those who sang my song,' she says.

It's poignant, and she makes the pose – but, now she stands before me – really short. Another question of aesthetics. A punishment awaits, I'm sure: she's having hers ... her height. Mine – it will come, for prejudice, discrimination, all the rest.

'Yes!' says Melissa. 'There you go, you, your friends – you stridulate, you fly, you fornicate, you flee and you intrigue, you build your worlds, you blow them up ... and me? I work the trains. What would it cost you, as you swarm like toads for sex in seconds, frolic like hares before the bullet – to help me out? Just for a day...' I hear her out.

'It isn't hares they kill with bullets, my dear friend,' I say. 'They use a blast of peppery shot... Pellets.'

'At least,' she says, 'no one goes looking for me, puts me on their list. It's you they're looking, asking, for. They always catch their hare ... you'll end up as a *lièvre au poivre*, my *Hasenfuss* – in a jug – jugged in a jail – your brain, your perfect dialogic instrument, a braised mouthful, hare-brain: – they'll hear your case, you'll end up cased, skinned nude and crude...'

I'm terrified, of course. Everything I've ever done has never crossed the line: yet they're searching for me: 'Hide Gino's scheme,' I say.

'I haven't eaten, Vince,' she says. 'Maybe the future's tasty, peppy, even...' and she pretends to swallow ... everything.

'Who's been asking, Melissa,' I ask. 'Military? Aviation? Forgery? Trafficking – or abandonment?'

'All of those,' she says. 'Do be calm. See, I've learned to play the *dutar*. Lutes – you go all over – in time, for centuries back or more, to Africa, to Samarkand...'

'Melissa,' I interrupt. 'That's niche. You could be singing in a bar, making them cry. Here, you're a lost soul...'

'Then here is where I am, and I belong,' she says. 'I see everything you don't. I'm full of silent folk – their journeys mostly short, uncomfortable, preoccupied. I watch. I am the eye of God, dear Vince,' and she laughs. 'So – put your obol in my cup, mean bastard. Or stay and watch with me...'

'What else, Melissa?' I ask. 'I'd watch, but there's no end. They stand, they reach somewhere, impassive they push their way ... they disappear, and we go on. We reach the end, but it's eternity – it all starts off again, the different people, impassive, in a rush, the scenery like it's painted on, and tunnels with those fairy lights in case it all breaks down and you must stumble on the track...'

'Yes, yes,' she says. 'We know about the trains. You must feel your presence more. You and I needn't leave, not when the others do. But you'd be poor, dear Vince. That wouldn't suit. Hungry too. No water, and no booze, and no one offers anything. The song repeats, and when I'm dead, it will go on, another mouth will hold it for a while – without a consolation, saying exactly what there is. Short people with short lives.'

I say, 'That was your choice, Melissa.'

'Look at all the choices you have made, dear Vince. You're terrified now,' she says.

It's true. But she is not the eye of God – that's what the semi-destitute believe. They think where they are's the best that they can do ... some gods are happy with stale cakes, of course, don't climb off those pedestals...

'I don't run,' she says, 'not from anything.'

'I don't run,' I say. 'I make choices, for the best.'

'Then go!' she says. 'Leave! Who wants you?'

★

'You can paint me any colour / I can be a clown', the music says. It's exactly right. This is freedom. Everyone in the bar seeks it, and now we're free, floating up, leaving our skins and boots, up in the smoke. You put your quarter in the box, music – and you're free.

I've told the guy beside me about my life – 'To me,' he says, 'it's absolutely normal.'

I'm abashed – 'I thought my life was vital,' I say.

'People come in every day,' he says. 'Ideas: not always wisdom. Jetpacks. Ranches. The big project – the street is full of them, and all for sale. Down in the alley, they're divvying winter coats – it's hot as hell this summer – but you take a dozen...'

'You buy into everything?' I ask.

'Of course,' he says, 'and I do it all. What else is there? It's my expression does it: they think I'm a fish, a *pollo* – so, I am. A dolphin with a stash of Spanish gold, a cockerel that scratches up cut diamonds... In my window, it tells you: "Broker". No one believes it, just how broke... You can't put "brokest" – it's not grammatical.'

'This way, you don't survive,' I say.

'It's not Italy,' he says. 'It isn't organised, you don't burn saints' pictures, don't cut your thumbs. It's business. So, you don't die young – no one need be loyal to anyone.'

'There must be rules,' I say. 'For not living long.'

'Right!' he says. 'If you want rules – don't quote. Always be original. Be proud – any one of those chickens,' and he points, six turn naked, glumly, in a hot case – 'Could have written Shakespeare. Always have a line. If they say "Are you an idiot?" you say, "No, I'm not an idiot." That way, you'll see – you'll make out fine.'

'It sounds so easy, Mike – it is Mike?' I say, 'I'm sure there is a further knack or two.'

'Keep your distance. Imagine tight places – aggression without singing and without hitting people – that's rubbish,' he says.

I tell him about Icaro, my bird friend, looking down on fields of flowers. Migrating – knowing exactly where you have to go and running into eagle scouts along the way...

'Men and woman,' Mike interrupts, 'that's a problem. Our sensibilities have diverged, over the millennia, nothing to be done. Making up? History. That's not sharing a ciggie when you've enjoyed someone. Best not to try adventuring.'

'It's all feeling,' I say. 'Perception, not cognition. If you don't go along with that, you end a bigot, old hat. Some old dogma. After the modern comes surrender. It should be sweet.'

'All your friends,' says Mike, ignoring this ... what does it mean anyway, apart from making a career and lots of cash with saying it... If you're migrating – feeling's not enough...' 'They're Christians – or else they came from that Village. Except the Muslim ones – they're from a village very similar. No one comes from those now – if you did, you're empty, like a sardine can you bring home from the picnic, empty, a bit oily...'

He talks on about sardines, what they're made of, how he may have been a whale in life – and thinking of the can, and being soldered into it, I find my bladder's full, and wonder if he'll still be there when I get back...

He's talking to a guy – I hear... 'I'm Apollo,' the sardine riff, and he's spliced in some of me. 'Mike,' I say. 'You're a product!'

'No,' he says, 'I'm buying...' but the guy has moved away. 'Don't be jealous, Vince,' Mike says. 'Nothing anywhere belongs to you. And I'm not going anywhere... Do you have somewhere in mind, that you'd like to go?'

'I know about it, Mike,' I say. 'Migrating, you don't go anywhere.'

'You might be eaten before your time,' says Mike, 'or fall down out the sky; or netted. Shot. The timing's everything. My behaviour, Vince – it's all consistent. I'm not looking for a drinking friend that I rely on – charred with alcohol and dead before I've had my fill.' He whispers, 'The guy that I was hooking on, while you weren't here – we could roll him when he goes outside. A kicking he'll remember and get sympathy for years. A bad surprise that turns out profitable.'

I don't react. He says, 'Or – we could do a tour, old time. Two hundred US cities, me on spoons and you on comb and paper. That way – you learn a good profession, and geography as well.'

'Look, Mike,' I say. 'I'm more into the exotic. The things that change the world – at least reveal the lava dawdling in the cracks... "Wings beating softly, the windows flew away." Like that.'

'I told you,' says Mike. 'Don't quote. It makes you seem an idiot.'

'If I bought it, it would belong to me,' I say. 'Like an ex voto – it might cure something, thank someone.'

'That's foolish,' Mike says. 'Exchanging invisibles, your gods, for more invisible – the capital behind your cash. Think how complicated it must be, your dimes and quarters, what lies behind all that? Nothing? – it can be so intricate, the invisible, like what's behind the dancing in the fire, poking a pointy stick right through your tongue, sacrificing fluffy animals. Down on your knees – who sees? The invisible. Counting your coins – in your pocket, caressing, over your groin. Who sees? Not you. Don't let it out, the secret. How much? How close to the big pot, that lets you buy your dream? Maybe the invisible, the sightless one who trusts in God, who struck them up, each dime, and gifted them to you – and lets you buy a cake, a shot – of bourbon, maybe, God save all those weedy kings...'

'You're inconclusive, Mike,' I say. 'It all coheres. It's a mobile – you hang it on the ceiling. What for?'

'We should rob that guy,' says Mike. 'Most people don't understand their teachers, or don't like their badger smell.

We take his cash. Then, he finds he belongs to the world: cops, offices, surgeons. He'll thank us, and we can buy more drinks. It's a lesson not everyone gets: or else – it takes a whole fucking war, an occupation, a tyrant, smashing buildings, peeing in wells, diplomats, infanticides... we're teachers, Vince, not into politics. I could beat up on you, if you're squeamish about strangers. Your lesson, unique to you, learned, and all the benefits.'

'I'll think about it, Mike,' I say.

'Yes, you will, Vince,' says Mike. We drink some more: 'But you should follow me more closely.'

'I always follow close,' I say. 'Hawkett. My boss. Andy – mooching, in a bar, like this. Steve, the hard man, melting off. Maya. The lovely miniature – Melissa... I follow – where do they lead? Is it all a pack, that pick me up and cast me down, because they see a destination in my eye that they won't reach, will never see...'

'Oh, my friend,' says Mike: 'You're the best case I have seen. A paranoia growing in a celadon, so fine and whispy – the grey, the green... beneath, percussion swishing to uphold a voice of pure disinterest... Your innocence, dear Vince, cries to be violated. Watch your back, your front, your sides! It's not just you... The flowers – grow by themselves: if they get picked, it's chance – there's no conspiracy, no plot.'

He laughs, and other guys join in – my brothers...

'So, to be sure, dear Mike,' I say, 'you love my company? There is no other interest...'

'Who would mislead you? You've no cash – except for picking up this tab,' he says. 'Maya had nothing, Melissa – even less. Not everyone who's nothing wants to cheat you, Vince. Trust your imagination,' he staggers, nearly falls. I hold him up.

'You see,' he says, 'the holy fool, compliant Sancho, pilgrim in the bog – who see the golden walls, the crystal city – those types all die when destiny's in sight. Or – suppose – they just get sent to jail for vagrancy, resistance ... or there is no city: those are tents for refugees. Come home with me,' Mike says. 'You can't keep sleeping on that train.'

He's right. There is no plot. It's true – I have the paranoia ... it's a gift, an alpenstock as I climb up the hill, steeper and steeper, thicker swarm the clouds...

'Pay the bill,' says Mike. 'Sleep over in my chair. You're not wanted, are you? Not a deserter? Those boots look like military – give them here, I'll get you sandals. Used a wrong word about a war?'

'Oh no, Mike,' I say.

I miss the train – you could lie out on the seats.

The stairs in Mike's house, a continent – 'Don't get sucked in here and there,' he says... 'They have to eat. There's couscous, steam boat, and I don't know what that is ... there's timbals, pine nuts...'

'Did you notice, Mike,' I ask. 'The house is listing?'

'Yes,' he says. 'It's following a trend. Big places, countries – swallowed into sink-holes. And now we have the new religion, spreading here and there – roots, leaves... Soon everyone will have a new one too – all different, and militant. If you can't choose – or haven't thought – just keep on climbing, mind your step, your hold – right up... I'm in the attic here...'

'Who knows how it will end,' I say, making conversation, as the stairs are steep, some break away.

'Of course, you know how,' he says. 'But then – who cares? Short lives! The best choice, and inevitable – but things get denser, faster – so you'll never know if and when it finishes... So many dramas, left incomplete – Lulu, Moses, symphonies – someone will finish them, if not – we live with that, the inconclusiveness...' And panting we arrive.

He takes my jacket and my boots. 'There,' he says, 'your chair. I mostly don't have stuff. You never know when you may have to move. Those plastic bags prepared – less ostentatious than a suitcase, Vince.'

There seems nothing to eat. 'Time to sleep,' he says: 'My! Those suppers smell good,' and he's gone.

I pass the night up and down the stairs – each floor tilts differently. Maya. Maybe she's lodged here, a hard-shelled creature in the sea-wrack. Mostly, people have left, to work, to clean. I saw them on the train. Others sleep as long as possible. On the bells, no name looks like it's just been changed.

Mike says, 'I've just eaten – you weren't here. One meal a day – the house rule! If you do fancy stuff – you'll need to knock: go down a floor.'

'Where are we going, Mike?' I ask. 'Are you taking me somewhere?'

'Don't be pathetic, Vince,' he says. 'I've already given. Now – it's your turn.'

'It's not my world, Mike...' I say.

'It's too early for the bar,' he says. 'There's no one interesting. We could sing. Duets. Berber songs – we'd need no orchestra.'

'Without camels, it's not the same,' I say. 'I know a song in Farsi, and that's it.'

We stare at each other.

I say, 'This is a tree you live in, Mike. Each with their branch, a different fruit.'

Mike is morose, he says, 'The fruit is pinched and sour. The leaves – they're poisonous. Where's the water for the roots? A broken sewer, maybe, metres down. No, Vince – your age, and mine – the age of doubt, precariousness, of curiosity – it's over. The people here – they'll grow apart until they're different species – a monkey, lemur, eagle, vulture... each eating various stuff, and fighting over it. Some in fur, some in feathers – some with bare bums aflame. When everyone has their new faith – a balance will be reached. To some the fruit, to others – others' flesh. Each against all, dear Vince – that will be it. No time for languor, sex, or telling tales.'

'You'll find your twig, I'm sure,' I say. I'm not so sure.

Is that a tear? This, the old dispensation – mean, squalid, on the run – does he regret...? 'Yes, I regret,' he says. 'It could have been quite comfortable. Mean spirits – that was us. Frightened, ungenerous. Our symbol was the tank. Steel cans – you fry inside.'

'You're quite the moralist, dear Mike,' I say.

'It's living with the fear of death,' says Mike. 'Morals don't come in. Play before you die, they say. But – fear takes the upper hand. It makes you need strong stuff – belief, a God. It's quite a paradox – this God is death. She used to be a mother too. No more.'

'Then – short lives,' I say. 'Is just a strategy. It's realism; it's what you get, not what you want.'

Mike pushes me towards the stairs. 'You owe me for the night,' he says. 'You didn't sleep, and so you pay. Since you can't pay, I'll show you how to live.'

'I don't want a job of conning drunks, Mike,' I say. 'I don't want to end up working for some stupid strongarm hood. Besides – you're stuck on your metal: sardine cans, tanks. It's against the common view, that seats each in their carrel, jollying along with all the rest.'

'You have to work it out,' says Mike. 'I'm right. Guys in the tank – Laszlo, David or Saul, Elroy and Mahomet – of course they get on. They're comrades, all in love. "Pass the shell," says one. "Right away, my sweet," the other. What I tell you, Vince, you have to think about it. That's where I differ from all the rest.'

'It isn't always easy, Mike,' I say. 'It doesn't always make a sense.'

'You see, Vince,' Mike says. 'You like my little caricatures. You love the dialogue. All powerful people – love to talk, they talk to everyone. It doesn't mean a thing. They love ingenuous guys like you: you think you're smart, you flatter them. It doesn't mean a thing. If I were to sell you, Vince – what would you fetch? Something? Nothing? A nickel for your conversation – your yes and no. It's dull, dear Vince.'

Mike scuttles down the road – in baggy brown – he's a shameless mutt: appearances? If they matter – they're irresistible. 'Come on!' he shouts, 'I'm the one whose legs are short. Run! Everyone – look – they stand back!'

Running after him – doesn't make a team of us.

Melissa – the tiny solid figure in the core that gives the matrioshka meaning. Someone must know what that meaning is. Foetus? Saviour? Someone knows. Or – everybody knows but me.

'Mike,' I ask, 'Is it riches? Is that what you're looking for?'

'I don't want to be a rich man, Vince,' he says. 'But yes – I guess – rather than inner life, it's cash my reasoning and my rhetoric are hitched to... Why? The poor all think like me... In my way, it's them I serve...'

'But Mike,' I say. 'Suppose we have a different scheme. All in the middling sort. Maybe a tawdry prize for thoroughbreds – a book, a frock... Everything you do – transformed. Equality – will bring fraternity...' He leaps in:

'No, no,' he shouts, 'it isn't so. Do you want fraternity, Vince? You're not the sort. That needs a different route. But I seek purity, dear Vince. Abnegation, sacrifice.'

'And paradox?' I ask.

'Of course. That's in my schedule. It's the part I most enjoy. It takes real effort: the drunks, the ignorant – those are easy. Maybe I disappoint you so?' asks Mike. 'If I transform the world – does that make me useless? If everything is changed – poor into rich or middling – I'll be changed too. But it's not. I am as I am. Exactly. Not forgetting who I owe, and who owes me.'

'You're not my train, Mike,' I say. 'You don't take passengers.'

'Only the poor understand purity,' says Mike. 'Because they live a life that's absolutely not. If you're rich though – you don't entertain the thought.'

'Is it good, Mike, being pure?' I ask. 'Or is it just a thought – like being equal. Is that good? When they have something like it – people don't enjoy. Is it a good, Mike?'

'I've really no idea,' he says, hurrying away. 'I think it's like the fire for you. I don't pester you for that.'

He pushes open the pub door – there's a roar of welcome, maybe just a roar. He turns,

'Your mission, Vince...'

'Yes, Mike?' I say. 'Yes, I have one, like everybody else.'

'Here,' he says, 'here's my parting gift.'

A magnificent kazoo, a little rusty, but the rest shines like the moon. A moment of epiphany, though – suppose, that everything Mike told me was a con – the wars, his doing without furniture, the charge for sleeping over... 'The house, Mike,' I say, 'all your invention?'

'What do I want with furniture?' he asks. 'And people make their millions for people sleeping in their beds. Civilised people – always need a pretext for the greedy things they do. I'm not greedy, Vince. I do best exactly what I do. Holy fools, like you, Vince – they're old hat. The walking on the water, flying donkeys, power to the imagination – or was it the working class? – those Jews, those Arabs, were they gullible, taken in by holy fools – or making fun of Romans who were there to stay? Inventing things, dear Vince – it leads to terrible revenge. Don't do it. It's an explosive. Remember Dostoevsky, following his lucky fairy – the wheel of fortune, hobnob with the kings and queens, and slap them down... Beware the knaves, my friend. You know they're there, but on you go! They're waiting for the deaths – then they'll be kings themselves.'

He plays the huckster: 'On my left – the water-walkers: on my right – the flying donkeys! Ladies, gents – a contest never seen before. And after – for the title – imagination, up against the working class!'

He laughs, he coughs, he spits.

'No, Mike,' I say. 'It's all two centuries ago. I have no truck with all of that...'

'Then tell it to the people in the house,' he shouts. 'And if it's really all for cash and land – then give them some of yours!'

He's gone. A cruel shot from the great bow no one can string but him. He never told me how to live – I didn't want him to, but it's something more that I have missed. All the other creatures scurrying by... I'm a pliant tree, silent in their forest ... some rub on me and leave a clot of fur, or urinate, sharpen a claw. It's nothing special – this wearing down my biteless bark – is all my day and most of nights.

*

'Hey!' the shout: 'Stand up, no pathos.'

Here she is, Tara – a long blue stick for walking, but not in urban lanes. She's blue – her arms, her neck. 'Don't stare,' she says, 'I'm not a leaflet. I'm a parchment – gives you rights, takes most away.'

'Don't explain,' I say. I wait for her Gennaro – the usual jealous type – he's in the shadow there...

'Armand!' she shouts. 'Come out, salute this stranded wreck. We'll pull him off the reef.'

'Oh no,' I think. 'There's been the past, with Andy – a hard landing – on crutches. Grounded, flight annulled. Steve – the present – fleeing with the desperate, their faces lit like in old movies where you cranked by hand, all under-speed, Maya cloche-hatted, kohl-eyed ... Mike – and the future: all manacled, aligned and humble in a chant...'

'No time for that, she says: 'That's old stuff. Past, future, forget all that: a short life has this beauty – it's all at once. The past – not composted; the future quite improbable. And what you have – is not the present, with its layerings of all the rest, the pallid lives all round – all the unknowns, the unpresentables, the virtuals, the severed heads on plinths. Forget the swish of time: that's tinnitus for you. You have so little time – best to assume there's none.'

'It makes sense, Tara,' I say: 'But my adventures ... no more roofs or wings of styrofoam...'

'Quite right,' she says: 'You've no time for accidents. I know – we blue people are a scarce resource. Those men of the desert – they were napalmed, then deprived of everything. Some was an accident, mostly malignity. Best avoid sand, stay schtum and near a bus route...'

'Your cash?' I ask.

Tara looks like she's had breakdowns, like the bus. You need to find another going well, and get a part from that... Maybe it's sex-shows they put on... Or painting bodies.

'Oh,' she says, 'if you don't think about it, cash keeps coming in. And if you haven't thought and then there's none – your mind's quite free. There's no burden from what's not there – that's a scientific law as well. You have to keep within the rules in something – and that's a good and easy one. "Nothing is from nothing made." It's poetry.'

'I'm sure you're right, Tara,' I say. 'But filling even a short life – especially with something huge... it needs a take...'

'I'll start way back,' she says. 'It started bad. The Germans – they devised an epic: a foundation myth. Those, you know, must end in "all goes well". The guy commissioned wrote the music too. It was an evening's show, with tunes. His bigotry – maybe it underlay the tragedy. You never never say "it all goes wrong". He did. It all fell down, for everyone. The trenches, the massacres, the camps... His Ring – it turned out just a ring of corporations...' and on she talks. Armand has heard it many times: he says, 'Tara thinks to write it as an elegy. She'd have done the epic right – but it's too late. That's why our lives are short...'

'No, Armand,' Tara says. 'There's more than that – but there's no time to tell it now.'

'There's no hurry, Tara,' Armand says.

She hurries us along. The stick is used to point to crenellations – 'Hohenstaufen or Hohenstollen?' she asks, chuckling ... or to raise mail flaps... Maybe there's a letter there that she could read... 'Out of date, out of time, Tara,' Armand says.

She pokes at nests in hedgerows – 'A pipit, a poppet... What a lark, if only there were birds alive...'

So, we roister down the street: 'You're an intellectual, Tara,' I say: 'I don't know how to deal...'

'From the top you deal, you mutt,' she says: 'God wasn't an intellectual. A simple soul – if there was one of those attached. But if You are the Star – when you die, there's nothing left.'

'Always the joker, Tara,' Armand says, unenthused. He says to me. 'She can't celebrate. Nothing has a terminus for her, no consequence secure. It's her affliction.'

'Her body isn't the beginning and the end, like it is for us,' I say. 'There's always a commentary to be drawn on it.'

'From it,' Tara says.

'Tara is broken,' Armand says. 'She's lost her substance. Only style is left.'

'I've not seen this before,' I say. 'I'd want that for myself. Substance – it doesn't make you friends, and weighs you down.'

'Energy,' Tara says. 'It's having much too much. It lifts you up, it wears you out. That's what has no substance. People live many years – but still their lives are short. Mine will be shorter still. The time you feel alive, that is. What shall I do? What do you want – help someone you don't know? End their misery? It would take a century, then you're both dead, gaga, speaking different languages – not well – not having travelled round, seen the mountains, the sanctuaries, the skittery blue and yellow beast beneath the rock the instant when it terminates, its whole chapter, its file, drawer in the laboratory – all extinct, tossed into the furnace...'

'It's what I've been asking, Tara, on and off,' I say. 'Those questions.'

'You need a question for that answer,' Armand says. 'I think we shouldn't be burdened with you, Vince.'

'What burden?' I ask. 'You have money.'

'They pay me to look after Tara,' Armand says.

'There's nothing wrong with her,' I say.

'Look, Vince,' he says, pushing me aside. 'You think they pay you, just because you are alive? One of you must be sick, real sick, before...'

'It's the last day of your life, Vince,' Tara says. 'How do you spend it? You could shoot that guy over there – right through the eye – the left one, closed; the other's aiming at you. No one wants this piece of scrubby land you scrabble over, but who aims best makes everybody rich, they'll eat sheep's tails, they have good lives, and holidays to see the pyramids. That copy of Le Cid you brought along and never read – who'd you want to have it? Not me, I don't hold with it...'

Dark and misty, we hear the siren in the rushes: 'There's a river-boat,' says Armand. 'I wonder, will it go to Krems?'

'If the river's long enough, it will go to Krems,' says Tara. 'The monks will give us two white cells. I'm sure I know the captain – it won't cost.'

'Do you need have faith to get a cell?' Armand wonders.

'The Sufis were wonderful,' Tara says. 'But they showed themselves too much. The dance – it always makes me cry, to watch, and think of genius revolving, slowly raise its arms.'

They go aboard: they don't take me. Tara cartwheels up the ramp. There's no one else about. Armand picks up Tana's stick, carries it after her, as he's been taught.

How valiant they are, Tara and Armand. Forget Indians and robots, those straight faces, our brothers that we'll never see, our silent selves... Those two stride out alone, disconnected ... not taking sides, because they don't believe enough to do what must be done: destroy your enemies, go bowling with their heads, throw roses at your warriors.

The money... Is it really tossed to them, so they can roam? I should have asked.

⋆

'We're tired of being poor,' says Whitney. 'We're passing it on. That's why you get to rent the room.'

'Remember it always,' says Dolores. 'If you don't, it's not worth the money.'

'I'll make a start,' I say. 'Maybe the bed's broken leg will mend, if I take my time. And – where will you sleep now?'

'You have a niggly mien,' says Whitney. 'The earth is made of broken things. The moon – that just spun off. No use to anyone – but people go on and on...'

'Fine,' I say. 'I guess the money's for your useful things.'

'We're going into action,' Whitney says. 'Soldiers or doctors – whichever seems the best.'

'They're both mortal skills,' Dolores says. 'They interdepend, and both are lined with goodness.'

'I don't need your justification. Give me some pegs to hang my memories on...'

'Don't be clever about the garden,' Whitney says. 'It's not for fine writing, nor for snootiness. A dead lady left the furnishings – you wouldn't throw them out.'

'I might,' I say, thinking of Mike, not gathering stuff – and Maya, needing it.

'It's not about taste,' Dolores says. 'We fit right in, for size. We're all normal in this street. You don't want to empty out. Someone might call.'

'Or mistake our house for theirs,' says Whitney. 'Then, there's burglars. If you've nothing to take, they kill your cat.'

They move into another space, giggling over me. Whitney is a frizzy blonde, Dolores has red ends – for sure, I'll remember everything.

'It's good,' I say. 'You don't want to start anything or analyse – just to do good.' It's a thing you say, to make friends, reduce the rent.

'Oh no,' Dolores says, 'we want to do good by doing bad.'

'Underneath,' I say, 'you want to do it together – maybe there's love involved. They say when all else goes, love remains.' That's another thing you say.

'They say that, do they?' asks Dolores. 'It's crap. Love's dying all the time. A grope, forgotten date, trench mouth: you're on your own – no sympathy.'

'Interesting lives, you have,' I say.

What does that mean? – that there's someone else involved – somewhere. Your own life doesn't interest you, not in that way.

'Our lives?' Whitney asks, looking for some repartee. 'We haven't had them yet. And when they're done – we can't talk to you about them.'

'That's why you must remember things,' Dolores says. 'Dimensions, smells – start with the room you're in. That should be simple – most people here – have rooms. Others have a jungle, or a desert, and no rooms – that gives your memory a feast, but not more happiness...'

'That's what we'll probably find out,' says Whitney. 'When you've something larger than a room, with no happiness – but what?'

'Remembering,' I say. 'That's what transpires. But, Whitney, this doesn't seem to tilt you where you want to go. You're back to poor people in a space.'

'Yes,' says Whitney. 'But this time we're looking on.'

'I get the scene,' I say. 'Saving bad lives – or living them. Which do you prefer – being killed before your holiday – or after? Not so easy. You might save the fare, the threat of rain...'

'That's if you go away,' Dolores says, giggling. 'If you're at home – the question's only one of time.'

'Jolly people, Whitney, Dolores. I've been meeting lots like you – moving along, questioning the inscrutable, not caring much about response...' I say. 'It's disappointing.'

'Oh, Vince,' Dolores says. 'We're not benevolent. You can't relax with us. We might do to you what we might do to anyone. More – since you have lodged with us. Most things that lodge in you – must be cut out or burned away.'

'You don't talk like doctors,' I say. 'I wonder, do you know more about soldiering?'

'The basic's much the same,' says Whitney. 'You bring relief. Bad news – it's seen as your intelligence. That doesn't mean it's easy, either way, but it's been done for centuries...'

'And like the song says, "Everybody dies",' Dolores says, and laughs.

'You're dangerous,' I say. 'You've no brakes.'

'Ah,' says Whitney. 'That means speed. It's a real puzzle – you think you're going fast – but it's just turned into light, here in your skull.'

Dolores interrupts, 'We thought a lot about the invention of time. At first, it wasn't. Things just came round. There was duration – but that went on and on, colourless and flat. It's only recently that people learned to chop it up – long lengths and short, like spills...' 'Spaghetti,' Whitney interrupts. 'We were into Buddhism – a drama seconds long, a drum, a fan, a long white gown, black buttons.' 'Like a surgeon's,' says Dolores.

'There was long and short, and also where you were, and we were outside it, so we wanted something more. Our time,' says Whitney. 'Doing what we want in it, without an end, without an interruption. War and peace – it's all the same. No one to tell you which is which.'

'This place,' Dolores says. 'They go to lots of wars, and tell you when they stop, and some they say will never end. So – if they can do it, so can we...'

I lie down on the bed and hope they'll go away.

They won't go away. They live here – I don't. I hear them laughing – they're both much larger than me – if there's a fight...

Dolores shakes me – 'You've been trained,' she says. 'A recruit.'

'Yes, I joined, to find a person,' I tell her. I don't mention boots, or pills.

'We have a friend,' Dolores says. 'Mister Bongo – from the Congo. We wouldn't call him that – he does.'

'That's a place they might want you both,' I say.

Whitney's too chubby for a long march. Dolores is tall enough to see above the bushes. A sack of rockets on her back, precious as a baby, so they say.

'Mister Bongo's quite delightful,' says Dolores. 'I love *frites* too, though it's not clear to me – were they an African invention? Or an importation? We know potatoes came from there. All that, the horror, it's all part of us. We sent it there, they've sent it back. No one is cured, not ever. Ostend – Oostende, they call it – where Christ came in procession, to make us beautiful – in an hour, you see it all, *frites* a-plenty. It's a friendly place, if you're not from there. They remind me of Slovaks, in a way.'

'I don't see you in the Chinese army, though,' I say. 'You live on intimacy... Your take, your world...'

'You're right,' she says. 'Two of you, of us, can't stand in line, in order. It would look absurd. No action, then, for us. You can't fool around with scalpels, either – the Chinese are demanding, do things quick – tick-tack, before you know.'

'Dolores,' I say. 'You've got it wrong – your side, it would be here. You'd not go anywhere. Not needed, not wanted. The enemy, it would be them: for them, is you. Your future – exactly what you have right now, here in this house. Short lives, but not heroic, not what you'd want.'

'It may not come to that,' she says.

'I've nearly memorised the room,' I say.

'I told Whitney having someone in would fuck up everything,' she says.

In the morning, they've gone away. Their note says – 'Put the rent in the pig, Pig.'

I don't see any pig.

*

'I see we're brothers,' the person says – it says 'Anna' on her badge: we're stuck, not glued together – something's broken down. 'You realise,' she says, 'it's odds and sods that govern us. However they get in ... election or the warming pan. You'll not be rid of them. We're in a primitive stage. You either stick with them, or you develop or transform. Minorities – they help. The Jews made German industry, Janissaries helped the empire float... Syrians, Iraqis – they have history behind them, and they're smart...

'Guys like you – they're quite deluded. I bet you think that people, places – they are interchangeable. It's mostly true. It isn't wholly true – so it's not true at all. Hotels – they look alike, even if you holiday on Mars. And people – they're all equal, as you know, and yet – like the hotels, we see each one is different within – like chocolates in a box. Yours are illusions, friend! You have to come to terms with difference – although it may not matter much, my dear.'

They winch us back. We start again. It's a relief – anger's no use, when you're halted. Outside, there's a noise of sabres clashing, long sparks.

'The trolley came off the wires,' says Anna. 'And the points are never true. That's why we're lurching forward.'

'You can't steal a tram,' I say. 'And the passengers – they're special. They don't carry notes, only small coins. On every trip you glimpse goodness, how it could be if the tracks were straight.'

'It takes a bright city to have tramways,' Anna says. 'You need to know where people want to go.'

'Guys tried to fly centuries before they thought to lay a track,' I say. 'Our brains must be put in the wrong way round...'

'That's not at all the way to think,' she says. 'Don't stand so close. What makes you think I'd want to see you another time?'

'Nothing,' I say. 'Just to hang on to, while I decide my future.'

'Exactly,' Anna says. 'In your obtuseness, you're quite smart.'

'It's about perfection, Anna,' I say. 'This ride on the tram. Many people have the tickle: the meeting, the performance. Finding a companion. I have, many times.'

'Sex and perfection – those are different things,' she says. 'When you reach perfection – it's the end. The fall, the splash – they think it's a fish, that silver leg with gold stubble going down. The flesh – it flakes off like soaked bread, the eyes flat – like dimes. They don't bug out. And go pop – it's inaudible anyway. If you have it all inside you, everything there is up to now – and no doubt you have – why let it out in a display, an airshow? Look at us all here, in this launch, motoring along, on our rocking stream, knowing it all and letting nothing out at all. Getting off when it's our time. Mostly we don't pay the fare, but – we keep schtum. Try it.'

'Someone gave me this stick,' I say. 'I've ways to go.'

'There's many shops sell those, Vince,' says Anna. 'Gift means nothing special. It's over. There's nothing more for you to do. Forget the hanged man and the tipping castle – it's been done. The guys here – have everything on their screens. Balloons, floating up and down, not like the real thing – that's the game you have to play when it's all revealed. Revelations are infinite, minus one ... near to infinity, it must mean there's one to suit. Believe or don't – what's there is what there is.' She laughs, as I have no reply. 'You wanted destiny, poor Vince, that sat beside you, fit your plan. I am your fate, Vince, and I'll drag you down. I'll put my suckers in your eyes and suck your stomach out and make you spit your lungs... No tears – the sea is what you've wept. No sleep, I'm bells inside your skull...'

'I don't deserve you, Anna,' I tell her, crumbling. 'I never did wrong to anyone, never anything by myself...'

'Oh, my dear,' she says. 'You're in the web, your little thrashing legs are sticky with your sentiment. Don't be afraid – I fly, I don't spin and weave. My wings are black – but you will never see them.'

There's always a way out – those millions we've forgot, and everything they did ... although – behind the wall – there's rumbling, mining going on. Maybe my boss – a plan, a motor, pushing us along...

'There's always that,' says Anna. 'You make your walls without a crack – no windows, then the beast arrives, opens the plaster with its horn, you see your garden's all been gobbled up, it's holms and furrows, armed men springing up.'

'That's the poetry,' I say. 'There must be more, not just potato skins.'

'Here's the trick,' she says. 'You know how runners fill themselves with someone else's blood – spiked up, maybe a phial of Alexander's, San Gennaro's – well: the guys who move the scroll along and let you see what they have drawn, and where you are on it – they have a special blood. Replete with that – they have short memories. Short lives – those don't appal. They don't feel pain – above all, yours... They make the story, invent it as they sing an aria so full of air, it bears you to the clouds, it lands you on an attol ... everything's unique, the centre's smoking, there's no fire ... most things are poisonous, but you can live on nuts ... there's promises of slaves that's washed ashore that you can eat or set to work...'

'I see all this, dear Anna. But...' I say.

'The greatness lies for some guy who can make the blood,' she says. 'Mostly it comes from holy warriors,

funambulists and human cannon-balls. Since everyone
aspires – what you most need is synthesis: an artificial
boost, available to all. Or, better – available to just a few.
You set the price...'

'It doesn't work like this,' I say. 'The great men filled
with Lethe blood ... it's just a fable... The scroll – it's set on
automatic – it comes out with scrawls and runes already
formed...'

'No,' says Anna.

How beautiful she is. The skin – what you see here on
the tram, is limited – I bet it goes all over...

'No,' she says. 'You keep the fear, it's an essential. But
cut out the pain.'

'Then it's what runners have,' I say.

'No, no,' she says. 'When you run, you mustn't flap your
arms, or pound your fists, or think of things to say. Simple
arithmetic, daggers behind the tapestry ... what bosses do –
all that is special, must be added on.'

'I guess that long ago, people had their sage, their seer,
their queen, their warrior. A shaman, too... One by one,
they pass by, the tall poppies, their pictures drawn, they
smirk, and scan the portraitist, easy on their elephant, the
donkey trotting by ... but now...' I say.

'Yes, yes,' she says. 'You need them by the thousand –
nature's not equipped.'

'We could concoct the stuff,' I say. 'Or denounce the
use. But, since meeting you, Anna, and underneath the
love, desire, that accompany this ride – I feel an
overwhelming anger and despair. The vanity – oh, the
vanity – it puffs your veins and shrinks your arteries...'

'Exposing the trick is easy, quickly done – but earns us
less than manufacturing,' she says.

'Well,' I say. 'Here we both are. In a place where nothing grows. Nothing for me, nothing for you – we're sterile. We can't pick each other's flower. Or stick our prick inside its dust.'

'We can't be in the place where nothing grows,' she says. 'Things grow everywhere. It can't be us that isn't in the place that can't exist. We're stuck, that's true: here is the fence – but we want more, and different. You, Vince, want what you can't have – it's easy to stop wanting it. And if we make the artificial blood – you think it's not for us...? Are we so stupid that we'd sell the stuff?'

'It all seems crazy, Anna – first, the flying, now the blood...' I say.

'No, no,' she says. 'Think Blériot. They're all called mad until they're millionaires.'

'They say the Russians had those first machines,' I say. 'Harassing their enemies as Moscow burned. Wings fur-covered – then buried in the permafrost. They couldn't dig them out.'

'Exactly so,' she says. 'Your business model must be fur-covered too, or else you don't get first prize.'

'This is the business, then, as they say: *le business*,' I say. 'Odds, sods, and tarts. They're the strongest, they're the motor. No compassion, no fine comprehension quite misplaced. They win because they're winners.'

'You sell so you can buy,' says Anna. 'Yourself first and last, the rest, as they occur. Remember – all heavens are disfunctional – Olympus, Valhalla. Come on, Vince, little soldier, raise your banner! That Mount Atheos – how those monks quarrel over what vegetables to plant! Listen to the songs – they'll tell you all the stories you want – "*O weile, weile wandellos!*" "stay, don't change" ... even when you're dead – wow! how you change when you're a corpse! On

your horse, Vince! Remember – it's not only wolves that
howl – you've the whole sky to raise your muzzle to... That
song – "All I really want is to be wonderful" – that's the
spirit! Your grail – it's that crucible of dragons' blood. See
it foam and seethe. You'd change that for a frolic on used
sheets? With me – worn thin as I am ... Insane!'

'There's no feeling in us, Anna,' I say, 'But you know
how to raise me up. It doesn't matter, if it's hate...'

'Yes,' she says. 'The strongest potion you have in you –
that is the thrust.'

There's something here that's going to fail, to wreck. 'I
don't want all of this,' I say. 'The thing we'd look for – it's
like what those endless movies seek: another Ring, even the
tunes. They're pits I won't fall in.'

'It's true,' she says. 'Most people involved in them, those
films – they don't survive. Armour, space suits – all heavy
togs. You see the trembling hands – is it the weight they
bear? The guys that hold the camera – their grip is firm.
Maybe it's them that brings the drugs and guns. The
others, actors all, both sides of the lens – they don't survive:
they fall off wooden rocks, pop the wrong stuff, are cut
down on divans ... they're knifed, they have destinies
bizarre with animals... You're right. Maybe it's not us, not
our scenario. A past rouged up as future – the holiness has
been sucked out ... the stars, the knights, the dwarves – all
fascist kitsch.'

'Anna,' I say, 'let's move away from that. Forget the
holiness – it doesn't suit.'

'You're right,' she says. 'Inventing things. Empowering.
Making a name and cash. Power to the people, all fired
with the same blood... It all sounds innocent. Innocence –
they won't believe you, and it isn't true. Everyone distrusts
the claim.'

'What then?' I ask.

'We renounce our invention,' Anna says. 'All its consequences. It's buried in us. We'll forget it. The game, that one – it never started.'

It's a fine idea: I look closely at her. Those aren't furrows on her face – they're lines – a net, scales – drawn with the finest pen.

'It isn't age,' says Anna. 'That will come – the lines here are a plan. A city that I shouldn't want to live in.'

'Just lines?' I ask. 'It's a tarmac, runways for airships deviating with the breeze. Where are the buildings?'

'Oh,' she says. 'It's painful, walking in that space. You need a car – but driving's such a bore.'

'That – could be a castle – a copy of those blown up or down,' I say, running a finger over.

'No,' she says. 'That's a nose. Not war damage – those are nostrils.'

'Expressionism in the purest state,' I say. She runs on – 'Or the plan, the face-space, might be of rooms – trapezoid. Traps – rooms full of dirty people, shooting up. Who'd want to spend a weekend there?'

'If you knew exactly what your plans meant,' I say. 'The knowledge might kill. Get you thrown out. This way – you're safe. It's all – on your face, inscrutable. No transgression, and no destination. Nowhere you would want to go, but only yours, no danger, not communicable.'

'You think you're clever,' Anna says. 'You've no idea – why the city was blown up, who's squatting in its spacious ruin, where those airbags are flying to.'

'I don't need to know,' I say.

'There,' she says. 'You've got it. If you need anything – write it on your body. It can be rubbed off. The spirit of it all, of everything, in miniature. No bass trombones – a tiny box, let into your armpit – that will do the trick. Abnegation. Know everything – keep quiet about it. Live everywhere – don't pay the rent. Life – a sip, a sniff – releases every countryside and every fruit, the sweat of every harvester. Have truck with forms, with wholes – what they call the telescope's wrong end – that shows true distances, how far you are from everything.'

I kiss her – the top of her head. She turns her face, illegible beneath the *craquelure*. 'There,' she says, 'that was it. The everything. You'll remember it for all your life.'

We'd long since left the tram. 'Up high – you see them come. Down low – you have more chance to run away,' she says. The building only has two floors.

Her days are long – some hands of poker on the screen – 'I've friends who give me numbers,' Anna says. 'On the plastic card and on the hands. We split the winnings: losses, they don't count.' Then, it's the baseball channel, into the night – 'That diamond,' Anna says. 'It's the best I'll ever have.' I have no comment.

'It may disappoint, all this,' she says, 'but every wrinkle's clear...'

'Remember, Vince,' she says, 'apes are born to be sad. In the jungle – it's hetero heaven, but how glum they are. Picking themselves all day.'

I don't speak, don't answer that infrequent speech. I'm not missed, it adds nothing. There was Bianca – the lady who disappeared, without a shadow, no cry. I should feel bad. No doubt they come looking, for me, the people who do that. I don't feel bad at all, but I don't want them to catch me.

'The best thing,' says Anna. 'Is you don't need meet those people – the poker, there's no one real. The baseball – those little guys in uniform, you know exactly how they are. It's arithmetic – their money's not for things or services. Just swing the bat and multiply.'

'We're out here on the periphery,' I say. 'More village than a *banlieue*. It's hard for me to move around.'

'Poor albatross,' she says. 'Your long legs don't let you flap those little wings. Try walking. Not on the water – the sharks are waiting.'

'There's nothing left to say,' I say.

'Exactly – that's the goal. That's the accomplishment,' she says.

'There's guys round here,' I say. 'Who want another chapter – the one about the fire. I know all about the flames – those that burn out, and there's nothing left... Their fires, though – they blaze throughout the night, the desert's black with smoke and soot ... the earth is eaten like a lump of coal.'

'There's nothing new,' says Anna. 'It isn't you or me, the gangs who try to ride the world. You know how to keep clean, Vince. Remember when you walked the line, the 8s, the 18s. And now you're here, at peace, bored as you've never been before...'

'It all changes, Anna,' I say. 'Another system creeps in, imposes – we don't know what to ask, what it can do. The guys that fight it – they fight us as well.'

'You chatter, Vince,' she says. 'Silence was better. I have everything here set up just right.'

Nothing holds me here. I could just walk away.

I walk away – that was the invitation. I'm free. Except – you have to bear those coins, moist, hot in my pants. The heads of spirits that I don't believe in. That no one does now – yet, they persist, the myths that you can't live without. Maybe they unite us in our disbelief – not that I care about that stuff... I could sign up, fight for freedom,

death to the occupiers ... but I'm free. Doing all that –
requires I'd not be free. That's far too much ... and firing
guns or digging holes. Not good jobs, for sure... All that
obedience...

The walking wears you down, is all.

★

'I have experience,' I say. 'I know, everyone does. Maybe
it's not always bad, admitting it. You still need a job,
despite it all.'

The lady laughs, as though I am ingratiating.

There is no war. People are recruited, off they go, some
with a band. Corpses return. There's shooting around, not
where you are. It's normal, like it was, as long as I
remember.

I tell the boss – 'I fear I need some work.' He's
thoughtful, not like the other guy, boss, who wanted to be
told he should get out, forget the vanity.

'It's not the money, Vince,' he says. 'That's to stop the
squeaking wheel.'

Oton. A Kurd, a Bosniak? Or both, or turned by cash to
something else, a hybrid, in between, more shaded, more
anonymous.

'There's two systems, circling round,' he says. 'A global
one, with guys in suits and jeans. And guys contesting.
What do they wear? All kinds of stuff – disguises,
uniforms... Do you believe the story, Vince? The epics?
Ancient stuff, at war with ancient stuff... Does it make
sense to you?'

'Oh no,' I say. 'You mean – old-time religion? Clans?
And dancing?'

'That's it, Vince,' he says. 'Then there's the bigger scene
– survival, saving the bees. Digging up everything.'

'I know all that,' I say. 'That's what I think about. I
know it all. But knowing ... everybody knows.'

'The systems touch...' says Oton, vaguely.

'Oton,' I say, 'I'll save you cash. Give me an envelope,
full of notes – I'll save you time as well. The system's one.
Its history means it isn't round, circular, nor like the Greeks
thought, an ellipse. It's one: it's us who don't know how to
deal with it. That's why you ask. You'd like to plan a
paradise where you feel safe – but to get the rocks and
palms, the sand to set them in, you have to sell...'

'No,' Oton says. 'I could buy, instead. And build, and
add security. A new system; an oval wheel. One based on
guilt, not expiation. I hate socialism, knowing what's wrong
and doing right – I see us wandering on the evil path –
wearing my red trousers, copied on to every one of us,
whistling my song, living in my black buildings, praying
together to unnamed gods... My priests: my atlas:
colonising my planets – playing the santur, the koiré...
Abjuring me and mine, spitting on my image, pinning dead
field mice to my shrines... Do you see it, Vince? The
colours and the space? Only accept, Vince! Nothing to do
with me – it's raking the mosaics, harrowing the pavements
... living by night... Are you there, Vince?'

'Yes, Oton,' I say. It will take time.

'No force, Vince,' he says. 'No power. Just people doing
it. Do they want to do what they do? No! Do they gladly
give their power to other guys? Of course not. It could all
be open. Philosophers, up till now – they've always tried to
entertain the people: now it's time to have them wander
down another path.'

'I see that, Oton. It's something I've doodled in my head,' I say. 'For me, animals have a special place.'

'Of course, we'll have them too,' says Oton. 'It's unavoidable.'

'People will ask about the poor, the mines,' I say.

'Well, why ask me?' asks Oton. 'I'm a rich guy – that's how I seem. What would I know about all that?'

*

'Wait here, see if he likes you,' says the lady. 'Here's the new pitcher of Manhattans.'

'This is like paradise,' I say: she pours.

'That means you don't know why you're there, how long for, and what you have to do,' she says.

'It's early for so much alcohol,' I say. 'Watch out for your job.'

'Making them – it *is* my job,' she says. 'Well – he doesn't like you. You can stay. He wants a woman, who'll replace him, do his work. You're not that.'

'It's good,' I say. 'I don't understand. Nothing.'

'People want to do something,' the lady says. 'They pay us. You tell them how.'

'It's so easy,' I say. 'It's a joke.'

'They're original things that come to us,' she says. 'You digest. They become your idea – you and your team.'

She takes the pitcher in to Oton. There's shouting. I tell her, 'I don't think I want to work for anyone.'

'They're ideas coming through the door, not people,' says the lady. 'I'm about to take over from Oton. Now, you've resigned? That's not a good sign.'

'I liked Oton,' I say. 'But not the outfit.'

'If you stayed,' she says. 'You'd always be Oton's man. That wouldn't do.'

'I have loyalty, though,' I say. 'That's good. You just need other things to make a winning whole. A desk, perhaps.'

'What you want a desk for, Vince?' she asks. 'No one's even told you about their plan.'

'Claudine!' shouts Oton. 'I'm unhappy!'

'He loved being boss,' Claudine, the lady, says. 'Now I'm boss, I think we ought to fire everyone, start over. Maybe re-hire...'

'I'll go out on the road,' I say. 'Do the job.' I'm quite drunk, but it's still early. No principle's been compromised.

The road forks – there's a knobbly path up to a hill – in this light it's varnished, vaguely Trecento. A wider road – Quattrocento comes to mind, with trees, some pines, some bushy-topped. A guy falls into step beside me – we strike out towards the landscape, the more recent one. 'I'm doing fieldwork,' I say to Roger, trotting along beside. 'You want opinions, then?' he asks. 'Peopling your field?'

'No,' I say.

'You must be from a charity, a state, a church,' he says.

'We do our biz with all of those,' I say. 'They say they're for the poor, but all they teach is self-reliance.'

Roger cuts some staves for us. We tramp the dusty road.

'The one place you're not poor,' he says, 'is in the army.'

I'd tell him it's not true, I was enrolled – but, then, I'm a deserter too. We walk along in silence.

I feel bound to tell Roger what I'm doing here. He's smiling left and right, in this painterly scene he plays the artist. What's the question I'm resolving? Nothing occurs to me – except the solitude of Oton, his tumbling mind, his military service – blows given, received, recorded, lost.

'In the opera,' I say. 'King Roger was a mystic, and became a monk.'

'I never heard that,' Roger says.

I speed up, leave him far behind. I'm sorry for the snub, I guess, though if I apologise, it's not a snub.

Redress. That's my subject. What ever redress is there?

No. There's no redress, not for anything, no dirty deed, nor leaving things as they are, not your fault, or anyone's. Redress – what form? A resurrection? Something from the insurance? A tree planted, a song sung, ribbon cut...?

Roger catches up.

'Nothing personal,' I say. 'Just your banality, those set phrases – how they irritate!'

At least, I blame myself for nothing. Nor my relatives – all honest fearing people, no victim and no perpetrator, no massacre, no genocide, no disappearances, no sentimental trips to places razed or redeveloped, memorialised. No regrets, no apologies – the family of perfect lives, no blot or smear, anonymity pursued, achieved. A tree of forbears, honey in the forks.

'My brain's as full of kinks as yours,' says Roger, prodding with his stave. 'Suppose we meet the aliens – some, shaped like wild turkeys, and you say "Good morning" – if they can hear you in your rubber tent, the air in bottles on your back... They maybe have a morning every hundred years, as they go circling round, without regrets, without the massacres... Or some – medusas, feed on stomach acid – while you sleep, they fold in through your nose and live down there, as quiet as quiet... You want to swap equations with them, do they go to concerts, wave their arms...? The vanity, of wanting to make friends, like at a conference. It all comes from our cinema, our hope to be unique and kind...'

There is no answer ... what might Maya, Anna say? They're both on their planets – one spinning fast, it looks like a dust devil, and Anna's, slow as if it's stuck in nothingness, a space no one would rocket to...

*

'I'm boss now,' says Claudine: 'Come back at once.'

Roger's the hero, he must plod alone ... he'll find the garden, the teasels burning with immortal fire, the sunflowers like old gasfires, upturning, scorched... What then? You find burnt flowerbeds. I could hear him whisper, clueless, 'Ah! Hohum.'

Claudine is in her room. 'If you're boss, why aren't you in there, where Oton was?' I ask.

'Oh, he's in there still,' she says. 'He thought to close the chapter. You would have heard the shot. He thought he'd end the sadness so; the quarrelling, the tortures, the regrets. It's not been so.'

'Perhaps he felt a new defeat,' I say. 'From you, Claudine. You closed his road.'

'Oh well,' she says, 'we'll never know how things turn out. That is the beauty of the tale – there's no end yet, and when there is – no one will know...'

'I'm working on redress,' I say. 'What you must pay for what you've done, what you might gain, if bad's been done to you.'

'Well,' she says, 'stop it at once. "Done"?, "bad" – you all have specious claims, who knows what's wrong, what can be reimbursed, what punishments to set against rewards... Best have a ritual, a sorrowing, and not delve in.'

'Oton took me on,' I say.

'He didn't like you,' says Claudine. 'How are we to use you anyway? Redress – it must be put in money terms, or time. In jail, or suffering in other ways ... and Oton – surely he deserves redress? We've not been in to him. What would be the point?'

'He might be waiting for his pitcher,' I say. 'Did you think of that, Claudine? What if he feels you're persecuting him, his vision...'

'That's so,' she says. 'He is the only one who has a plan. Is that a merit, or a fault?'

'A vision like that,' I say. 'The grandeur – it leads to frustration, knowing you won't make it, not ever find a mate to help...'

'Well,' says Claudine, 'some mates! ... I'm really shocked – you and Roger, fighting, with those staves. They were meant to keep the dogs away.'

'Roger was frustrating too,' I say. 'He's one who wouldn't punt your vision up a hill... They weren't real weapons anyway.'

Roger was like Oton – a mind in full flower. But Oton knew the answers, and that they didn't help. Roger – didn't care. All he wanted was more road to trudge down.

'You're stood down now, my boy,' she says, grinning at me. 'Nothing boisterous! I'll cut you in – there's orders come from China now. They're running low – ideas, the soil ... all that scrabbling, now it's hit a rock, maybe it's coming to an end. So soon... It's temporary – just like you.'

There's photos that she shows – the earth is black, then in a bucket down you go, it's dark, and when you reach the end, it's black again. China – it's name suggests fragility, and bulls – who enter, smash, and run off out.

'Cut the crap,' shouts Claudine. 'Oton shot himself – he's gone, I'm boss. Now, money talks, our heads are clear and empty, waiting for our clientele. We could be lovers, Vince – it would be unethical to have you as an employee. Our problems that way would be solved...'

'I'd not get paid, Claudine,' I say. That body, blued and sweaty like a gorgonzola – alas for her, I'm not attracted.

'It's true,' she says. 'You don't attract. But – it's solutions that we seek, not things that fit.'

She's undone a button on her blouse: we clench our jaws, both of us, tight – the opposite of hungry – angry – beasts. 'You and Roger,' she says, laughing. 'Two pilgrims, turning into devils, squabbling on the mystic road.'

'No, Claudine,' I say. 'Not like that at all.'

'And walking out, across a desert and a mountain – a hostage, spy, a special soldier, Vince,' and she laughs some more.

'It wasn't me,' I say, 'another person quite exceptional, I'm sure.'

'The Chinese customs – they can smell your breath,' she says, 'and when you enter – they can tell if you will last for long enough to leave. We could send them round the world – sniff, sniff – a diagnosis everywhere, and people with short lives can do the fifty things they wanted to ... and we might take a cut, dear Vince.'

'I heard it, Claudine – so has everyone. It's really not at all my thing,' I say. 'Roger was terrestrial. He's irritating. I need feel no shame.'

Chinese Customs. They must have every package, every shape and smell – wonderful creatures, never on a list, messes in celadon, dragons' breath in bags... The human hearts – those whiffs of methane they send up, from when we lived on other rocks with other stars – we go there in our dreams. And will they come – maidens in uniform, at last with pigtails all erect, to suss us out...

'Your visa – you'll expire before it does...' they'll say.

'Do we want cash from that?' I ask Claudine.

'Everything must have its point,' she says. 'Or else the whole is meaningless. Everything must travel, not see one thing, but two at least. Not to impinge – to 'ping' on some instrument, something that doesn't play a tune. Yes – the hour of death must mean a lot, dear Vince, or else there is no shape, no form or cadence, and no resolution.'

To me, that's ordinary words. 'Unfinished' – that's the work to leave.

'That's it, Claudine?' I ask. 'Chinese Customs.'

'Will make our fortune,' Claudine says. 'Mine, at least. You'll have to wait for trickle-down.'

'It's not what Oton sought,' I say.

'All the founders get things wrong,' she says. 'They want peace, it comes out war. Foundation – that's the nub. You sink the piles, stand back, are shovelled in some hole – and what is built upon your foundations – it could be anything. Power-station. Amusement arcade or betting shop. Oton wanted something different: we show it all ends the same.'

'I knew that, Claudine, long ago,' I say. 'Even Roger knew... And yet – it ended premature for Oton, by his will. What's built on his idea, Claudine? Where did that go? Wearing red trousers. All the other stuff I don't remember well...?'

'Oton's will?' asks Claudine. 'His hand, at least,' and she giggles. 'These Chinese wizards – they'll tell the truth. Life, short or long, rich or poor – it's just a breath, a breeze, a zephyr from the south – sandalwood and mangoes. It takes so little, for the professional...'

'They couldn't have foretold Oton's end,' I say. 'Not from his lungs.'

'No, no,' Claudine shouts. 'But from his eyes!'

Chinese customs: letting things in, keeping them out, stripping the leaves off bundles, poking into spicy dusts, the ginger, the paprika – all contraband hidden within – the bones incised, the white dishes... Holding the border – *douaniers*: the peacock – Krishna – and Radha the milkmaid – setting the boundary between us and other creatures, us and the gods – the frontier where the naked man fights with the lion, both on their back legs, both valuable...

'Thirty coming in tomorrow,' says Claudine. 'Can I trust you with them? Colors and faiths – not your best shot. You only know guys like yourself...'

We put them on the métro. They're not liked – to be sniffed, and told you have an hour to live – it makes a panic. What use is it? 'It's all made up,' says Wei. 'There's big dogs, tell what is your destiny, but they can't talk.' She laughs.

It's true – the Italians call their boundary a *dogana*.

Mostly they want to start a business, those custom people.

I ask Wei, 'All frontiers, then, are in your hands – life, death, for instance. Flying and walking, fire and water, things you can't and things you want. Custom and – what? Mobility? Hard edge? Ideas? All these?'

'Oh yes,' she says.

'And what criteria?' I ask, insist. 'There must be boundaries that limit the contraries. Over ground and under, to take your customs as they're said to be. Underground, there's fire and water – that's not opposites. Is it the same for others too – that they may coexist in some dimension – maybe on a scroll, a white pagoda-jar.'

'That may be so,' she says. 'But don't exaggerate.'

'I need you for a guide,' I say. 'I'm not ready yet... I need to map the frontiers – see which are permeable. Stay over there, dear Wei,' I add. 'Don't get so near you smell my breath or look into my eyes. Like the inscription says – 'you today, my comrade – tomorrow, it's my turn.' Do you, your officers – each morning, smell each other's breath, to see if you'll get through, arrive to do some overtime, or...'

'That's what you find out if you join the service, Vince,' she says. 'I don't see you're a good recruit. You're even listed somewhere as a guy who's on the run, although long legs don't mean you can run fast.'

I don't implore. It's the first day – there's time for that to come.

'Listen, Vince,' she says. 'I know you've met most people who live outside the Wall. It's true – we've spilled a bit and taken in the shamans too. You can believe everything we say – but you can't trust us. We don't have a side, and so we're not on yours. I know you'd like to see what's in and what is out, what passes, what is halted, what comes in on golden wings. The problem is, dear Vince – to understand the movement – you must have a territory. If there's no bounds, there are no customs, Vince.'

'No, no,' I say, 'that's pure conservatism – romantic, sentimental too. It's reaction, Wei.'

'I didn't make it so,' she says. 'But look at all the other beasts around. Not there to become clay effigies. Look at earth and air – without the air, there is no earth...'

'That's not what I mean at all,' I say. 'I know about apocalypses, all that stuff. I looked for something sage, dear Wei...'

'I'm off now, Vince,' says Wei. 'I have to earn Claudine's cash, Down in the Underground...' And off she goes.

In or out. Dead or alive. Maybe – not the most important questions. Interesting, though. The book says – we've a serpent in our belly – it fires us, we're its crucible, but when comes the hour – you smell the poison billow up. That's it!

In the evening, Wei says, 'Everybody cheats, a little – friends try more than enemies. What does the cheating do? What do you have, so precious – that it's worth a risk you'll lose it? I'll take it, if it's precious – but it won't gain you a day on earth, if it's taken, or you get away. The people here – their mouths are closed, they don't like me looking at them. What's to be lost? The risk is only – knowledge, of how long they have to go...'

'I don't follow, Wei,' I say. 'There's an accident. All the healthy guys are pulped – and you and they would never have believed...'

'Exactly so, dear Vince,' she says. 'It's all a trick. But – maybe you have never worked a week, a month – you can't believe the satisfaction that it gives to guys like me, to have a secret, break the monotony, be seconded here...'

'It's true,' I say. 'Easy money, moving about – it's granted me indifference to many things. So – tell me, what's your scheme?'

'Claudine clings to everything,' says Wei. 'She knows the project – Multiple Longevity. She brought us in because we know the lines – where they are, what they're made of. What can be taken in or out. Who can stay, and who can leave. As for the rest – all have short lives. Most are full of suffering, we don't have time to meditate, exchange our suffering for wisdom, so she is convinced we are the experts.'

'The wisdom, though,' I say, 'it's not for you.'

'Oh no,' she says. 'We're just the guys in uniform who know the tale.'

★

'People are terrorised,' says Claudine. 'But they don't come to me and pay. They weep, instead. No one will trade intense short life, success, for tedium, decay...'

'My career...' says Wei. 'This doesn't help. I might stay here...'

'You're not my responsibility,' I say. 'Don't count on me. I love these capitals – but I might move on... If everything is slowing down, maybe an alp, a stream, a pitcher and a goat, enough for me.'

'I need my hands, my arms,' Claudine says. 'More of them, and everyone ... my attributes. My pitcher and your goat. The cops will come – they say my diagnosis is a threat, the death of each is my revenge. They haven't even found poor Oton yet...'

I say to Wei, 'You could desert. If they find you – it's no tragedy. There's always people looking for your job – the wars they have now, means killing everyone. Peace is the same.'

'Poking into people's cases – that's no life,' says Wei, brightening.

'I could tour,' I say, 'with my kazoo.'

'Is that why you wear red trousers, Vince?' Claudine asks.

'They're russet, Claudine,' I say. 'It's for Oton.'

'That was his joke,' she says

'That's not a bad memorial,' I say.

'I wanted to be interesting,' Wei says, 'Even if I'm not.'

'It always takes someone else to make you that,' Claudine says. 'Me – I'm safely into history. Vince! – I guess you're still murky in the gloom?'

'We're much nearer where we don't want to be, Claudine,' I say.

'I haven't started with you yet, Vince,' she says. 'And, Officer Wei – I haven't begun to finish with you. Neither of you runs. You're not a pair of legs.'

We'd like to live for ourselves, Wei and I – she has a common sense, adaptability, all that. It's unbearable. A mile of that – more than enough for me.

'Wei,' Claudine says, 'sniffs out short lives. If you're a terminal case, the guys in white coats take you away. If you've planned some violence, you're resigned to die, or thrilled by it – then you take the other route. Terrorists, or terrorised, and sometimes both. The métro – mass diagnosis – that was scattershot. This way, there's cops, free drugs involved. We'll work out then how visible we are, the credit due, to take or bury...'

'It's a horror, Claudine,' I say. I'm pleased I have no part in it.'

'No, Vince,' she says. 'You are the expert. The wayfaring lads – those are your speciality – the sick and the committed. Both have the look – the eagle, diving like a suicide, or to feed. To kill, that is. Their eye, dear Vince. It's much like yours.'

'It may not be a good idea,' says Wei. 'I see lots of trouble. I'd be much exposed...'

'Nonsense,' says Claudine. 'Those who aren't wage slaves – they go mad for schemes like this. And all the good you'd do.'

'Oh,' says Wei. 'The good part – I can take all that as read. It's the rest – the doing, the not doing, things not working out.'

'I could have you sent back home, you know,' Claudine says. 'That wouldn't suit, that wouldn't do you any good.'

You can bet on that.

'People believe these legends,' Claudine says. 'You can bet on that.'

'You could ask my colleagues, they know rules – but only those they came with. It's all a puzzle – you go from place to place – some cities claim they're lay – then there are some where everybody has their sacred book and tries to bend its rules,' says Wei.

'Come, Wei,' Claudine says. 'How you exaggerate! You're not called on to understand a thing – just go down the line: some will survive, and others too – but not for long. Then other guys will do the work of wondering how the shaky ones will end.'

'It's all a matter of degree,' says Wei. 'I'd love to help – but "soon", "inevitable end", "afar" – they're terms you find in poetry, not in breath.'

'You needn't fix a date,' says Claudine, turning red, frustrated. 'Just think "afflatus" – poetry is borne on zephyrs' breath – or used to be. There's nothing can't be measured by the air – life and death, for sure, the space that's empty, and the space that's full of us. You need philosophy, dear Wei. A feeling for the economic side would help...'

'I'll cry, Claudine,' says Wei. 'If it would help. It's not in character at all...'

'You're beautiful, you two, Vince, Wei – and as you know, beauty seeks beauty, like flows to like. But,'

Claudine says, 'I have this corpse to dump, a cover story too to spin. Poor Oton – ever anxious to help out...'

'He never was, Claudine,' I say. 'It's true he wanted the impossible, but that was just his plan – to sunder everything that is, to spin the spheres like fruits in the machine, and have them cartwheel up the hill – and have the payout made in venerable grains from Babylon and Ur...'

'That's not the point,' says Claudine. 'He's a corpse that I can't shift.'

We move away. 'Of course,' she says, 'I'm not involved – it's just a bad scene. I need to see if there's some moral fence to climb, while I drag you after, Vince.'

'There's no problem here, Claudine,' I say. 'The question of your guilt is yours. Do you feel guilty? No? It's settled, then. Did you do the deed? That's technology, just a fact the whitecoats probably get wrong, blame it on some travelling man. The same goes for Wei's diagnoses – the timing of our death, the how – and what it does for living... The answer is, don't stand in her line – no test! The problem disappears. Knowing it all, when you depart, especially where to – it's all unanswerable. Maybe she's wrong. Maybe you are. Forget it, like the song says.'

'You're right,' Claudine says. 'We'll leave him as he is. And we'll deny.'

'And I'll deny I know you too, Claudine,' I say.

'I'm armour-plated,' says Claudine. 'Businesswoman of the century. I'll pay a guy to bioengineer – block out the sun, have rain and snow all year... Saving our habitat – a medal's in it, that's for sure. I take precautions – eat no food that's harvested. I take my holidays when it rains – better watch porn movies in your room than go to work in thunderstorms.'

We're not impressed. Claudine shifts disaster so it falls on us.

'We must make Oton disappear,' I say. 'The finger of suspicion points – at all of us.'

'I'll settle this,' says Wei, 'as a favour to you all, that I'll exploit, and that's for sure.'

We crate poor Oton, born in Split, and now for ever refugee.

'Send him by sea,' says Wei. 'Far, far away. And we shall sing a song.'

We label him. Wei instructs, 'Put "Tiger" on the box, when he arrives, he will be tiger bones. Everybody knows that's a Chinese quirk, a custom, quite above suspicion. Send him to the States, in memory of his anti-system dream.'

We sing, off-key and awkward, 'If You're Going to San Francisco...' and Wei sticks a chrysanthemum in his hair. The bullet hole's invisible, amid the rot.

Claudine says, 'What if there's misdirection...?' so we sing 'New York, New York', just to make sure. We label him – 'To await...'

'Oton didn't fit,' Claudine says.

'I don't fit either,' says Wei. 'Not here.'

'The question is – where does the "here" fit in,' I say.

'I read old books,' says Wei. 'I know this isn't Istanbul – there's places there I'd really like to see.'

'You've seen them, Wei,' I say. 'They all fit in, within the walls. Over the water, you can watch the wrestlers. Now, it's quite another scene.'

'There hasn't been a single country, just the world, for many many years,' she says. 'Not since we were all in Africa. Now, you have to fit in to tiny temples, backyards, blood on the grass and in your mouth. I've done my years as border guard – oh, what a bore!'

'You're fragile, Wei,' Claudine says. 'Forget the dewy dream. A word, a stamp, a visa – resolving life and death, enter, exit. Now, it's goodbye to you, precious as you are!' She leaves, making the effect.

'We must pretend,' I say, 'that it all matters – the flag, the family, the character that makes us all be different and yet fit in ... shoulder to shoulder, fellowship, good cheer and bottoms up in prayer.'

*

'I never knew Oton,' says Wei, 'but I suppose he saw his slice of history and wished it had been different.'

'Yes,' I say, 'he couldn't draw, but he could see, and what he saw he painted – it was what there was, and what he saw, both together. And he must have seen far off, all the named people, the big cheeses, striding and strutting. He wasn't afraid to talk to them, though it didn't seem to matter, or at least we don't know what was said. It was mostly him you'd want to know, to remember what was said.'

'That's sugar,' says Wei. 'You didn't know him at all. What you say gets said of everyone.'

'Listen, Wei,' I say, quite exasperated. 'You may think you're born again, starting off afresh, because you've jumped your ship. But here – you can fall, quicker than a baby. Your character doesn't matter, you can be strong or weak, left or right. You fall exactly at the same speed. It's physics.'

'I don't have a character,' Wei says. 'Not yet. I wonder – should I shop Claudine, tell the police?'

'Do you think she's worth all that atttention?' I ask, thinking of the trouble it would be for Wei, none at all for Oton, and even more for Claudine. And for me.

'You're not courageous, Vince,' says Wei. 'I guess that leaves you time, free to do the rest. I don't blame at all – it is a point of view. No one leaves a smudge, even if they take it out on other people: in their grave there's no responsibility. It's those who've suffered, they're who ought to be remembered.'

'That's sugar too,' I say. 'They aren't.'

Later, she says, 'I didn't know Oton painted. I didn't see anything like that.'

'It was a metaphor,' I say. 'He left bits of talk – he might have done better painting it.'

'It's the rage in China, painting. They say the market's saturated. That'll be some fall!' she says.

She's put a red *mèche* in her hair – she's fitting in. That snaky green and yellow dress – it fastens up the side, not what you'd expect.

'I like going out at night,' she says. 'It's always been a sexy time for me. And it's certain – in the end, the light will come... It's not uniform, the black, it unrolls from the pianissimo, and makes a tower before it all spins off to lands you'd like to see, even at nightfall...'

Inside her dress – her body's side – I think of pig's ribs, of the pig, slung up on hooks, its grin... 'You won't guess what I know...' he says. I remember them, the pigs, picking over fallen apples in a garden – not many pigs nowadays so lucky that they have an orchard... Another death, pig of a day for someone – like the Greeks – 'some guy told me you were dead', it goes... it ends, surprise, that this dead guy had written poetry – his nightingales – they all did that, wrote poems, whipped their slaves. But there's no poem –

'on whipping my slave' – and if I'd been the slave obeying orders, even maybe not – captured in war – better a captive *plongeur* than hanging out the flags, as back they trudge, survivors, with a slave for each to do the dirty work...

'Vince!' says Wei, 'you can't be thinking what you've started off to do! Concentrate, or let me be!'

'Another time, dear Wei,' I say, fastening her up. 'Suspended, not abandoned. It's our corpse I'm thinking of, and memory – in with its scythe and grin. The short sarcastic life of pigs...'

'Your trouble is, Vince, you don't play the game. Don't chase the ball, even when you know it's going out of bounds,' says Wei.

'You mean I'm honest, Wei?' I say.

'No, you're not that at all,' she says. 'People play and chase the ball. It isn't what they want. You won't even play – that way you'll never have what it is you want.'

'No one does, Wei,' I say. 'Wanting's a hydra. It means destroying time and planets.'

'Then – for you, it doesn't even start. Don't look, you say, you'll never find. You won't strike gold that way,' she says. 'Anyway, my *mèche* – it works, my flame, my red light. It says "sex" in seven languages.'

'It's hit and miss, Wei,' I say. 'That stuff. It's more complicated than you'd like to think. You need be a brave little soldier.'

'I've been enrolled, Vince,' she says. 'You should try something courageous yourself. Deserting is brave, joining up again – even more.'

'I'm a coward, Wei,' I say. 'It's an obstacle.'

'Nonsense, Vince!' she says. 'That's just your lame foot – who was it had that? Oedipus? Achilles? It stops you running away.'

'I could stick here,' I say. 'My hand's impregnable. I've counted out the deck. If no one talks, or gets publicity, I'm safe. Good gods, bad gods, bigoted, indifferent, an ethic quietist or progressive, mankind marching to extinction or to electronic brains – I win.'

'They change the game,' says Wei. 'And people love to talk.'

'Help me, Wei,' I ask.

'Don't be weak,' she shouts. 'New lands! I know all about frontiers – every kind. The metaphoric ones, the geographic, and the kind you guys are squabbling about. And I'm a communist – I don't believe in them! That's why I'm here. Why are you here, Vince?'

'I told you, Wei – I'm moving on.'

'And I told you, Vince – I guarded the frontier – it's like the state and Lenin's cook – simple administration.'

'I shan't be around, I hope,' I say. 'When you're proved wrong.'

She presses on, 'You could start a militia, Vince. Everybody's doing it – you need some weapons, and there's people ready with the cash. You can run when they start bombing you. It could be – the Castilian Revenge, the Zoroastrian Resurgence... You can be prime minister, fix your own pay. Saint Augustine – there's a model! Off with the heretics! The Iron Guard, or those French torturers...' and on she goes.

'It's history, Wei,' I say. 'Everyone's buried all that. Besides – I hate looking ridiculous, and saluting at parades.'

'You wouldn't need to think about sex, Vince ... you'd concentrate on the price of beans,' says Wei. 'It seems here it's all soldiers, spies and sex. I'll see how good the latter is,' and she swishes away.

She thinks sex is disorder, a dropping of the guard – it's not; at most a smuggling, an incursion across the border. Those provinces – they have no sovereignty. Remember the little book – that says the best frontier is a railway line, too valuable to all sides for anyone to cut, and once cut, easily repaired. A line that no one crosses, runs from my town to yours.

★

Wei's soon back: 'You're right,' she says. 'Sex here draws much from soldiers and from spies. I hope your guys don't come to my house, to save me from myself, bring disorder, steal, partition.'

'Your work,' I say, 'must have been like spying.'

'Not *like* anything,' she says. 'It *was* spying. Most things are.'

'You're full of conclusions, Wei,' I say, 'but nothing concludes.'

'I'm young,' she says, 'I've seen it all.'

'Well,' I say, 'I don't want an end banal, but somewhere between revelation and a crash.'

'We mustn't talk about those things, the ends,' says Wei. 'Some are just starting off.'

'It's all in mathematics, Wei,' I say. 'Locked in.'

'You could say it's unlocked in ... or by,' she says. 'We knew all that. What gets in, or who ... it's all an algorithm. That stuff about the breath, the document – it was our joke. The same result – you'd get by human random. That job – the customs – is so dull... We'd do the test – then guys would feel so happy, or so sad, when we told them they would die before they could return ... or wouldn't die at all.'

'It's not a funny joke, dear Wei,' I say.

'Oh no,' she says, 'it's of the cosmological kind. The thing that adds an element of chance – it's bombs. Think of those people – they get called the Arabs, whether they are or not – and they get bombed, and bomb you back as best they can... Well, Arab just means "warrior" – a joke of ancient days. It leads people on... You must be, you must believe, what you were called – when you walked out of Africa. Everybody wants a piece of territories that go down – it's sharks at hungry-time. The mathematics doesn't work for them – it's scattershot and run! Shrapnel or swallow – yours the choice.'

'Don't say that here,' I say. 'In other parts, it's easier – you're how you're born. And that decides it, all for ever. Here – you have to read the papers, watch the things you say. Be loyal. That is your freedom now.'

'Oh, Vince,' she says, 'it always was.'

'We should investigate,' I say. 'Go where they wouldn't let you out, or let me in. And – those guys... the sex? I'm curious, Wei, quite morbidly.'

'Guys with their trousers off,' she says, 'look very stupid everywhere. That's my universal truth.'

'That's why Oton wanted them in red, kept on,' I say.

'They wanted to know what I believed. Not what I thought – believed. They had the hope – convert! Thought and belief – they're different chapters in my book,' she says. 'Belief – I've never read that one. Maybe back home we're born without. It's not like you, Vince...'

'You have me wrong,' I say. 'I think, and so I don't believe. That's what the poet said. You believe to make time pass: thinking tires, and leaves you as you are, or thinner still.'

'It's best to stick to flowers, primped in an ancient vase,' she says, 'or sages sleeping in the mist, their fishing rods lost in the fog, the carp, rejoicing, sing...'

'The mathematics – that should let us in or out – we could go anywhere. See the Uighurs. Take along professors, people of that kind,' I say.

'That's only ever about us, not other people, those people being swallowed up,' she says, and – 'You're not jealous, Vince? Of my fat pig? My, how he grunted, seeking something – not to be found, he didn't find, but all that breath! And if he'd died on top of me, he'd have been my marbled slab.'

'No, no,' I say, 'amuse yourself, dear Wei, and be enjoyed. Maybe your porker was a holy man, a theologian, speleologist into the cave to find a primal purity... Those hungry guys, sitting round, can't eat because the elephant meat's tabu, belonging to the gods, who're always late...'

'Listen, Vince,' she says, 'the crate with Tiger in – that's real. And us being paid by Claudine for our cover-up – essential.'

'Or we could walk away,' I say. 'Like nothing ever was.'

★

That is what we do. Tiger's carried down the stairs. We walk away. Claudine waves the notes we'll never claim.

'If we take the money, they'll think we did it,' I say.

'If we don't take the money, they'll think we did it,' says Wei.

'I come away with my integrity intact,' I say.

'I'd like to see how Claudine ends,' says Wei. 'It's a story that can shake the world. I want to lift the curtain, see the next scene. She has her integrity as well – she could win elections that make us all bow down.'

'We'll be well and far away before all that,' I say.

'Suppose the people here – they decide to massacre. A group. Say – Arabs. Lock them up. Expel them. Or – Asians, say. What would you do then, Vince? Would you lend a hand?' she asks.

'Of course,' I say, not knowing what's expected. 'We'd not be here, at all events. We've just to decide where.'

Wei's bemused. 'I look into the faces, it's my trade – and I'm not sure. Maybe the faces are all different – that's not the point. It's the intention, the use they make of them – the eyes, the mouth, the nose. They keep the future buttoned up. Locked in, you'd say. The history calculations – they're not good. No one likes what they think are people new, inspired... I don't know where the frontiers are. What people, peoples, might do, or be induced. We could go back – the primal – but we've all been different since the dinosaurs ... there's no question here of keeping people out – they're all inside.'

'Of course we think that way – it's necessary when you come into a place,' I say. 'Look around. Of course, they all look hostile. No one is carrying anything, Wei. You can't ask what they might have hidden, to declare.'

'You could be a hero, Vince,' she says, 'You haven't been that yet. A saviour.'

We jostle round some stalls. 'Oh, crispy, I love that,' says Wei.

'The food here's not so great,' I say. 'Nor is the company.'

Some guy's dog jumps up at her. 'Hey!' she shouts. 'Your fucker wolf just ate my duck.'

'Come away,' I say. 'Before the insults start. That guy respects no foreign culture, you can bet.'

'No, no,' she says, 'I've every right...'

'Of course,' I say, and pull her after me.

'The duck and I,' she shouts, 'are from Canton...'

'Of course,' I say. 'The customs recognise all dialects...'

'Not dialects, you idiot,' she shouts some more. 'They're languages. They're tongues,' and she sticks hers out at me – a brilliant red – the duck must be spicy too...

'You've dropped, Vince,' Wei goes on. 'Once, you resisted. Now it just took that denatured dog to have you run... Dogs not allowed,' she shouts to all the crowd.

'Oh, Wei,' I say. 'I used to know them all. When Rodney Hawkett was alive ... the ministers, the chiefs – I found them unimpressive, on their leads and in their kennels, robotic...'

'I'm alive to that,' says Wei. 'The smuggled animals, inbred and hybrid, the wolf brought out in dogs, dogged up indeed... Robots – all the rage, that fight the wars now...'

'Everyone is blameless here,' I say, but there's a crowd, and cops are sighting on us, their caps, the yellow covers, turn like sunflowers – but still she remonstrates...

'If that's an attack dog, or wolf – that's what we need,' says Wei, and waves a scrap of spicy crispiness: 'Nature follows its own track.'

With one bound, it is beside us: the wolf is ours. Our soldier. Its trainer stares, his lids, heavy as stones – 'We are the guard dogs,' Wei shouts out, 'This toothy mutt is one of us!'

We run.

Concentrate. And run.

...Cerberus, Anubis – the pointy ears, the porous nose – best have them on your side, remember space wizards, their ears – spice magicians from the starry isles, rocket dogs, empires rested on them, enduring dogged dog days, their gods coming, going, putting on their dog, my lungs sounding wolf notes ... beware the empires of the dead ... run, ventilate and pant

...we're both exhausted, though the wolf is not. 'We need some nature, something sliced fresh out, that knows the right way from the wrong,' says Wei.

We don't put a collar on it. 'A lead would dissipate the energy,' says Wei. 'It will walk ahead, and if it runs away – that will be its choice.'

'You'll bet on that!' I say. 'I shan't intervene. The guy, though, whose it was till now...'

'He's had enough,' says Wei. 'It's clear. Over. And the animal, you see it loves its Cantonese – that was a gesture of good taste. I'm maybe its epiphany, a terminus, its end.'

'It's true,' I say. 'It recognises you, your skills. The dog-wolf perches on a frontier. It's prey – it preys. The dog protects, the wolf invades. It's enemy and friend – it strolls, it slinks. It's like our world – you cross the frontier – and it's war. You trade across it, empathise – there's comradeship. But Wei – you're not at ease with our new guard, whether it is dog or wolf.'

'Of course,' she says, 'It's my protection and a threat. That – I resent. It is my weakness and my strength.'

'Food, Wei,' I say. 'It steals its food, and runs away – it follows who it's stolen from. A puzzle, Wei.'

We exchange views on jackals, and coyotes.

'We seek the moral core,' I say... 'The dog looks on, maybe measures out its time with us, evaluates how we go on, and how we navigate...'

'The moral code? The dog's cuisine? You worry about things you won't be punished for,' says Wei. 'Because your

prospects are so slight. The sages give examples of how you
ought to act, always at crisis points – the crux, hard cases
settled in a single stroke. They never touch the life, the
years, creating situations where you might have doubts and
fears. Ought we to do, or tell, confess, betray? Dilemmas
pass away, like they were gunshots.'

'We don't have tricky situations, Wei,' I say: 'So, there's
no moral case to make or drop... We are becalmed, our
moral gristle's gone to fat.'

The dog goes out, no glance, no sign, and comes back,
smelling strong. 'Nasi goreng,' says Wei. The dog sniffs at
her breath, then comes and sniffs at mine.

'This room,' says Wei. 'How do we pay? There's lots of
others here, like we all had emergencies.'

'We leave the customary sum,' I say. 'We're all in transit
here – see this as a bridge.'

The wolf – it leads us on. It can show the right path, it
lights up the end, the hotel, hospice, anywhere for decent
sleep – 'This will do,' says Wei. 'We'll doss here. The dog
will be our star – but not tonight. I'm through. Our Tiger's
in the hold by now, and on his way. The moral compass –
it's boxed up too, high on the bridge, the captain
unconcerned with us ... we're exonerated, Vince, forgiven.
Whatever we should do, have done – it's on the ocean
swell, a crate within a crate, no address, labelled "to await"
... Who'll claim them, Vince, those bones? Don't you have
a friend in LA?'

'No, Wei,' I tell her. 'Let's not bring others, in – the
pardon should be ours alone.'

'Vince,' she says, 'I burn, I burn – not to be
extinguished, but to blaze. Will no one see the beauty of my
flame, its ferocity, the colours? You were a fireman – you
should know. Our Tiger's dead, he's on his way to being

ash, the world is full of disappearing beasts, the people with the banners dead, retreat is everywhere, Vince, there's no stability – one step forward, two steps back. I'm burning, Vince – set me up high...'

'A guide will come,' I say. 'Right now, I'm at a loss.'

And so – we never mention Oton, nor his death, again.

*

'We've had some intimate talks, revealing everything,' says Wei. 'We can roll up together in this carpet, just for warmth – but keep that dog away.'

Our carpet is a fine Tabriz – faded, but the underside, its red and pink, blue and green, is like a painter's floor. The dog goes round the others, sniffs their sleeping breath, and goes outside. My head sticks out the cylinder, Wei's all inside.

She kicks, as she sleeps. I wake her – 'I'm on the crest,' she says. 'Looking down is mist and leaves. I've distances to trudge – I'm not sure you have, dear Vince. It's all a picture – the Long March. Did it all happen? Shall we do it all again? You, Vince, for sure – you'll not be there.'

In the morning – there's no one left but us. We struggle to be free. Wrapped up like Mongol warriors, ready for the execution, trampled so as to spill no blood. Wei asks,

'I heard the people from inside the carpet, praying. Or were they soldiers?'

'They're the revolutionaries, Wei,' I say. 'No one likes them, or to call them that. They're the dragon's teeth – martyrs, crooks and desperadoes, naive and saints ... corporals and brigadiers, growing scattered in thin soil.'

'You can't imagine,' says Wei, 'the poverty, the masses, the abandonment, the love of death instead of nothingness...'

'It's nothing we have made,' I say. 'It's not our scene'

The sign over the window says – 'For your safety – don't look out.' And over there – the wheel. A priest that says, 'My child – if you don't believe, it won't go round.'

'Watch out,' says Wei. 'Standing there – you are a perfect silhouette.'

'The wolf,' I say, 'still at the door.'

'It's no bother,' Wei says. 'It'll be with us till the end.'

'I'm sure it will,' I say.

★

'You could protest,' says Wei.

'I'm an artist, Wei,' I say. 'Creating, not consuming. It's all thinking and complaining, unless you're making pots.'

'I don't see what you create,' says Wei. 'You could make a scene... The warplanes here, overhead – always buzzing off. Indifference, profligacy. The helots, and the scrabble. The values hoarded by the rich.'

'Creation is a smoky thing,' I say. 'What ends up on the paper or the canvas – that's just its ghost.'

She's not convinced, but she's been quietened, and it all spins on.

I tell her, 'The universal plan, they say – was beautiful. But lay it out in rocks and sparks, it's lost to view, the lamps keep going out, the paint's too hot and spurtles off, the surfaces dissolve, the magma underneath cracks out in steam – then, there's the infestations too. The slimy things, the fish with feathers, lizards disproportionate. Then, Wei – it's us! We can have ghosts, because we're ghosts of ghosts.

The primal beauty, stuck in the sponge behind our eyes –
we glimpse it – take our brush and ... there! it's gone.'

'I know all that,' says Wei. 'I meant a different thing. In
China, we have rich – they're good at making lots of cash.
That's it – no celebrations, and no flags. But here – you let
them run the theatre, say what's the good and bad... Does
it irk, Vince? Once it was warriors – now it's them...'

'Just ghosts of ghosts, I told you, Wei,' I say.

We go down, walk around in the street. There's an army
of people, mostly poor – that's how they look to me. 'You
see,' says Wei. 'There's not enough rich guys here to let the
poor guys have their heads.'

I'm not sure it works like that.

'I'd be an artisan,' I say. 'That's how art ends up. The
spirit takes its form. That's it – the end. For me, no
ceramics and no dance. I'd fancy maybe goldsmithing...'

'It's out of reach,' says Wei. 'Vince! How do we go on?
We can't hunt – and gathering, we call it confiscating – the
people here don't carry stuff. They all do different things,
you can't tell what, they look alike because the clothing's
poor...'

'Painting and books,' I say, 'those you can tout around.
It's sculpture – what you've not sold takes up your space,
and clogs your future ... marble blocks won't fit in the
trash.'

'We could sell eats – that way, what you don't sell, you
eat,' says Wei.

'No, Wei,' I say. 'That's too conservative. It gives no
leverage. I'm sure, too, there is a flaw – it's hunger, Wei,
makes you hallucinate.'

'We can't beg,' she says. 'That means you've reached the
end. We might ask for loans... But here, you borrow, and
you know that it won't grow. It's just a weight. Here – it's

all heavy stones, you have them on your back, humps – they fix your gaze down on your feet. You're tired of history, you guys. It's painful. You hope it stops, your terrifying story, and it will. You polish it and dust it – it's your furniture.'

'You've seen – I'm not like that. I always choose the hardest way,' I say. 'It's my training, my challenge.'

'Is that it, your quality, your point of view? Yes, I'm full of stories too, I'm made of them,' she says. 'I can convince you, because you've no idea...'

'We could start a café in Russia somewhere. Or China. That's where the philosophers go, and you would have your cake – to sell or eat,' I say.

We'd each prefer to carry on alone.

★

There's a sign, says 'Feed the hungry.' 'There!' I say, 'they are our sponsors.'

'I'll pledge a million. If I have it, I always keep my word,' says Wei.

We are the only hungry ones – the sponsors all are sleek. There are brioches – silent, we eat.

A tall captain embraces us. 'Ah! Hungry people! How we need you!'

'Too late!' says Wei. 'I'm full as eggs.'

'Vince!' shouts the guy. 'One of Rodney Hawkett's men. What a benefactor Hawkett was!'

'He gave his body to the fire,' I say. 'Mostly, we do that.'

'A message,' says the guy. 'Around the world – you'd give them hope – information, at the least. Where you all are, the hungry, how many... You'd represent the famished, everywhere...'

'Oh no,' I say. 'I'm not a humanist. We can't save all us animals – some already slip away, and some we step on heedlessly. Many get bombed, incinerated, flushed when they become a drag... The hunger's something we all live with – no more hunting and gathering ... there are laws, there's property...'

'You're not religious freaks, I hope,' says the guy. 'Endure the suffering – maybe get rewards ... feeling good...'

'I've not been born for anything particular,' says Wei. 'Avoid the pit, cling to your passport – that's my rule.'

'Look into my eyes, Alex,' I say to the guy organising the expedition. 'You'll not have noticed. Right in the middle of each one, there's a black hole. It leads straight to our core. Nothing comes back out. It's a cave entrance. Everything enters. Nothing emerges. It's a depository, of everything, all that goes on, it leads to shelter, to nothing. A black hole, like the universe is full of...'

'I understand, Vince,' says the tall captain, Alex. 'You're not willing. But you ate our cakes, so you owe us. And you'd be paid.'

'We'd go everywhere?' asks Wei. 'And do anything, be anyone?'

'Of course,' says Alex, 'I'd go myself. But I'm not hungry, not like Vince. And I've not renounced my frontiers, my charge, not like you, Wei. All you have to do – is be hungry. Show it to all the rest. Most will recognise it, not everyone will have the right react. Explain how it's all getting better, help will come...'

'What are we looking for?' I ask.

'Everyone knows that,' says Alex. 'Don't fool with me, Vince.'

I don't press him. For sure, we'll find out. It might involve the slash and burn.

It's a great idea. Just right for Wei.

'You can't take the dog, Wei,' Alex says.

'It's his,' she says. 'Vince's.'

'It's best for you,' I tell her. 'Symbolically – you'll wield a hoe – a spade, a sword. An invocation. You'll call it work – it's nearly the freedom that will come when we'll do nothing, maybe we'd criticise a little, drop our line into the carp-pond, catch, toss them back in ... shoot brown shadows on the forest verge... And, Wei – you'll do the good, I'm sure. While you're alive – it's immortality.'

She's happy and she's sad – that is the best. For both of us – adventures separate.

'The ship is ready, Wei,' says Alex. 'Bring me back some curious things – white gourds that taste of tripe, and persimons that make you laugh...'

'Oh Vince,' she says, 'come and trek the world, the poor, the powerful – we'd be both of those, magnificent in rags...'

'It's right for you,' I say. 'It's just not me...'

There's nothing more to say: 'Off to Cythera, dear Wei,' shouts Alex, pushing me aside. 'Press the right button, and your instructions will pop up.'

'Farewell, dear Vince,' she shouts. 'This interlude will last until we both forget...' The waves are blurring her, the sails, the helmsman – the movement jiggles her about, the outlines go to grey and cloud, we both get small, so small there's no point in waving more, so strong's the swell, the wave...

The wolf trots off, and I am close behind.

Off she sails – away, away. Peace and freedom, far from the borders and the laws, the magistrates, police ... away the Party, away lines of longitude – there's only latitude, sweet twenties for the galleon, the super-junk – a cargo bland and tempting – bullseyes and cats' tongues, a voyage like the Chinese used to make – discovering America, away on tiptoes – spaghetti woven into belts, offloaded in Genoa...

I weep. I should have gone. With her, the life, the paradise. 'Feed the hungry' – there she will be, a nacreous robe, a gentle smile – distributing the taffy, blowing clouds of sherbert... The winning sign – 'No animal was harmed in the making of this dream...'

Alex is staring: I say, 'We're changing the colours – yellow, grey. Sand and slush. Making a planet like the Martians did, with them all dead or underground and out of sight – the place unlivable. Maybe all the planets started so – quivering with bees and butterflies, then they were killed and filled with acid dregs by feisty suicidal aliens...'

He mutters, 'New frontiers ... we must suss them out...' Then, 'Vince – Wei was too fine for you.' Silence: 'We had you pencilled in as captain, Vince,' he says.

'I don't navigate,' I say.

'Someone else does that, I think,' says Alex. 'For you, a role imposing: there's funerals at sea, walking the plank, and mutinies. They require a lofty presence.'

'I'm not sure about giving orders, Alex,' I say. 'That's been a problem.'

'If there's a storm, no island near – the ship will founder, that's for sure,' says Alex. 'The water – it'll bind the cargo into floss and send it down. We send them out, those paper boats, ambassadors who love mankind – they turn to cannibals on the rafts ... those reedy sails are torn, the keel of sturdy osiers – it doesn't serve...'

'They do good...' I say.

'We robe them. We send them off. They do good. They don't come back. Mostly. Often,' Alex says.

'You came back, Alex,' I say.

'Doing good – it's a human urge,' he says. 'You get recruited. Some get eaten. Some find a hut and stay.'

'Recruited?' I ask.

'They live well, they get bought off. The mission's altruistic. Before there was money, there was food – so food is money, mother and son, or so you'd think. When no one's hungry – they will still need cash.'

'I understand that, Alex,' I tell him. 'But – say there's a tempest... I should have gone – I know all about island monsters and their powers.'

'You don't know about wind, dear Vince,' says Alex, 'Although a storm of it comes out of you.'

'When you're in the sea,' I say. 'On it or under it – you're like the fish – death is all around ... Without the air, we are a poor design. A hook, a mouth, a rock that walks, eels electric, smothering – a paralysing flower... It sucks you in – past no teeth, a ribby tunnel like a man o' war's hold – you see your destiny, the anus... Your boat's gone down – you flounder, give up your soul...'

'Oh, sometimes you survive,' says Alex, offhand. 'You need allies,' he says. 'They will protect you. You're like those little fish that clean the sharks – a thousand sorts of shark. How many sorts of men are there? They all need cleaning, you can bet!'

'Once landed, Alex, I don't see why it's dangerous,' I say. 'You give out food. That's it.'

'We give out agriculture, Vince,' he says. 'We mobilise the marginal, identify the poor, and help. That's the provocation – it's not the candy bars.'

'I can imagine, Alex: I'm not just stuck on waves and fish,' I say

'Women, Vince,' he says. 'They grow the food, they buy it, and prepare...'

'I know all that,' I say.

'Who buys the land and hires the hands, and sells the seeds, expropriates,' he says. 'Comes from afar, and sets a price... Is men.'

'I'm not insensitive, Alex,' I say.

'We send them off,' says Alex. 'The angels. They're judges for the end of time. If time it is that ends.'

'I see them judge,' I say. 'But – the time, the time they work with: it's limited, but not the end, not yet.'

'They leave,' he says. 'No one comes back. Nothing; no cargo comes to us. Maybe it ends up...'

'She went down?' I ask. 'We don't know – at least, we don't know how.'

'We don't know why,' says Alex. 'Was it my fault? Ours, Vince? A broken contract – at least, agreement that we wanted her to do exactly what she was sent to do, and what we wanted her to want...'

'It all sounds inconclusive, Alex. Maybe you're mistaken, not responsible at all...' I say.

'Oh,' Alex says, 'Unless we have some news, I'm not responsible. Rather, it would be you, the captain of the ship who didn't step on board.'

'It's neat, Alex,' I say. 'You come out well.'

'You're not happy with this, Vince,' says Alex. 'It's evident. Men and women. A rift in history – maybe it was normal to be hungry: – then the hungry were to make a revolution... But – suppose they'd been fed. No longer hungry... Where do they stand?'

'I see your point, Alex,' I say. 'Where does that leave me?'

'Oh, Vince,' he says. 'I've really no idea. Poor Wei – she went out unprepared, like all of them. If she died, she died too soon, her time not come.'

'That kind of time – too soon, too late – is quite beyond me, Alex. Are you sure you went? You seem the precious type. Clothes nonchalant, the cultivated beard...' I say.

'Oh yes,' he says, 'I made big friends – not great pals, you understand. The size was overwhelming, though.'

'You did a deal, a dirty deal, you dirty boy?' I ask.

'They have the power, the land, the seed,' he says. 'Then I played the other side – sending them off, the naive angels. That's life.'

'Maybe it's not,' I say. 'If the boats sink. And – after hunger. What'll it be?'

'Oh, hunger will come round again,' he laughs. 'Not just as metaphor. We'll eat the beetle stew, grass sandwiches and Coca Cola on the croquet lawn... And then? We are that way, dear Vince, and me and you ... the same. We love the edge, the void, limit, the emptiness. We climb up in the spire – then – there's the urge – to jump. Over with it all. It drives the mystic guys to make a poem, a critique – new ordering of revelation. Enough of made-up chronicles. A vision, oratorio. New chosen people, without territory, without a clan. A tool, a song and dance, to reach the truth, a diet of veracity – a text that weaves the threads of all the worms... they glow up there, dear Vince, among the mulberries. See – they excrete – the red, the blue, the green, the orange. It's beautiful, it's foul, it's homicidal, it is salvation – saving us from no one, nothing, from ourselves – a nimble fiddling with the dust we live on, that we are – but in the end, the truth is – has been – always there. At the beginning.'

'But Wei!' I ask, 'why sacrifice her, Alex?'

'Oh, I expect she wanted the same impossibilities as you, my friend,' he says. 'The more you flap your wings, take off – the steeper is the fall. The greater is the height that you come down from – fewer hear or see the splash.'

'For sure, she wanted what we want,' I say. 'That's not my point.'

'Come to my house,' he says. 'It's up a hill, it's true – but that means nothing special ... if it overpowers you, the slope, bend your head down. The road appears quite flat, and so you positively fly!'

The house is full of people, coming, and, by definition, going. It reminds me of those ancient times, of Dolores, Lady Bea – their projects and recruitment; through the tall windows, we can see forays of trespassers across a handkerchief of grass: a stand of bamboos, sharpened into stakes. There's some books – a *History of God* – I thumb it through. Alex says, 'What an eye! The binding – quite exceptional: a sheep in sacrifice.' There's games – balances – 'Those I distrust,' says Alex – swings, copied from Fragonard. A swinging trunk for two, a ride, goes round and round – 'The sun and moon,' says Alex, 'those are kissing cousins clinging on it.'

It's a marvel, the house, full of brown furniture, with trompe l'oeil corridors, commodes stuffed with the testaments of kings, parleys of trumpeters at ease, things to be guessed at – a babble of ill-meaning businesses...

There's two and twos, couples of strident arguers with fluty voices, making a context for a text, exchanging insults, insisting on a point...

'There,' says Alex. 'That's the house. You'll have some time to see who's who, who I am, who are you, dear Vince, how do we fit the story...' and he laughs. 'You'll hear them working upstairs, adding some higher floors, beneath you – the stables and the cellars – the rumbling means a filling in, a tearing down...'

'I'm surprised,' I say. 'You keep no animals.'

'Oh Vince!' says Alex. 'Naughty boy! They're full of dirt, you know. You must admire my cleanliness, with all these people going in and out, the dust clings on to everything ... they all pass through, disputing – what a crew! – the sponsors, benefactors, friends and enemies from all the world. Some have the news of those sent out – the struggle and the difficulty...' His tongue frisks lightly, confidentially, in my ear – 'The others, Vince. They own the land, and we have nothing; like it ought to be – but how do we assert ourselves? How do we make our mark?'

Dear Alex – how you want to love him, though you can't.

'Do you want the good, the true?' I ask. 'Or just hop on the roundabout, start a big thing, your epic, all the drafts and cancellations, stories for grannies, pointed arms for youths... A state of plenty? Or obedience? Of flagellation, refectories where books are shouted out – no true food, just rabbit bones to suck?'

'Yes, Vince,' he says. 'Exactly right. You have imagined all those things. You lay the keel, the fragrant lady with the wine – baptises; down the rollers goes the cruiser... Where does it go, where does it end? You're right, dear Vince – you imagine all the ports it may approach – greeted with gunfire or with tarts, all on the house... A sailor's life is that! In your heart, Vince, you've done all the trips. It's for your useless imagination that you're prized – my guslar, my minstrel singing of the all and less... That is your role, my friend.'

He hugs me. I avoid his kiss.

'Where are your people, Alex?' I ask, moving away. I see small animals crowding at the fence – marmosets and hares – as curious as me.

He says, 'You mean, because these are so quarrelsome? They're all my people. Otherwise we'd all be dead. We'd slug it out! If you undress them, you'll find they all wear my insignia: *in hoc signo* Vince, remember. Of course, there's good and evil, but they all profess the truth. I don't ask you to join up, Vince, not with me, not just now – but, be very very careful whose team you end up on. No one gets a long life, guaranteed – the thing is, remember that your cause was just. That way, it all smooths out. That's the best life you can have. And as for Wei – she's a good shot – they train them so. She'll resist it to the last.'

That's good for her, I guess. He goes on, 'This house works perfectly, just like it should. There's games. There is security – some guys come here to die in bed – they know it's peace to come. In the next room to them, high up those stairs, there's couples come to screw, to scrutinise their bodies, say what they've done that's good and not... The bourgeoisie's women, they are had in common. It was in the book. Now it's their men: in common too. You're not a bourgeois, are you, Vince? I guess your women come and go, your men as well – hardly you remember them, not as complete existences, if that is what they were – just encounters, Vince. There's many here that don't believe in what we do – gathering the people, and the cash, sending them out, accumulating more – you need a steady gaze for that. If you don't believe, you can't enjoy the house, the people setting out, new ones recruited...'

'I can't live up to that, Alex,' I say. 'I'm grateful that you think I can – reach the standard. But I can't.'

'It really isn't up to you,' he says. 'The standard's stronger than your weakness, Vince.'

'It must be "no",' I say.

'Look around,' he says. 'There's women here as well – they're open books. You've been ingenuous, dear Vince, you thought you'd run for ever, blundering and tumbling, leaving and being left. Now – look around...'

He draws out someone from the mass – I guess she's an assistant. Cinzia. She says, 'I've read how our machines, like us, will all be made of helixes. That's the saliva in your cheeks. All mankind fits in a two cubic metre box, buried in Siberia – alongside the mammoth bones. And it will last for ever. Digital: that's counting on two fingers, Vince. All the info about hunger. Yours. Maybe your lust as well.'

'Suppose that's metaphor?' I ask.

'Oh,' she says. 'I'm sure it all goes in. When you're dead, perhaps someone will search – and there you are. Hunger and metaphor together.' We all laugh.

'It sounds like paradise,' she says.

'We're all reactionaries,' says Alex, laughing more. 'Here in this house.'

'I'm already full of information,' Cinzia says, going off to store some more.

'She's your sort, Vince,' Alex says. 'She's passionate about eternity. We wouldn't send her out – she'd sink her ship with knowing what she knows. Me – I'm not a humanist, and so – I know it all already. Just think – in Venice there's a thousand miles of shelves, a million tons of different sorts of paper: each individual, every transaction for two thousand years – all stashed in a thimble now. Down it goes – a deep hole in Siberia. A mammoth's graveyard. You dig it up, you find out everything of people that you never knew.'

I wonder why he wouldn't send me out. I'm not like Cinzia – I don't know anything.

'It's a complicated enterprise you have,' I say to Alex. 'All sorts get in, and do all sorts of things.'

'Oh yes,' he says, 'and Cinzia has the names: recruited, infiltrated, sacrificed and willing. It comes out the same. It's to your credit, your protecting her. But – she's just a jar. A sweet person, a heart of candy. You might say – a door ajar. It goes in, comes out. Everybody's satisfied. Almost everybody. Vince – she was right for you. You didn't make your move. Too bad.'

I'm at a loss. 'She was old for me, Alex,' I say.

I don't want anything to do with her. My name – a deserter's, tagged in her.

'There's safe houses too,' says Alex. 'Ready for an idyll. Practice an instrument there – no one will ever hear.'

I could make a trip alone: to a safe place – not by sea or air.

'Of course, Vince,' Alex goes on, 'you've been close to other deaths. Very close. "Responsible" – what a tough word! The sentence, as you know – it's always "Death"! That's irony! Death wipes all other things right out – it's the great pardoner, and the worst punishment,' he laughs.

'I didn't do a thing...' I start to say.

That's maybe worse. A waste. An indecision punishable...

'I never set out, Alex...' I say, 'Not to be close to the end of others...'

'And yet – they happen all around you! Known, unknown, with heavy weight or fillet-knife,' he says, and laughs.

'Then send me out!' I say, daring him to set out the criterion.

'Oh, you're not ready yet,' he says. 'Vince – you may never be. Always on the edge – how does that sound. The "always", naturally.'

'To me, it sounds quite good,' I say. 'The moment that you test the air – and will it bear, and lift you up? The moment on the roof, on the wheel – will you resist desire, to throw your body down, see if you've a soul, and if it wings away...'

'Exactly so,' he says. 'Vince – we are at one. That is my view entirely. Best wait and see, and send the others out. It's even statesmanlike. But – you can't do it here, with me. We can't have two of us the same.'

'That's most unfortunate,' says Cinzia, who hears everything – her ears deep and cool, like arum lilies. 'It's a paradox. Those don't register, except as an anomaly, and over time – they're sanded down, away. They're dust, detritus.'

'She means,' says Alex, listening in, 'there's no more dialectic. That's a state they once called "God". Myself – I don't believe a word – precious though Cinzia is,' and he cuddles her.

Alex is a prince – he's offered Cinzia, but all she knows is other people's news. 'You're banal,' she says to me. 'Banality's my trade – but yours is instinct. You're like the animals – you think you're omnipotent because you do everything you want.'

'There's something off-key,' I say to Alex, ignoring Cinzia. 'All over here. There's no bar...'

'That's what you're looking for?' he asks. 'You could do that. Even take a cut. I'd send you to Siberia, you'd learn to make that hooch, the samogon. You could bury Cinzia's boxes while you're there, cover them with bones.'

'No alcohol, dear,' Cinzia tells Alex. 'Remember your scenes.'

'I'm just the dispatcher,' Alex says. 'Being lucid doesn't enter.'

'You have a great capacity for love, Alex,' says Cinzia, holding on.

'And sacrifice,' says Alex. 'I love them – off they go, in the name of doing good. Do they do it? I shan't know. But Vince – I don't think you're capable of love. And you don't sacrifice – you've nothing to do it with.'

'That makes us equal, Alex,' I say. 'Except you seem quite rich and I am temporarily indigent.'

'Don't forget your dog, Vince,' says Cinzia, pushing me into the garden.

'It won't forget, Cinzia,' I say.

'Oh come!' says Alex, 'we can't lose him before we've decided what's to happen to him.'

Cinzia says, '*L'art de vivre* – the art of living – remember that? It was the rage, those old guys all gone now ... the art once mastered, living can be over shortly. Maybe that is Vince's thing.'

I remember Maya wishing that her life had never started. Once wound up, though, it rolls and rolls.

'You're the tough virgin here,' I say to Cinzia. 'Not Alex.'

'See! I thought you'd work things out in time,' she says.

'You two,' I say, 'it seems you haven't reached the core. You send them off, and that's their destiny accomplished. What have you learned? There's always more volunteers?'

'Oh, the hell with it, Cinzia,' says Alex. 'Let him go. Let him take to the waves. Let's be done with it.'

'No,' Cinzia shouts: we're standing on their little rockery. There's rocks the size of heads – she pelts me with them. This could end real bad. 'He's not worthy. Every dog must have its day – not him! He has no right to time, to chance, fulfilment, joy and misery. He's a butterfly. His wavering course ... can lead to no assessment, judgment – why's he here, not there? He doesn't know – no one can tell what drives him, lifts and drops him... His cycle – quite absurd: a fritillary, a metamorph – from crawler into aeroplane, worm into bird – affront to nature. Reason too. To have a mission! Choose, be chosen. How do you earn the right, Alex – tell him how...'

'I'm not sure I know,' says Alex. 'I did this and that, I am the one, the only; you are my spokesperson, Cinzia. That's it – I have the key, mine is the signature, I have the automatic pen that thanks the correspondents for their wish.'

I run, I leap the fence – not from fear, of course, but – this is real punishment! – I run as self-defence. This is not the answer – but it fills the moments. Cinzia bursts from her blouse, her pants, to run, to throw. In the second of the glance, the revelation of the impossible – she's desirable, she's the huntress huntable – the bloom, the wasp, the ripe peach ... she's chasing me, out of the garden, menacing ... her brown juicy pitcher's arm...

*

'...and so, my friend – no alcohol, so you get stoned.' This stranger steals my line. The guy – he's not my friend – we're neighbours anomalous, on bar stools, like random letters, strangers mustered on a keyboard.

'No,' I say, 'we were all sober, lucid. I knew – I know – exactly what I had to do. I've always known. That's not the secret – making decisions, following a path. No – the real life – it's everything I haven't had.'

The bar is dim. In one dark green alembic, there are pickled eggs, and in another – horse cocks. Either pricks the hunger and deflates...

'Founding a city, curing a disease, fighting a war – those are the adventures that can justify a life of any length,' I say. 'Well – everyone's at war. Enemies, brothers, neighbours – fathers, mothers, sons and all the rest ... the sun, the moon, the rain, all threatening, the poachers and the insects, the drugs that cure, that cuddle or arouse... As for diseases – you must identify and give a name. And, you're dealing pills. The cure, the genocide – the motivation's parallel... Besides – you need a life for war or cure – existence ends before the battle's joined... That leaves the city.'

I should have told it clear. I shake the guy beside me – Mirko. I say, 'You find a river, with a bend – a view of mountains...'

'Sounds like old Titograd,' says Mirko. 'It's no discovery; no novelty is there.'

'No, no,' I say. 'The mission. That's the point. A Faustian enterprise – the draining, damming, planting. Transforming nature, bringing reason, science to mankind...'

'You need a refuge – not another heap of bricks, and guys all doing different things – like bagging bentonite,' Mirko says. 'The way is clear – we should belong beneath the water. That's the element in full expansion. There you can learn to live a new, a slower life. Your lungs? The bobbing up and down, and blowing air – that's not for creatures serious. What we must grow's not longer, fatter lungs. It's gills.'

'I see,' I say. 'You take a bowie knife and slash them in?'

'Don't make me regret telling you,' Mirko says. 'It's quite revolutionary. Not all the details have been pencilled in. As for you, Vince, I'm disappointed. You say the good life's everything you missed: why not say it's "justice"? I'm sure you've not had that, and nor has anyone. And yet – it's what they say they want.'

'I know all that,' I say. 'My life's more street-pastoral than abstract, than an aspiration. You're right, of course – lives are all too short to do what guys had hoped, although some say when they are about to die, there's nothing left to do, they've done it all, and satisfied!'

'My plan,' says Mirko, 'is on the stocks. All it needs now is someone with a blade. And cash – to pay them off.'

'This is my laboratory,' he says. The lake is huge – grey and white, and down below – blue watery shapes of currents; on the shores the smoke from husks on fire, more white on white.

'This is Aurora,' Mirko says. 'And this is one man and his dog. Vince.'

Aurora looks quite grim. Her eyes are hungry, like an owl's.

Mirko takes off all his clothes. 'Strip off, Vince,' he says. 'Down there, I have another house – you'd say a lean-to, though there's nothing there to lean against.'

'I can't swim, Mirko,' I tell him.

'I'll show you how,' he says. 'Remember – hold your breath.' He's gone. We watch his white shape change to blue, then disappear.

'This is the village,' says Aurora. It's iron-grey. There's nobody around – 'Where are they all?' I ask.

'Oh, their crap jobs,' Aurora says, offhand.

Three ladies come out of a church, their heads in scarves, the Mediterranean way.

'The cellars here are deep,' Aurora says. 'See how it's all designed, built on a hill. There is a backbone street – runs up, right to the citadel. There's little curvy alleyways on either side, like ribs. Then, there's the walls all round. We're mostly refugees round here. That's how they settled here – millennia, and metal ages, layered down, from bronze to plastic... We can take over too,' she says, and takes my hand and drags me round. 'This here's a good defensive point,' she says. 'You hold them here and then run up – each moment is stronger than the last. You wear them down... Think of a matrioshka – that's what the old guys had in mind...'

'Does Mirko plan to live down there?' I ask. 'A new life, submarining? You, together – where do you live, what do you do...?'

'Oh, he eats the loathsome things, down in the mud,' Aurora says. 'The eels. He slithers round, makes friends with them, and then – inveigles.'

'This house of his, beneath the drift?' I ask.

'Oh, his religion lets him have women from each element,' Aurora laughs. 'There's his mermaid. Then the fire – he's longing for that one.'

'I know,' I say. 'Of course he – anyone – would long for that.'

'There's the air. When he takes off – behold, a filmy one. I'm the earthy type,' she says. It's true – her face, a well-proportioned stone, clay the lips, the eyes a pale and scurfy blue you find round minerals.

'You can't mean to take the village, hold by force?' I say.

'It's history. That's how it's all renewed,' she says. 'You take these shabby houses, add a floor or two – then others come and chase you out. They settle in, you have their kids.'

'They'll bomb you. They won't fight from street to street,' I say.

'Then we'll go in the cellars too,' she says. 'Like they all did. Our cause is just. The people here – they're senile. They've forgot the story, so – their time is up.'

'I see all that,' I say. 'It's not my scene, of course – but why take on a place like this, so dank and crumbling, no road in or out?'

'You have a sugar heart, poor Vince,' she says. 'You need a history that toughens you.'

'Money, Aurora – you need lots to make a stand,' I say.

'We may have to change our names,' she says. 'That way, they'll send cash. Who can resist just causes? There's enough that can't.'

'I understand there's prejudice, Aurora,' I say. 'You're a novelty. You don't fit with Mirko... Maybe you'd do better on your own... Mirko can prosper from the elements...'

'It's just the same for me,' she says. 'I'm straight – I get the same deal as him. One man, from each element – or woman, if I wish. Turn and turn about – our religion can accommodate. Live the good life, that's it.'

I could be the fire. The fire man. I can't imagine how we'd live.

'The disenchantment was complete, a century ago,' she says. 'Some whitecoats try the incantation even now – we can be saved, in peace, longlived and bland. It isn't so, Vince – we're desperate for space and water, our subsistence...'

On she talks; down in the lake, I see Mirko, the seeker after wonder, renewal – a simple cut beneath the arms ... plunging and surfacing, longer the intervals before he takes a breath.

'Oh no,' Aurora shouts. 'The water's spewed him up!'

He's beached. We pump him out.

'We're not a glam couple,' says Aurora, 'but together, we'll get somewhere, change it all. Separate directions. You could join me, Vince. You can't swim. Mirko's not for you. You don't care if there's a future, and the water's cold. You don't want a mermaid. It's to me you should belong.'

'Yes,' I say, 'you're right. I'm your fire – but I've demands. There has to be first person. Action. Me. I can't find a perspective, stand back, cogitate, write it up, or down. That's sterile, teaching dead stuff to sceptics. No – it has to be adventure, and me the principal. With you, it won't work out. They'll bury you alive, Aurora. Maybe you'll be a torturer, or hang a row of people. You could change the rules – retire, and have men for all seasons: Mirko would be winter. Me, I don't have a time, a temperature. I know reality – it turns out wrong. Or dull. It's a paradox, Aurora – you, I, take the lead, you have to believe in what you're doing, or it wouldn't turn out right – and yet ... it won't. Someone will trip it up, the history you're about to make...'

...and that's the best bit.

'I don't want all that,' she shouts, kicking at me. 'I need hands, sharpshooter's eyes, not a lolling head.'

'Are you sure, Aurora, you want a conquest? Maybe a house would do instead,' I say.

'No, no,' she says. 'First comes the battle. Then, of course, you settle in. We all forget the massacres, and if you live the good life – we can all be friends.'

I see Mirko on the shore – with his nail gun he's shooting plastic cladding round a crate. 'It's an expedient,' he says. 'I'll live here under. I'll search out the treasure, and the dwarves...'

'There's no window, Mirko. When someone goes to Mars, they can see the nothing all the way,' I say.

'Oh, I thought of that,' he says. 'See!' There's pictures all around inside, of sharks, and treasure – bullion, mermaids, their hair in golden fillets...

'This is science, Vince,' he says. 'I'm trained. If these nails don't keep the water out – I'll hold my breath. It's circular – the oboists are used to it. Breathing like that – it makes your face go baggy, but the air goes round and round...'

'Aurora isn't prepared for this,' I say.

'She's just another heretic. She'll change one heresy for others. That's what we are, Vince – your journeys must have shown... We are heretical monkeys. We've been cast off. Once there was truth, they say. And who told us that? Apes, Vince! In the beginning was the slime. You end in dust, my friend. Add water – and you're slime. That's the truth, Vince. Apes told the story, and we wrote it down. That's why it never is the same – each ape embroidered, got things wrong. They rhapsodised. They looked higher up the tree, they saw the shadows flickering round – the nymphs, the demons – look! up where the fruit is always ripe and tempting...'

'I'm reaching that conclusion, Mirko, on my own,' I say. 'The story...'

'It doesn't all conclude, dear Vince,' he says. 'Until you pull the switch. We each have one. And there's a big one, for everyone. We're not into sadomas, I'm sure, not you and I, no flirting with the end... Aurora, though – she'd do anything to get her house...'

He fires the last nail from inside, shouts, 'Push me out, Vince. Have a drink on me!'

I push, submerge him. His air bubbles out. The crate says 'Aurora: To await'. Of course – so far, she's no address. On the side, there's a stencilled gun.

The dog – it's not the swimming sort. It's loyal, I guess – it makes no rescue moves, it trots away.

Here's two adventures – Mirko, Aurora – in my sights, both missed. Neither was for me; quite alien. I didn't need an ape to tell me that.

Aurora stands in the village square. There's nondescript youths around. 'Help me,' she shouts.

They don't know how to load a magazine. We did all that at school. I show them how. I don't approve.

The eels will have revenge on Mirko – though there's no satisfaction for them there. They could expect to live a century or more – until he came and carved them up. If you believe in poetry, the importance of the things you see, the sport of words, drug-free, professional and measured – all, any of these – it's hard to fit in eels.

You don't see Icarus beneath the waves – Aurora doesn't see the scene at all, of Mirko launched and disappeared. He and Icarus, those pioneers – they scarcely made their splash. To history, they're failures – and – yes, they're failures, the biggest there can be. Mirko, Icarus, eaten by the eels.

Aurora's band moves slowly up the empty street. They have no flag – if they had asked, I'd have designed a beauty for them – even though I don't approve at all. If Icarus had made his flight, been a success, started the fashion – Aurora might have the aeroplanes she needs...

They could divide the habitat. She on one side ... like the
18s and the 8s. Doing what she says – you'd be as safe as
with the other crew.

There's not much time. I'll find an attic room, it's cheap,
and if you look down on the street, your head will swim. I'll
write out a version of my life – short, packed like an egg –
and send it out. There's tall poppies around, bosses of all
kinds – they think there's a secret, or a mystery, in how they
got to where they think they are – they need a follower, one
with a project ambitious, transforming, in their head – but
one who'll serve, crouch down before the chair.

Be loyal.

ABOUT THE AUTHOR

John Fraser has lived in Rome since 1980. Previously, he worked in England and Canada.